D1527135

Low-Hanging Fruit

Fruit

A Lemon Sisters' Adventure

Phoebe Richards

ISBN- 9798546881078

Bolyn-Codhi Publishing
phoeberichardsbooks.com

Dedication

To Debbie and Diane, my inspiration, and to Phillip, my constant.

Chapter 1

Everything's fine but call when you get a chance. I'm okay. Really. Just need to talk.

Maggie stared at the text. Interesting. Her oldest sister, Rhoda, had been radio-silent for almost two weeks. Never a good sign.

"Miss Lennon?" a smug, pimple-faced, fifteen year-old waved his hand from the back row. "You said we're not allowed to have cell phones in class. How come you can have one?" The rest of the class snickered.

Why did the biggest rule-breaker always remember the rules? "Sorry. You're right." Maggie pocketed her phone. "Go ahead and take out the most recent draft of your research paper and exchange it with your neighbor. Using this checklist," she passed a stack down each row, "check off all the items you see in the paper." That ought to keep them busy for a while.

A text from Rhoda didn't always mean trouble, but the last time she said, "I'm okay, really," all three of the sisters' worlds had been turned upside down. Maggie had traveled from her comfortable home in Greenville, SC, to Rhoda's trashy trailer in Florida. What a nightmare that turned into, especially when

Rhoda's husband, Lute, went on a rampage and pulled a gun on their other sister, Cheryl.

Then, poof. He disappeared. Was that what she wanted to talk about? Was the crazy bastard back?

After an eternity, the bell rang and the students exploded from the room, leaving Maggie three minutes before the next class. Good to hear from you finally. Is this an SOS, or can I call on my way home this afternoon?

No SOS. TTYL. LU

She needed to check in with Cheryl before calling Rhoda. Cheryl was the link-in-the-chain, or, more accurately, the grape-on-the-vine among the three sisters, since she called or texted each of them daily. She'd know what, if anything, was up.

♦♦♦

During lunch duty, the siren's song of an incoming text again buzzed in her pocket. Her fingers itched to check her phone, but she didn't dare divert her eyes from the kids in the cafeteria. She'd made that mistake her first year and picked peas out of her hair for hours.

What if Rhoda really was in trouble? If Lute returned, who knew what he might do to her? A second vibration broke her resolve. "Hey, Dan," she called to the other monitor in the room. "Can you spot me for a second?"

Never breaking his surveillance, Dan nodded yes and held up two fingers to indicate how many minutes she could be gone.

She slipped out into the hallway, hidden from

the students' view, to check the message.

Great news! I have a HUGE surprise! I know you're at work, but call me as soon as you can. I'M SO EXCITED!!!

Typical. A cryptic yet ominous note from Rhoda and an effusive one from Cheryl. Eeyore versus Tigger. Somehow, as much as Maggie loved her sisters, they could ignite her anxiety in twenty-five words or less. No matter. There was no dealing with it now. She had to drag through her three remaining classes and a staff meeting before calling either one back. She put her phone on airplane mode, reentered the cafeteria and followed the trajectory of a flying carrot stick. Pimple-face. Shoulda known.

The minute she started the car, the phone rang. She looked at the media screen on the dash. Rhoda. Damn. So much for getting the scoop from Cheryl first. Maggie hit the call button. "Hey, stranger. Where the hell have you been?"

"I know. I know. I'm sorry." Rhoda's voice sounded more like Eeyore than the text. "Things have been kind of rough lately." Big sigh. "Just didn't feel like talking."

Maggie heard Rhoda's voice crack. Things must be bad. "What's going on? Are you okay? I mean, you aren't sick or anything, are you?"

"No. Not sick. I shouldn't have called. I just wanted to hear a friendly voice." A sob came through the speaker.

Maggie shifted to high alert; she could count on two hands the number of times she'd seen or heard Rhoda cry. "Rhoda. My God! Is it Lute? Did he come back? Has he been bothering you?"

"No. I've never heard another word from Lute. It's like he just vanished off the face of the earth."

Maggie heard a gulp. Uh oh. She'd heard that sound many times before. Was Rhoda back on pills? "Take a deep breath and tell me what's going on."

Rhoda's voice hitched several times. "Ben left. And he didn't just leave me. He left Eugenia."

"You're kidding? What happened?" Maggie never knew Ben was Rhoda's lover until after Lute disappeared last year, but apparently their affair had gone on for a while. He seemed like a nice, normal guy—an unusual choice for Rhoda.

"I don't know. It's a big mystery. I thought everything was going great. But the last few months he got quiet and sullen. He seemed anxious, too. Jumpy."

"Did something happen at work? Maybe a malpractice suit or something?"

"No. He would have told me about that, plus I snooped through his emails. I didn't see anything unusual."

"Do you remember exactly when he started acting funny?" Maggie heard Rhoda gulp again. Maybe she was just drinking iced tea.

"I don't know. Seems like all of a sudden, he got real interested in cleaning up my old trailer and the lot."

There was only one reason anyone would mess with that crappy trailer and yard—to look for more gold bars her conspiracy-mad husband, Lute, had buried. "Was he after the gold?" There was a pause while Rhoda inhaled. Obviously, she was still smoking.

8

Low-Hanging Fruit: A Lemon Sisters' Adventure

"Well," long exhale, "I wondered about that, but he said he wanted to clean the place up so no one would wander onto the property, get hurt and sue me for negligence. He went over there a few times without me. Said he just wanted to clear junk out of the yard. It was like he was obsessed with the place. He even rented a concrete mixer and had me go help him fill in that sinkhole where the septic tank used to be."

"That is strange."

"I know, right? He kept looking toward the swamp, mumbling 'where'd it go' as he raked the whole yard free of debris."

"Weird. How do you know he wasn't after the gold?"

"He dug it all up before he cleared the place and gave it to me."

"Wow. How much was there?"

"I don't know. I haven't figured that out yet. It was a pretty good haul, though."

"And then what?" Maggie was losing interest in whatever caused Ben to run off.

"I came home from my women's circle last week, and there was a SALE PENDING sign in his yard. The house was cleaned out. He left me a note that said he just couldn't take it anymore. Asshole even said, 'It's not you. It's me.' I haven't heard that shit since junior high."

Maggie was glad to hear anger replace the despair in Rhoda's voice. "So, what's next?"

"Screw him. In fact, screw all men. They're nothing but trouble. I've temporarily moved back into the junk-heap, but I'm going out today to buy myself a double-wide."

Typical. Rhoda had a trunk load of gold bars but moving up meant buying double-wide. "So you're okay?"

"Yeah. I just needed to talk that out. Thanks for listening. I'll send pictures of the new place. Love you."

"Love you, too. Good luck."

Chapter 2

It was an innocent mistake.

When Lester Nusbaum was hired as an Upscale Security Officer by the Jacksonville Wackenhut Corporation, he assumed carrying a weapon was required. Neither the job description nor the application explicitly stated "no weapons allowed." Security Officer screamed armed, in his mind.

He was actually surprised when he got the job. The application had been intimidating. In addition to the minimum requirement, a high school diploma, there was a long list of qualifications:

- Meaningful and verifiable work history in any field
- Minimum of one year verifiable and successful security experience
- Associate's degree or higher in any discipline
- Service in the active duty military, military reserves or National Guard
- Service in auxiliary police or police cadets

Rereading the instructions, he realized only one from the list was needed. He certainly had a verifiable, though sporadic, work history. The rest of the must-haves were simple—operate radio or telephone equipment, identify critical issues quickly and accurately, possess active listening skills. Hell, his sister's two-year old could do all that.

The first day on the job, he was given his assignment.

"Welcome to the Wackenhut team, Mr. Nusbaum." A towering hulk of muscle shook his hand. "Officer Weismueller."

Lester craned his neck to look up. "Nice to meet you. I'm looking forward to the job. I've always wanted to be in security."

"That's what we like. People with a desire to keep our clients safe, so their businesses can run efficiently, which leads me to your assignment. You will report to the JaxPort Access Control Center. Do you know where that is?"

Lester nodded that he did.

"Excellent. Your duties are uncomplicated but critical to the organization. You will be required to stand guard by the boom barrier at the point of entry for cargo trucks, where you will observe all incoming and outgoing vehicles for suspicious behavior. Do you understand?"

"Yes, sir."

"If you see anything that might be considered a threat to security, use your walkie-talkie to alert the guard in the control booth. Any questions?"

"Will I also be in the control booth, sir?"

"No. You'll be outside where you'll have an unobstructed view of the entire area. Understand?"

It would be hot outside. "Yes, sir. Thank you, sir."

"Good. From here, you'll go straight to our state-of-the-art training room to complete the two-hour online course relevant to your position. You'll receive further instructions at that time." Officer Weismueller pointed Lester in the right direction, then turned on his heel and left the room.

Lester drew back his shoulders and held his head high. There were sure to be cameras everywhere. He didn't want to lose this job before it even started.

A week after completing the training course and receiving his Wackenhut uniform (59/34 pants; 5XL shirt), he began the job with his Ruger LC9s secured in the homemade belly-band holster he fashioned out of his ex-girlfriend's sister's maternity pants. Lester, an ardent member of the NRA, believed all situations called for concealed carry.

The job went smoothly for three weeks, though the hot Florida sun and the even hotter asphalt made standing for hours difficult for a man of his girth and fitness. On one particularly sweltering morning, he positioned himself next to the pivot assembly and counterweights that hoisted the barrier arm.

Traffic had been slow. By 11:00, only three trucks had come through, and for lack of movement, Lester's lower back began to spasm. To get some relief, he rested against the gate assembly and leaned over to stretch his cramped muscles. Though his uniform was custom made, the waistband rode down his hips while the stretchy holster stayed in place. As his back pain started to ease, he heard the rumble of an approaching vehicle. When he snapped to attention, the belly-band caught on the pivot assembly, pulling the holster above his waist. The motion freed the gun which landed on a rock just large enough to discharge the firearm into the base of the security shack.

"JESUS CHRIST IN THE FOOTHILLS!" The supervisor inside screamed through the loud speaker. "Hit the ground. NOW. Arms over your head."

Lester dropped to the ground and raised his

arms.

The burly man yanked open the shack door, and, reaching Lester in two strides, jerked him back to a standing position. "You could have fucking killed me, you moron." Without waiting for a reply, the super ripped the badge from Lester's neck, grabbed the walkie-talkie, and picked up the gun. "You're dismissed. Immediately. Leave the premises and do not return. Ever."

♦♦♦

Maggie barely made it to the bathroom in time. Just as she settled down to business, her phone rang. Google Duo. Cheryl, of course. That woman had an uncanny knack for calling at inopportune moments. She'd ignore it, but Cheryl would just keep calling. Angling the phone for the least revealing shot, Maggie answered. "On the john, Cheryl. Can I call you right back?"

"Oh, sorry. Sure, sure. I just had to share my good news with you, and I only videoed so you can see the proof. It's just all so exciting. I can't believe it's finally happened. I mean, I thought it was all over after last year, but here it is again, my…"

"Cheryl. Take a breath. I'm on the toilet. I'll call you back." Jesus. Maggie loved her middle sister, but trying to break into the conversation when Cheryl was excited was next to impossible.

"I know. Sorry. I'm just gobsmacked about the whole thing and wanted to share it with…"

After hanging up and finishing her business, Maggie ripped off her work clothes and bra. Time to get comfy in her standard chill-at-home clothes, a well-worn USC Gamecocks tee shirt (Go Cocks), and stretchy Eddie Bauer shorts.

She could feel the tension of the day draining from her shoulders and jaw as she headed to the kitchen for a snack. She loved her little house, a single-story, shotgun with a wide front porch and a tin roof. It was only nine-hundred square feet, with two bedrooms and a bath, but it was all she needed and all she could afford. The kitchen opened into the living room, so she could watch TV while she cooked dinner.

Finally relaxed and settled with a beer and some chips, Maggie prepared to call Cheryl. She settled in her nest, a sleek, faux-leather recliner, and hit the Google Duo button. "Hey. Sorry. You caught me at a bad time. So what's the news?" She sat back, sipped her beer, and watched her sister talk.

"So," like Cheryl had never stopped talking from the first call, "you remember I was first runner-up last year on *Florida's Hidden Treasures*?"

"Yes, you did gr…"

"All I got was that 'lovely parting gift' Best-of-Florida food basket. What a slap in the face. Nothing but a bunch of stale coconut patties, gator jerky, and saltwater taffy."

"That was disappointing. You definitely deserved to win over the redneck with the trained rattlesnake."

"Right? Apparently, we aren't the only ones who felt that way. I got this letter," Cheryl turned the camera so Maggie could see it, "that says there has been a public demand for a *Tournament of Treasures*. And I got picked to be on it!"

"Wow. That's great, Cher." Maggie hated TV

15

talent shows, especially the ones that showcased talent other than singing, but she knew how important it was to Cheryl. All three sisters had to suffer through her disappointment at losing. To make matters worse, Cheryl's boyfriend, Ed, the shithead Hollywood producer who got her on the show, dumped her when she came in second. "When is it? Where is it? I'd love to come, unless it's during school."

"That's a problem. It's in two weeks here in Tallahassee. But you can stream it on your laptop. I just don't know what I'm going to sing or wear. What do you think? Something upbeat like 'Gimme That Old Time Religion' or something more serious like 'I'll Fly Away'? I mean, the song choice will determine my outfit, don't you think?"

"Do you have to stick with hymns and gospel? Maybe you should try something more contemporary." Maggie didn't know if she was up for another singing competition with Cheryl. The last time, she got so bored sitting in a church during rehearsals, she ended up drunk at a bar, necking with some stranger. On second thought, maybe she did want to be involved. Those few steamy encounters with Buddy Crapps had been the highlight of the last year. Make that the last several years. God, he was hot. Not that she'd heard from him since.

"So, what do you think?" Cheryl's voice brought Maggie back to reality.

"I think you have excellent taste and judgment. You decide which song you feel best singing and go buy yourself some ridiculously expensive designer outfit. Knock 'em dead, Sis."

Cheryl's face brightened at the compliment.

"I'll ask Rhoda. She knows which songs are best for my range. I haven't talked to her in a while, anyway. Have you?"

"Yes. Just today. Ben left her, so tread lightly. I'm worried she'll start using again. Maybe your news will give her a boost. "

After ending the call, Maggie stared, unseeing, at the muted TV, remembering the night she and Buddy made the "beast with two backs" in Rhoda's old Bonneville in the Starke Medical Center parking lot.

Chapter 3

Rhoda sat in her car outside of the Eugenia Medical Clinic where Ben used to work as a chiropractor. Pissed her off all over again. What the hell had gotten into him? They had been so happy after Lute disappeared a year ago. She tried to do Lute in herself by serving him all kinds of iffy chicken and oysters disguised with spices. Of course, the old bastard had obviously survived and took off for God knew where.

With Lute gone, she thought Ben would marry her, until he started acting weird—talking in his sleep saying, "… for you, Rho." Then, he'd lapse into gibberish and wake in a sweat. The current problem, now that the second assbag had left her, was how to get her hands on some Oxy or Xanax or anything that might help her cope. Her old stash was almost gone. It had been much easier when Ben still worked there. She needed to schmooze her way past her old friend, Linda, the pain management doctor, and into the medical supply closet. Thank God she had made a copy of the key before she quit working there. She looked in the review mirror, put on her best wide-eyed innocent look, freshened her lipstick, and headed in to try her luck. First, she had to get past the receptionist. "Hey, Janine. How are you?"

Janine looked up from the soap opera streaming on her IPad. "Hello there." She switched off the show and reached through the window to pat Rhoda's hand. "Sorry, sweetie, but still no sign of Ben."

Rhoda resisted rolling her eyes. She could use the sympathy to her advantage. "Not a word, huh?" She pulled a Kleenex from her purse, lowered her head and dabbed at her eyes. "I was just hoping, you know, that maybe…" Real tears rolled now. "Is Linda in? She's always been such a good friend."

"She just stepped out to run some errands."

Bingo. "Oh, shoot. Maybe I'll wait in her office. She won't mind, I'm sure."

"I guess that'd be okay. Hey, while you're here, do you mind listening for the phone while I run to the ladies room?"

Even better. "Sure, Janine. I'd be happy to. Just like old times, right?"

As soon as the receptionist closed the bathroom door, Rhoda bee-lined for the medical closet, shoved a handful of samples in her purse, and returned to the main desk just as the toilet flushed. When Janine came back, Rhoda looked at the clock. "Oh gosh. I forgot I'm supposed to go early to choir practice. Tell Linda I stopped by. I'll try again later. See ya." She was out the door and in the car before Janine could respond.

The Xanax worked wonders. The sun seemed brighter, the air cooler. She took a deep breath. This would be the year of Rhoda. She didn't need a man to take care of her. Between her disability checks and the gold bars, she could finally be independent. She certainly had more money now than she ever did when Lute was around. It was time to redefine her life. She headed straight for Mack's Manufactured Homes in Starke. Maybe she could trade in her old trailer and get a good deal on one of those modular ones that looked like real houses.

"Oh, that's a humdinger, right there, ma'am." The embroidered name patch read Larry. "The Vidalia is one of our best sellers. It's almost 1400 square feet, 3 beds, 2 baths, all for the incredible price of $88,599."

"How much?" It dawned on Rhoda that she and Lute had never bought anything new during their entire marriage. The trailer had been used, the camper attached to it was free and all the furniture came from church rummage sales and thrift shops. Even their appliances were second or third hand. She had no idea things were so expensive. "Maybe I could look at something a little smaller or used."

Larry threw his arm around her shoulder. "Don't let that price spook you. That includes transportation, installation, and connection of utilities. You can't get a better deal anywhere in North Florida. Let's go look at something more in your price range." He tightened his grip and hustled her toward another section of the lot.

After looking at smaller and used models and deducting the estimated trade-in value of her current home, Rhoda was still looking at over $60,000. She'd be flat broke. "I'm going to have to think about this, but thanks for your time." Undeterred, Larry clung to her through the lot. "I could prob'ly discount that new one."

"No, thanks." Rhoda maneuvered out of his grip and sprinted toward the parking lot.

Larry followed in dogged pursuit. "I got a used camp model—might be small, but she's in mint condition. An old widow-woman lived in it. Looks brand new." He was still screaming offers as Rhoda jumped in her car, locked the doors, and popped another pill. She needed a plan B. She'd have to go with a used model and not one from a dealer. By the time she reached Eugenia, whatever drug she had taken gave her renewed confidence. The answer came to her like a vision. Vernon Burwinkle's Pawn and Payday Loan. Vern and Lute had been good buddies. He'd help her out. She parked in front of the shop and went in.

"Well, hell, woman," Vern heaved his gut up on the edge of the counter, "you don't need to pay for no installation bullshit. You already got a foundation; your utilities is run to the old place, and you got a septic tank. I'm the one that found that big oil drum, and I personally helped Lute hook it up."

"About that," Rhoda said. "We had a small sinkhole open up and swallow the tank. I had to fill it with concrete to stabilize the lot."

"That's no big deal. We'll put in another one and run it out to leech in the swamp."

"That's great, Vern. Do you know anywhere I can get a decent used doublewide?"

"Let me check around. I'm sure we can get you all set up." Vern scanned the area for any eavesdroppers. "You hear anything from Lute?"

"Not one word. I try his cell phone, but it just goes to voicemail," Rhoda lied. She never thought twice about what had happened to him. "Have you?"

"Nothin'." He looked over his shoulder and leaned in close. "I bet THEY got him."

Jesus. Not the conspiracy crap again. "Probably. He tried to warn me—Mark of the Beast, you know." Rhoda poked a finger between her eyebrows, the secret password of the Brotherhood.

Vern returned the salute. "Sons-a-bitches. I hope he went down fightin'."

"I'd rather not think about it," Rhoda dabbed a tissue at fake tears. "Let me know if you get anywhere with that doublewide."

"Sure will. Old Vern'll take care of you. Don't you worry."

♦♦♦

After a night of erotic dreams starring Buddy, Maggie decided it was time to get back in the hunt. Maybe she'd have better luck now that she'd lost some weight and added highlights to her mousy brown hair. She needed a date, but she knew a man wasn't going to just drop in her lap again. She'd have to work at it. The whole idea made her stomach clench—the bar scene, online dating, singles groups, fix-ups. Some of her teacher friends had success online. She'd ask them during her planning period.

"Yeah, I've tried Match. It's okay, but you end up with some pretty long-distance choices. It's worth a shot, though. I've had the most success with Tinder." Lisa, the band teacher, pulled out her phone and showed Maggie the app.

Maggie looked at the faces of boys who could have been her students. "Oh my God, Lisa. They're babies. I mean, you're still in your twenties, but I'd feel like their mother. Have you had a second date with any of them?"

"Oh, no," Lisa giggled. "Tinder's mostly just for hook-ups. Which, you know, is sometimes all you need, right?"

"Right. I'll think about it." Not. She heard

22

Match and eHarmony attracted an older crowd. She'd start there.

Dan, the cafeteria monitor/assistant football coach, walked into the workroom. "Think about what?"

Lisa turned toward him. "Oh, Maggie's looking into online dating. Isn't that fun?"

Maggie felt the heat rise to her hairline. "No, I was just asking for a friend."

Dan smiled, gave the vending machine a good whack and grabbed the pack of donuts that fell out. "Good luck with that."

Chapter 4

"Break a leg, Sis!" Maggie blew an air kiss at the phone, hung up and turned on her computer to watch Cheryl perform on the *Tournament of Treasures*. Tonight was the culmination of a three-part series which started with twelve contestants selected through an online voting process. Cheryl had survived the first two eliminations and now stood as one of the final four vying for the grand prize. Only the judges would decide the winner. Cheryl had drawn the lucky straw; she would sing last.

Maggie fixed and ate dinner through a flaming-baton twirler/contortionist, a pianist not nearly as gifted as Rhoda, and a tap dancer who only lost her step once. After a commercial for the Florida Citrus Industry, it was finally Cheryl's turn.

"Ladies and Gentleman, please welcome our fourth and final contestant, the runner-up from last year's *Florida's Hidden Treasures*, Miss Cheryl Lennon from right here in Tallahassee!" Light applause sounded, punctuated by a Woot-Woot, no doubt from Rhoda. "Miss Lennon will be singing 'Crazy,' written by Willie Nelson and made famous by Patsy Cline." The announcer waved his arm toward the darkened center stage.

As the spotlight found her, Cheryl glittered in a black and gold sequined, off-the-shoulder sheath by Nicole Miller paired with Louboutin peep-toe heels. Her shimmering blond hair, pulled into a side-swept bun, accentuated her emerald eyes. Over the last two weeks, many discussions had gone into the perfect look. Cheryl wanted to stay conservative with her gown and music selection, but Maggie and Rhoda convinced her to go for broader audience appeal with a sexy, yet sophisticated dress and a popular song more people would recognize. The combination dazzled as Cheryl held the microphone close and began. "Crazy…"

Maggie was always amazed at her sister's ability to transform nervousness and self-doubt into strength and emotion when she gave a public performance. Everyone was transfixed. When the camera panned the studio, Maggie noticed Rhoda, front and center, gripping a hand-drawn "Go Sis!" poster, her jaw clenched as she tried to transmit success toward the stage. The rest of the audience seemed to ride Cheryl's voice through her loneliness and desperation. The camera returned to Cheryl as she lowered her eyes and whispered the heartbreaking final line. After a moment of stunned silence, the audience and judges erupted with cheers and applause. Cheryl's was the only performance to receive a full standing ovation.

◆◆◆

The raging sea crashed against the hull, but Marvin Whitcomb, knees bent, body braced against the wind and rain, merely chuckled. This storm was no match for the likes of him or his sturdy craft, the Pussy Galore. He throttled down, turned the bow forty-five degrees into the wave and tacked until he moved into smoother waters. "Pssshaw. Rough seas, my ass. Old

Pussy and I have weathered a lot worse, haven't we baby?"

"Excuse me?"

Slowly the clouds cleared and Marvin looked up to find a bony, angular woman standing at the counter with a china tea set. So he wasn't at sea, just at work in St. Augustine.

"This tea set is marked $10.00, but as you can see, it's chipped. It's only worth $5.00 in this condition."

For chrissakes. "Lady, I don't give a rat's ass what you think it's worth. This is a consignment shop. I don't set the prices; the vendors do." He stared at the woman. Her curled gray hair clung to her head like she still had on those roller things Ann used to use. At least Ann had combed her hair after she took them out. "Take it or leave it."

The woman placed a five, two ones, and various coins on the counter. "I'm tempted to leave it, you rude man." She inspected one of the cups. "It does match my china pattern, though. You can't blame me for trying to save a few dollars. I'm on a fixed income."

"We all are." He lit a half-smoked cigarette, took a deep drag, and let it dangle from the corner of his mouth as he sorted the change. Of course she'd pay in mostly pennies. Cheap old crone.

"Can you wrap those in newspaper for me?"

"You got any?" Smoke drifted across the counter toward her face.

"Oh, never mind," she said, gingerly placing the cups, saucers and sugar bowl in her reusable grocery bag. "I don't know why I come in here."

"Me either," Marvin said, putting the money in the cash register and handing her a receipt. "Have a nice day."

When the place was empty again, he took a slug out of the flask he kept in the desk, leaned his head against the filing cabinet and tried to find his way back to the sea, but it was gone. Might as well go through those new boxes #1434 brought in yesterday. It was marked "Tools." Finally, some interesting merchandise. Most of the stuff here at Ann's Cluttered Closet was nothing but fancy women's crap. What the hell was the point of a doily, or little porcelain Pugs, or a bunch of fancy crystal and china nobody ever used? Thank God he didn't own the contents. He just collected rent on the dealer booths. The crap was their problem.

Personally, he had no use for consignment shops and the like, but it had always been Ann's dream to have a little store like this. So, even as she made him do her bidding throughout their fifty-plus years of marriage, she guilted him from the grave into opening this place. Marvin considered selling it, but it provided enough income to keep him in booze and cigarettes. His social security covered the rest. Truth be told, the shop was a gold mine. It stayed full of merchandise from estates or abandoned storage units. The old folks here, mostly women, loved bargain shopping, so they came and bought useless junk that would cycle back through when they moved or passed on.

After their girls had taken Ann's jewelry, the good silver, and some of the furniture, he'd given the rest of her stuff to the church rummage sale. He didn't want all that muddle in the house, but he couldn't see putting it up for sale here. The important stuff, his TV, Lazy Boy, books, tools, and his bed, he kept. A nice Spartan house; that's the way he liked it. He'd even pulled up all the carpet. There was nothing wrong with that old terrazzo underneath; the stains weren't bad. Now, with most of the furniture gone, he could just open the slider and use the leaf-blower to clean the place out.

Sometimes he got bored sitting in the musty old place all day. That was the advantage of being the owner, though. He could open late, if he'd had a little too much bourbon and branch water the night before, or close for the whole week if he wanted. But it gave him something to do, and every once in a while, a hot little number would come through the doors searching for an end table or bookshelves. That's why he dressed up to come to work—crisp khakis, a pressed button-down and his favorite white loafers. God, he was lonely. Ann had been sick for so long before she finally…Well, he was ready to get back out there. He'd even signed up for the bereavement group his daughters told him about, "Moving Forward, Living Alone after Loss."

♦♦♦

"We have to call Maggie! I bet she's dying to be here." Cheryl propped the IPad on her dining room table and took a seat next to Rhoda. After a half ring, Maggie's face appeared on the screen.

"OHMYGOD, OHMYGOD, OHMYGOD!" all three sisters shouted in unison.

"Can you believe it?" Cheryl laughed. "I actually won!"

Maggie wiped tears from her eyes. "I'm so proud of you, Sis. I mean, I'm not at all surprised, but wow! You won. By unanimous vote. Not that there was ever any doubt. You were amazing."

"How did I look on TV? I recorded it, but we haven't watched yet. We wanted to call you first thing."

"You looked like a movie star at the Oscars. The light kept shooting little beams off the sequins on your dress and your hair and those shoes…"

"Rhoda, go cue up the show. I have to see it. Sorry, Maggie. Go on."

"You were fantastic, obviously, since you won the whole damned thing. And, what a prize—an all-expenses-paid vacation."

"I know. My choice of either a two-week motor coach tour down the AIA, or a six-day, five-night 'Fantastic Florida Rivers' cruise."

"I vote for the cruise," Rhoda said. "I can't sit on those damned buses for too long. Plus, you'd have to pack and unpack every night on the land tour."

"I'm with Rhoda on that one. Definitely the cruise. Who's going to be your plus one?"

Cheryl looked at Maggie's pouted lips and knitted brows. Then she looked at Rhoda. Same begging-puppy-dog expression. Ugh. Impossible decision. Too bad she was without a man right now. "I haven't had time to think about it. I'm still admiring my flowers and trophy." Cheryl turned the IPad toward a vase of roses and orange blossoms next to a golden treasure chest with a plastic replica of Florida on top. Maggie and Rhoda continued to stare. So much for stalling. "Okay. I agree. The cruise sounds better. Let me check into it. Maybe we can all pitch in for a third ticket."

"Yes!" Maggie fist-pumped. "I'm in. What about you, Rhoda? Do you still have any of that gold?"

"Maybe. I'm trying to buy that new trailer, but I can set aside some of it for the trip."

"Great," Cheryl said. "It just wouldn't be the same without the three of us there together. The Lemon Sisters ride again!" She smiled. Their mother would have been so proud, even though she had dubbed the three girls the Lemon Sisters every time they tried to sing.

"You're the best. Thank you." Maggie raised her beer toward the screen. "All hail, the Lemon Sisters."

"Yeah, thanks." Rhoda returned the toast.

Cheryl tapped the screen with her Vitamin Water. "You're both welcome. Now, enough about the prize. Let's get back to how fabulous I am."

Chapter 5

The intake counselor peered over the top of Marvin's file folder. "Mr. Whitcomb, do you know why you're here?"

He had to close one eye to focus. "You tell me. I was jus' min'in' my own business in my shop…"

"And you were drinking, heavily, weren't you, Mr. Whitcomb?"

Marvin grabbed the table which seemed to keep moving. "Like I said, min'in' my own business."

"You were minding your own business, getting drunk, until the customer came in, isn't that correct?"

"She interrupted me. I was having a good time, and that ole bitch came in and started bossin' me aroun'. Askin me to get that box a shit off the top shelf, then yellin' at me when I dropped it."

"And is that what provoked you to assault her?"

"I dint assault her. She said I was a worthless drunk and said she was callin' the cops. I dint want any cops, so I reached for her phone."

"According to the report, you lunged at her and knocked her to the floor."

Marvin snickered. "Yeah, but I got 'er phone."

"Unfortunately for you, Mr. Whitcomb, she was able to dial 911 before you got the phone. Do you remember what happened when the police arrived?"

"Achhhh. Stupid cops. I tol' 'em I was fine, just had a few highballs when that bitch came in. So they grabbed my arm and one of them went for his gun. I tol' 'em to go ahead and shoot me; might as well be dead, anyway."

"What happened next?"

"The cop gave me some shit about being dangerous to myself and others. Next thing I know, they dragged me in here. Where the hell am I, anyway?"

"You have been involuntarily committed under the Baker Act to the St. Augustine Halos of Help Detox and Rehabilitation Center." Her eyes shifted to the file from which she read, "You are required to stay and participate in both individual and group counseling for at least seventy-two hours at which time you will be reevaluated by our staff psychiatrist. She will then make her recommendation whether you should stay here or be discharged and access outpatient services." A light snort caused her to look up from her file. Marvin's chin rested on his chest as a string of drool darkened an ever-widening spot on his shirt.

She picked up the desk phone. "Take him to detox."

Marvin woke in a white, barren room. No TV, no radio, no phone, no furniture, except the bed beneath him. He had on one of those stupid hospital gowns that tied in the back. Where were his clothes? That was his new outfit, the one he bought for his date with Lorna. A knife stabbed through his temple as his stomach cramped. He looked around. No bathroom. He eased himself up to sit on the side of the bed, just as the door opened.

"Good morning. What's your full name?"

He squinted through the bright light. "Marvin

Whitcomb."

"Date of birth?"

"July 18, 1948."

"Do you know who the current president is?"

"Biden."

"Do you know what season it is?"

"Hard to tell here in Florida."

"What day of the week is it?"

"Shit. I'm retired. I never know what day it is."

The doctor or nurse or whatever made a note of all his responses.

"Where are my clothes?"

"Your clothes are in a bag that you can pick up at the main desk after you've showered. There's a community bathroom down the hall. We've contacted your family. They can bring you fresh clothes."

"And a razor?"

"No razors. At 9:00 a.m. you will meet with the staff psychiatrist to discuss the conditions that brought you here. She'll give you some Librium to alleviate withdrawal symptoms. At 10:00, you'll have group therapy. Your daughter said she'll come visit at 11:00."

"Shit."

Bunch of fucking derelicts. According to them, they were all shooting up heroin, living on the streets, stealing from their kids.

"Marvin, why don't you share with the group why you're here?"

"Hell if I know. I mean, I got drunk, but I had a damned good reason. It's not like I just sit around drinking and staying stoned out of my mind all the time. I run a business. I just had a bad day."

"And what happened on that bad day that caused you to get drunk and assault a woman?"

Marvin slid down in his chair and crossed his arms. "None of your business."

"By court order, it is my business. Proceed."

He pushed his lips together in a duck-pout. "I finally got a date."

"Go on."

"I haven't been out with a woman since my wife died. In fact, I haven't been anywhere for years, the whole time she was sick. We were both housebound. I had to care for her day and night, twenty-four-seven, every single day. Anyway, things got pretty lonely for old Marvin, you know? So I started checking out different grief groups after she died. I don't really believe in that crap, but they say there's more widow-women than men, so I thought maybe I could score." His eyes lit up as he leaned forward and rested his forearms on his thighs. "And sure enough, there was this real pretty gal, hair styled real nice, tight skin, perky tits. So I asked her if she wanted to go to dinner and damned if she didn't say yes."

"What happened next?"

"I went out and bought these new clothes. I'm kind of known for my style, you know? And then I thought, what the hell? I bought a nice pair of Brooks Brothers pajamas and a pack of condoms. You never know when you might get lucky. So, I got all cleaned up, put the bag with my PJs and stuff in the backseat of my car and picked her up. We had a real nice dinner— easy conversation, lots of laughs. Then, when the valet pulled up, he screeched to a stop right in front of us. When I opened her door for her, she noticed the bag in the back seat. It had fallen over, thanks to that stupid kid driver, and everything spilled out. She looked at me like I pulled a gun on her, slammed the door shut, and stormed back in the restaurant."

"Were you drunk then?"

"No. I was trying to stay alert and awake for the night's amorous activities. Clearly that didn't work out. So I went home, had some drinks until the sun came up and then went to the shop. You know the rest."

Chapter 6

"Oh God, Rho. I'm never going on a date again. Not only that, I can't ever go back to work." Maggie felt sick to her stomach after her evening with Dan the coach/monitor. Why had she agreed to that date?

Rhoda laughed. "That bad, huh? How did you end up going out with him, anyway?"

"He overheard me talking about online dating. He cornered me after lunch duty a few days later and said why take a chance with a stranger when there were perfectly nice people right here at work. It kind of made sense at the time. I should have known it would be a bust when he added, 'now that you've gotten in shape and all.' Ugh."

"Turd. So what happened?"

"He said we were going out to dinner, but he didn't say where. In hindsight, I should have just met him somewhere. Anyway, he picks me up and starts driving away from town where all the restaurants are. Finally, he pulls up to an apartment building, his apartment building, and says, 'Surprise. I'm cooking dinner for you. I'm a great cook.'"

"Uh oh."

"Yeah. But, I think, free dinner. How bad can it be? We go up to his place, which is a typical single-man pad complete with a Naugahyde couch and a cable-reel coffee table. I felt like I was back in the eighties. He hands me a beer, in the can, pops one himself, and then puts water on to boil for pasta. A jar of Ragu's on the counter. Good cook, my ass. We chatted for a while and ate dinner, which wasn't horrible. He was pretty much a gentleman so far. Then he says, 'I have a surprise for you for dessert' and scampers off down the hall."

"Oh, this is going to be good."

"I hear all this racket like he's tearing apart a closet or something. A few minutes later he comes out of the room, naked except for a camo banana-hammock, playing 'Roll Out the Barrel' on a monster accordion."

"You're making this up."

"If only."

"What did you do?"

"I Ubered home."

"I don't know, Mags. You might have been a little hasty. A good accordion player is hard to find." Rhoda could barely finish the sentence, she was laughing so hard.

Maggie, too, giggled at the absurdity of the date. "What's wrong with me? Why can't I find a decent guy?"

"Oh, Sis, you will. I don't know that I'd try the workplace again, but there's bound to be somebody out there. Or you could be like me and swear off men forever. At least you haven't had two men abandon you."

"Well, technically I have, but, I get your point. Let's talk about something else. Any more word on Cheryl's cruise?"

"Oh, yeah. She got some information on it. Apparently, we have a choice of themes. Wait, I have them written down. There's the American Contract Bridge cruise, Holistic Healing, Florida in Conflict: Conquerors and Chieftans, and, here we go, Boomer-GenX Mixer—Singles Cruise for Active Adults. That might be interesting."

"A singles cruise? Huh. It's probably just a bunch of losers," Maggie sighed.

""Hey, we're going on it. Plus, the tickets are too expensive; I don't think any low-lifes will be there. It might be fun."

Maggie warmed up to the idea. "You're right. Which one does Cheryl want? It is her cruise, after all. Please tell me she doesn't want Holistic Healing."

"She mentioned it, but I said it was probably a bunch of sick people. That scared her off. And none of us are any good at bridge. It sounds like the singles cruise is the way to go."

"What the hell," Maggie said. "I'm in. Hopefully, none of them play the accordion."

◆◆◆

Cheryl Cell: OK girls. We're all set. They did have a sailing during Mag's spring break, so we board in Jacksonville on March 28. We have a three-bed room on Ponce de Leon Cruise Lines *Forever Young* for the Boomer/GenX Mixer. What a hoot! Our share for the extra ticket is $560 each. I already charged it, so you can pay me. Do you want to meet in Jacksonville, Tallahassee or what? I'm so excited. Watch out world; the Lemon Sisters are on the hunt ;-)

Maggie Cell: That's great, Cher! Thanks so much. After my "Beer Barrel Polka" date, I need to disappear for a week. I'll send my share by Apple Pay in just a sec. Why don't I fly to Tally, rent a car, and we can pick up Rhoda? Then we'll only have one car at the port. Thank God you're talented. I love riding your shirttails! XOXO

Rhoda Cell: It all sounds good to me. I'll pay you when you get here. I should have all the gold cashed in by then. It'll be great to get away.

♦♦♦

Rhoda woke, fixed her coffee and reread Cheryl's text. She barely had enough money for a new trailer, much less some fancy cruise. Not that it mattered. She knew, if she procrastinated long enough, Cheryl and Maggie would cover her share of the trip. Still, she needed to figure out her finances. The gold bars were great, but they wouldn't last forever, and, even though she could work part-time on disability, she didn't want to. If she could sell her current home, that would help. The old junker wouldn't bring in much, but something was better than nothing.

She'd call Vern. He'd help her sell it. In fact, he'd probably buy it, though she'd get more if she sold it herself. It was worth a shot. When her call went straight to his voicemail, she used her best femme-fatale voice. "Hey Vern. It's Rhoda Mason. I just wanted to thank you for helping me look for a new trailer. I also wondered if I could put a sign in your window to try and sell mine." She let her voice crack. "You know, since Lute's been gone, I need all the help I can get. Thanks, again. You're a good friend."

Determined to make an attractive For Sale sign, Rhoda rummaged through a box of photos and news clippings until she found a picture of the trailer when they first got it. It showed the place just after they added the camper, the sleeping porch and carport. Wow. How depressing. The place actually looked pretty nice back then. She had painted it all the same color and even planted flowers (black-eyed Susans and daisies, her favorites) across the front. It only took Lute about two years to trash the place by dragging in all his "finds" from junkyards and pawn shops. The paint had peeled and the flowers suffocated under stacks of tires. Talk about a metaphor for her existence.

Depressed and angry, she finished the sign, grabbed her purse and keys and headed to town. First stop, Vern's, second stop, the clinic. She was running low on happy pills.

"Hey, Vern. Did you get my message?"

"Sure did, little lady, and I got a lead on a new place for you. I wrote the information down on an old pawn ticket." He patted his front and back pockets, then found it under a half sandwich by the cash register. "Here we go. It oughta be a good one. Old Missus Jessup lived in it by herself for years after the mister died. She didn't have no cats or nothin'. Her nephew wants to sell off all her stuff, now that she's passed. Name's Harley. He works over to the concrete plant near Green Cove. Nice guy."

Rhoda took the receipt. "Thanks, Vern. That's great. I'll give him a call today. Mind if I put this sign in your window? What do you think?" She handed him the poster.

"Nice picture. And I'd say $5000 is about right.

That camper gives you an extra bath and bedroom. How come you put your name as Lennon instead of Mason?"

"Well, as you know, Lute was in a bit of trouble before he left. I don't want any of his enemies coming after me."

"Prob'ly a good idea." Vern shook his head. "Anyway, I'd add that whoever buys it has to haul it off."

"Smart." She grabbed a marker off the counter and wrote, "Buyer responsible for removing trailer from site" and hung the sign in the window. Reenergized, she headed for the pain clinic. It wasn't unusual to see the parking lot empty, but the place looked dark. As she climbed the steps to the front door, she noticed a piece of paper taped on the inside of the glass.

United States Department of Justice
Drug Enforcement Administration
Medicare Fraud Strike Force

This office is closed pending investigation of the illegal prescribing of opiod pain medications for nonmedical use.

The padlock on the door rendered her key useless. Shit. So far, the Year of Rhoda was not going well

◆◆◆

"Get the hell off of those cockamamie video

games and look for a damned job. You think I'm made of money? That my goal in life was to support my slug of a son in his late twenties? I thought you'd be taking care of me!"

Lester took off his head phones. She was a human cuckoo clock. Every morning at 10:30, she'd pop through the door to the den and start in. "I know, Ma. I'm sorry. I've been looking online. It's just so stressful, I had to take a break. Most of the jobs require a college degree, so I can't apply for those."

"And whose fault is that? Hmmm? I got my college degree. If I can do it, you can."

"I know, Ma. But to enroll in courses, I have to have money, and to get money, I have to have a job. It's a vicious cycle."

"I'll show you vicious. Go bag groceries. You don't need a degree for that. What happened with that security guard job, anyway?"

"I thought I was supposed to carry a weapon, but I was wrong. They took the gun and fired me."

"Were you at least there long enough to qualify for unemployment?"

"No, Ma."

"If you ask me, you should sell all your damned guns and use the money to go to school. Or, here's a bright idea. Get a job." She turned and stomped from the room. "Oh yeah," she shouted from the hallway, "there's a letter for you from somebody named Wackenhut. What kind of crazy name is Wackenhut?"

Maybe they wanted to rehire him. He'd written to them explaining his confusion and asking for his gun back. He walked to the living room and got the letter off the table.

Dear Mr. Nusbaum,

We have reviewed your letter and your employment file. While we cannot reinstate you as a Security Officer, we have completed a thorough background check and verified the weapon is legally licensed to you. You may retrieve your property at our regional office in the JaxPort Cruise Terminal during regular business hours. Please bring your driver's license or passport, your Florida Concealed Carry Permit, and any other firearms licenses you may have.

Sincerely,

Malcom Bell
Operations Manager
Wackenhut Security, Jacksonville

So, no job. Maybe he would have to sell some guns. He had to do something to get away from his mom.

Chapter 7

"Excuse us," the cluster of elderly women rushed toward Cheryl outside the WEBT Channel 6 TV station. "Ms. Lennon? You are Cheryl Lennon, aren't you?"

Who could these women be? Were they patients of hers? Cheryl scanned their faces, and tried to place them. As a cognitive neuroscientist, she sometimes had a subject react negatively during one of her studies and they blamed her. She'd had some threats over the course of her career, but not many. She certainly couldn't remember a recent case that had been difficult. "Do I know you?" she said as she edged toward the door to the station. Surely there was a guard inside.

"No," giggled the woman in the front of the group. "We wish. We've been following you since *Florida's Hidden Treasures* last year and were so glad when you finally won the *Tournament* last month!"

"Yes," another said. "We started the social media campaign for the *Tournament*. You got a raw deal on that first show. Beat out by a snake charmer. Who wants that to represent Florida?"

The third woman, a tall, skinny, blue-hair with a porcelain smile reached in her pocketbook and pulled out a notebook. "Can I have your autograph? Please? And maybe a selfie with the three of us? We just love your singing!"

At first, Cheryl flinched when the woman stuck her hand in her purse. You never knew who was carrying these days. But the word autograph erased all fears from her mind. "Me? You want my autograph?" She stood a little straighter and her face relaxed into a smile. Fans. Real fans. "Well, aren't you all sweet? Bless your hearts. Of course, you can have an autograph and the selfie. I have to tell you; you're my first."

"Be sure and date it," blue hair said. "I want to show people I knew you before you hit the big time, and you will."

With her ego completely boosted, Cheryl gave a royal wave to her fans and headed inside the WEBT building for her meeting with the producers of *Florida's Hidden Treasures*. There were apparently some contractual obligations that accompanied the *Tournament* win.

"Good morning, Ms. Lennon," a portly man in a snug suit shook her hand. "I'm Chester Davidson, General Manager. Let me again offer you congratulations on winning the *Tournament of Treasures*. It was our highest rated show yet. Over half of the state must have been watching."

"Really?" Highest rated? Half the state? That must be close to ten million. Oh my God. She was famous. Finally. "That's incredible, Mr. Davidson. I, obviously, love the show, and I'm so honored to be a part of it. Thank you for the opportunity and for the wonderful prize. I'm very excited about the cruise." Cheryl tried to maintain some sense of decorum, though inside she was dying to dole out hugs and happy dances.

"As we discussed on the phone, there are some obligations that go with representing WEBT and the

FHT program. We will want you to be a part of the final episode of this coming year's contest, kind of like the reigning Miss America's last walk down the runway, but of course, we'll have you sing. We'll also use some sound bites and clips of your winning performance as promotional material, but you already agreed to that when you signed the contest agreement."

Cheryl couldn't remember signing anything of the sort, but she didn't object to more publicity. "Of course. That's fine. This is all just so exciting. Is there anything else?"

"Yes. It's actually why I called you in here today. The Ponce de Leon Cruise Line, as part of their agreement to provide the prize package, would like you to be part of the entertainment on the trip you're taking in a few weeks. I just got off the phone with the cruise director, and she said they will provide all the music, but want you to perform three out of the five nights. For a small stipend, of course. Here's the contract they sent over for you to sign."

Another chance to sing before a live audience? This was a dream come true. Cheryl signed, pausing for two seconds to read the fine print this time, and slid the contract back across the desk. "Thank you, again, Mr. Davidson. I truly appreciate the opportunity to represent WEBT and *Florida's Hidden Treasures*. I promise, I won't let you down."

◆◆◆

"Okay, Dad." Marvin's daughter said as she slid into the driver's seat. "I've already scheduled your follow-up appointment with the psychiatrist in two weeks. Also, you start the outpatient group therapy tomorrow, and if you miss one meeting, back you go."

Marvin looked at his baby girl. When had she turned from his little ray of sunshine into a controlling harpy? "They can't make me go back. After today, I'm voluntary."

"Don't be that way. We just want to you get better. Sis and I talked about it. Obviously, you're still grieving for Mom, and it's leading to these destructive behaviors. If this was the first time, maybe we'd consider it a fluke. But come on, Dad, admit it. You have to deal with this."

He lit up a cigarette and slumped in the seat. "I hate those group meetings. Bunch of irresponsible addicts."

His daughter lowered her sunglasses and cocked an eyebrow. "Well?"

"I'm not a loser like those others. I just got down. I thought I was ready to start living again. You know, go out and have some fun. But then I blew it. Who knew my date would freak out about the pajamas and stuff? I don't know how to do this. I'll never be happy again."

"Oh, Dad. I know it's hard, but you can't judge your future happiness on one date. You'll find somebody, if that's what you want."

"No, I won't." A long ash dropped to his shirt. "I always thought I'd find somebody else after your mother died." He turned his head toward the passenger-side window. "Turns out, there's just no one else like her." He exhaled a cloud of blue smoke at his reflection in the glass. The car was quiet for several blocks.

He turned when he heard his daughter sniffle.

Tears ran down her face. Damn. Now he'd made her miserable. He was a loser. Reaching across the console, he grabbed her hand. "I'm sorry, Baby. If it'll make you happy, I'll try all that group shit. You know I love you like crazy, right?"

She laughed. "Group shit, huh? That's the Dad I know and love. I'll make a deal with you. You go to therapy for the next few weeks, without missing a session, keep that psychiatrist appointment, and Sis and I will give you a big surprise."

"Don't go getting me anything. I'll go. As long as I can stand it."

◆◆◆

"Is this Miz Lennon?"

Rhoda didn't recognize the voice or the number. "Yes. Who's calling please?"

"My name's Delmont. Delmont Crapps. I was up to the pawn shop this afternoon and saw a sign for a trailer for sale.'Zat you?"

Finally. It had been over a week since she posted that sign at Vern's. "Yes. That's me. Are you interested?"

"Yes, ma'am. I was hopin' I could come and see it. I got me a trailer, but it's real small, and I'm gonna get married soon. I need a bigger place."

Rhoda looked around the house. Definitely not in condition for a tour right now. She looked at the calendar on the wall. "Well, I have to finish a little work before I show it. Can you give me a week? Maybe on the 25th?"

"Sure. We're not getting' married right away, so that'd be just fine, ma'am. Maybe I can come about

9:00 in the morning?"

"Sure. 9:00, March 25th sounds great. What did you say your name was again?"

"Crapps. Delmont Crapps."

Of course it was. "Okay, Mr. Crapps, I'll see you then." After hanging up, Rhoda grabbed a piece of paper and a pen and started a list. Number one—check all her old hiding spots for pills. Number two—pitch everything except the furniture, appliances, and pots and pans. Number three—call the number for Harley Jessup to ask about the doublewide for sale.

An hour later, sweat dripped off her hair and into her eyes. She'd wrestled the mattress off the bed, hoping some of her old stash was there. The three pills she found didn't look familiar, but were worth a shot. She dropped them in a baggie. Going through her dresser wasn't much more productive. She shook out all the clothes before throwing them in the trash bag. No drugs. When those drawers were empty, she turned to Lute's dresser. Even though rum was his drug of choice, maybe she'd find something worth keeping. If all else failed, rum would do.

In the last drawer, she unearthed his old dopp kit, and holding her breath, unzipped it. Ahhh. Hello, old friend—Smiling Dick's Erectite. Please, let these be the capsules I emptied and refilled with Prozac when Lute was around. It was worth a try. There were only three left. She popped them in her mouth. What's the worst that could happen? Raging headache? Orgasm? Definitely worth the risk.

Her search through the bathroom was more successful. In the hamper, under the false bottom she had installed, she found a half-empty bottle of codeine cough syrup and some diet pills. She'd forgotten about those. No wonder; they expired in 2009. What the hell. A little of this, a little of that, topped off with a mouthwash chaser. Life was good.

♦♦♦

"You're kidding. They wanted your autograph? That's amazing, Sis." Maggie put the phone on speaker so she could continue laying out possible outfits for the trip. She had ten days to finalize what she was taking. "Really? You're going to be the entertainment on the boat? Wow." Dear God. Maybe going on this cruise wasn't the best idea. She was thrilled for Cheryl, of course, but being in the shadow of "The Star" for a week would be tough. Even though she'd been working on bolstering her self-esteem—losing weight, getting her hair highlighted, wearing makeup and a bra most of the time—Maggie's insecurities were still very close to the surface. She'd always felt the need to compete with Cheryl. Unfortunately, in that race, Maggie usually crossed the finish line last.

"Hello? You there? I said, have you booked your flight yet? I can't wait to see you. I have all the cruise info for you and Rhoda."

Maggie came back to the present. How could you be jealous of such a sweetheart? Shame embraced inferiority. "Awww, Sis. That's so sweet. My flight gets in at 8:45 a.m. on the 28th. It'll take me a while to get the car, and then, I'll head to your house. I thought we could grab breakfast before we go get Rhoda. If I remember right, there aren't many good places to eat on the way to Eugenia. Unless you want to stop over in White Springs. There's a great barbeque joint there."

"Why don't I pick you up at the airport? You can rent a car right next door to my condo for a lot less, and we can eat something here. It'll take at least four hours to get to the ship by the time we detour to Rhoda's. She probably hasn't even packed yet, so we'll lose a good hour at her house. Have you talked to her lately?"

"Not since last week. Why?" Maggie worried. It was never a good sign when Rhoda went underground.

"I don't know. I haven't heard much either. I got a text from her the other night. You know, the typical, 'sleep tight XOXO,' but that's been it. I hope she's not using again."

"I'll try her today and see how she sounds. If she's acting funny on the boat, we'll have to talk to her. Let's hope it's nothing."

"Yes," Cheryl agreed. "Happy thoughts."

Pollyanna strikes again. "I'll let you know after I talk to her. I hope she's okay."

"Me, too, Mags. See you soon. Love you."

"Love you, too." Maggie slumped onto the couch. She'd been excited about the trip at first. The three sisters had such a great time when they vacationed together. But a fog of despair threatened to consume her. Cheryl would command all the attention, and all the decent men, on the boat. And Rhoda. God only knew what shape she would be in, but if she was using again, she would be furtive and erratic. Once again, Maggie imagined herself in the caretaker mode, supporting Cheryl's success and scrutinizing Rhoda's every move, as she, herself, faded into the background.

♦♦♦

The hot sun pierced Rhoda's skull—the skull that absolutely could not be lifted off the bed. She opened one eye and took inventory. She was on her mattress, but the mattress was in front of the window. In fact, it was hanging off the bedframe. Huh. Deep breath. She looked around the room. Drawers open, stuffed garbage bags in the doorway. Oh, yeah. The drugs. Note to self: do not take everything at once again. Ever. What day was it? What time was it?

At that very thought, the phone rang. She heaved herself to the side of the mattress and grabbed it from the dresser. "-lo?" Her lips were so dry she could barely form words.

"Hey. You okay?"

Rhoda looked at the screen to see who was calling. "Oh, hey, Mags. Yeah, I'm fine." She had to pull it together or at least fake it. "What's up?"

"Nothing. I just hadn't heard from you for a while. Have you started packing for the cruise?"

Shit. The trip. When was that? What day was it now? Again, she checked her phone. March 17th. "Isn't that like two weeks away?" She stood up and staggered toward the kitchen. Sweet tea would help.

"Eleven days, but who's counting, right?"

"Right." Rhoda gulped four Advil. "That's the 28th, right? What time will we leave?"

"Probably around lunch time. My flight gets in to Tally at 8:45 and it'll take us a few hours to get to your place. I think we have to be on the boat by 4:00 or 5:00 that afternoon. What are you, an hour from Jacksonville?"

"A little more than that, especially with traffic.

Jacksonville's the worst."

Chapter 8

His back flat against the soot-covered brick wall, Special Agent Marvin Whitcomb peered around the corner of the abandoned building. The alley looked empty, but the shadows were deep. Anyone could be hiding out there. Footsteps? His brow furrowed. Silently he pulled the Baretta from his waistband and fitted the silencer. The steps grew louder, the pace faster. He raised his weapon, squinting through the site ...

"Mr. Whitcomb? What are you doing with your arms up like that? Are you threatening me?"

Marvin looked past his outstretched arms and cocked fingers into the face of Dr. Antonio Martinez. The psychiatrist. Shit. This was supposed to be his last meeting. "Um, what? No, no," he laughed. "That's a calming pose I learned in my yoga class. I think it's called Barnavaka or something like that." Thank God that nut in his addict group told him about yoga.

"Interesting." The doctor scribbled something on his stupid pad. "I'm impressed. Yoga is a good way for you to control your emotions and focus on the present, like we discussed."

"Well, you know, Doc. I'm trying as hard as I can." Please, let him give me the Certificate of Completion. Please. "And I gotta say, I'm feeling a whole lot better. Much calmer." He hoped lightning didn't strike him right there in the office.

"Good. Good. I do think you've made some progress. It was a slow start, but it seems you're headed in a positive direction. How's the group therapy going?"

"Excellent. Great people." Bunch of bums. He didn't know there were so many kinds of addictions. Drugs, alcohol, cigarettes, even sex. That was the yoga girl. Nothing better than a flexible nymphomaniac. She's the only reason he kept going to the meetings. She wasn't much to look at, but, hey.

"Technically, you have fulfilled the terms of your release from Halos of Help, so I'll go ahead and sign your Certificate of Completion. However, I think you should continue with the group therapy and monthly meetings with me." Dr. Martinez slid an appointment card across the desk. "And here's a prescription for Celexa. That should even out the highs and lows. But be sure and give it a few weeks before giving up. It takes a while for your system to get used to it."

Over his dead body. "Sure. Like I said, I think this has all been very helpful."

After a strong handshake, Martin walked out of the office with the certificate. That, he would hold on to. At least until he met his girls for lunch. The appointment card was going in the trash as soon as he got home. He might as well fill the scrip. Might come in handy someday.

The breeze was light coming off the water at the Camanchee Harbor restaurant. He was tempted to order a drink, but decided against it.

"Oh, Dad," his oldest daughter, Maryann, held the certificate and wiped tears from her eyes. "We're so proud of you."

Lisa, the youngest, leaned down and hugged

him breathless. "We are. Three weeks sober. I knew you could do it. And, like I promised, we have a surprise for you." She handed him a thick envelope with a picture of Ponce de Leon on the front.

"What's this? Free admission to the Fountain of Youth?" Marvin hated when his girls bought him a present. It was always something feminine and fussy. Or stupid, like this tacky tourist trap.

They both laughed. "No, Dad. Open it."

Unsealing the packet, he found a folder inside with a picture of a boat on the front. He looked at them both. "A cruise?" Ann had always wanted to go on a cruise, but Marvin had begged off. Too many activities; too much shopping. Sounded like women's stuff to him.

"Yes," Lisa squealed with delight. "It's a small river cruise, only a hundred or so people on board. And it's only for five nights. But the best part is, it's a singles cruise — a Boomers/GenXers Mixer, see?" She opened the folder and pulled out the itinerary. "You said you were lonely, Dad. This might just be the thing you're looking for."

He'd actually been thinking about the nympho-yoga lady, but maybe a singles cruise wouldn't be so bad. "Well, isn't this something." He chuckled. "I'm really touched. But you don't need to spend your money on me. Let me pay for it."

"No way. We want you feeling obligated to us," Maryann said. "If you paid for it, you'd end up not going."

She was right. "Okay, okay. When is it?"

"It leaves from the port in three days, March 28th. You don't have enough time to come up with an excuse. You just have time to pack all your *GQ*-looking clothes."

"Where does it go?"

"On the St. Johns, the Intracoastal and the Tolomato River. It stops every day and most nights, and there are different excursions at each stop. One stop used to be a World War II naval station and another has a wildlife refuge. Right up your alley, Dad."

The girls were both so excited, he couldn't disappoint them.

"Well, it sounds great. Really." His eyes fogged and his throat caught. "Thanks. I love you both more than anything. You know that, right?"

Tears flowed as they threw themselves at him. "We love you too, Dad."

They looked through the information as they ate their lunch. Maryann read off all the activities available each day. "If you don't want to go on an excursion, there's a water painting class, a canasta group, and ballroom dance lessons."

Sounded kind of fuddy-duddy, but the dancing might be good. At least he could hold on to a woman for a while.

"Oh, look," Maryann pointed at the paper. "There's an AA meeting every morning."

There it was. He could feel his blood pressure rise. Deep breath. Just go along. They meant well. "Sure. Sounds like they have something for everyone. It'll be fun." At least he wouldn't have to present a certificate of completion afterward.

◆◆◆

Over the last week, Rhoda had hauled off trunks-full of clothes, books, electronics, and any salvageable junk in the yard and carport. She'd sold whatever she could to Vern and had given the food kitchen at the church the giant cans of baked beans Lute hoarded for the revolution. Things were going well until yesterday. Her Prozac, cough syrup and Ambien were gone; only a single diet pill remained. While not exactly the high she was hoping for, it served its purpose. Abuzz with amphetamine-energy, Rhoda cleaned the living hell out of the place. She scrubbed the empty drawers, closets, cabinets, bathrooms, kitchen, floors, walls, and even the windows. The place was almost livable.

Shortly after 9:00 a.m., Rhoda heard a knock at the door. On the stoop stood a lanky twenty-something with a stringy mullet. "Mr. Crapps?"

"Yes, ma'am. That's me. Delmont Crapps."

Despite the sweat-stained ball cap and the faded tee shirt, the kid had an earnest smile. Rhoda opened the door. "Come on in. Let me show you around." She led him into the kitchen first. One cabinet door was missing and the contact paper on the wall had started to peel. "The appliances are included in the price." She didn't mention that the refrigerator insulation was home to a large family of German cockroaches. "In fact, the place comes fully furnished, with everything you see here."

Delmont's eyes grew wide as he walked around the room. "Dang. This is a lot nicer than mine. You got lots more room in here. A four burner stove? And a table and chairs? Ain't that somethin'?"

And here Rhoda thought she had the worst

trailer in town. "Let me show you the summer porch." She led him down the steps from the kitchen to the screened and jalousied room that opened out to the carport. "This is especially nice when it gets too buggy outside."

Delmont's mouth hung open. "Wow."

The lack of questions and his awe at the beauty and splendor of the place led Rhoda to believe Delmont was not a working professional. He didn't even flinch at the plastic kiddie pool that replaced the shower pan.

"I wouldn't even have to clean that. I could just go get me a new one."

"So, what do you think? Are you interested?"

"Yes, ma'am. I never dreamed I could afford somethin' this nice."

Rhoda doubted he could. "Will you be getting a loan from the bank, Mr. Crapps?"

"No, ma'am. I don't trust no banks. I'll be payin' in cash."

"You know the price is five-thousand dollars, right?" Surely this kid didn't have that kind of money.

"Yes, ma'am. I'm all set."

"Where do you work?"

"I don't have me a job anymore, but my first disability check just come in the mail. I got hurt when the crabbin' boat I worked on blowed up."

Oh shit. He must have worked for Lute. It was just over a year ago that Lute had come home with another get-rich-quick-scheme, pulling a ramshackle crabber behind his truck saying, "I prayed to Jesus to show me how to monetize my love of the water, and next thing I knew, I found this boat for sale." She was furious at the time. He never had any money for her or the house, but he always found enough to invest in some fly-by-night scheme. The damned thing sank after only a few trips, and shortly after that, he disappeared. She remembered hearing someone was seriously injured when the boat went down, but when Lute left, she never gave it another thought. The boat hadn't been in her name, thank God. When letters from environmental and government agencies came addressed to him, she wrote, "No such person at this address" and sent them back.

Delmont puffed out his chest. "I can afford it even without that government money. My brother, when he left town about a year ago, gave me a bunch of gold bars, so I went up to Vern's. He told me they was worth almost ten thousand dollars."

Rhoda's inner radar screamed. Gold bars? There was definitely a Lute connection, but she wasn't going to bring it up. "That's just great. Are you able to move the whole thing to your location?"

"Yes, ma'am. My fiancé, Ramona Chance, she said her uncle has a big rig that can haul everything over to my place."

Ramona Chance. The choir director's daughter. The one Lute was accused of sexually assaulting. Jesus. She was glad she'd used her maiden name on the poster and especially glad this guy was dumber than a stump. He obviously hadn't made the connection. Yet.

"I can give you the money today, but I don't think I can get the truck over here 'til the first of the month."

Perfect. She'd be on that cruise while the move

took place. "Great. I've got the title here in my desk. I think we both just need to sign it, and then, you'll need to register it with the DMV."

"Huh?"

"The Department of Motor Vehicles. Even though it's a trailer, you have to register it through them. It's not a big deal. You just to take this to the office over in Starke and register it there." She looked at his blank expression. "I'll write down the address and phone number for you." She did not want him to get spooked and walk away. "Do you need a ride?"

"That'd be real nice, Miz Lennon. I don't have no car."

Chapter 9

Lester fought like he'd never fought before. After leveling up to Victor Charlie, he found himself in bullet hell, enemy operatives coming at him from all sides. One wrong move and he'd end up in the bottomless pit. He couldn't let his comrades down now.

The door to the den flew open. "Answer me when I'm calling you."

"BRB." Lester pulled off his headphones and paused his character, who was glowing red from a possible mortal wound. "Whaddaya want, Ma?"

"What's BRB? Some code? What are you doing?"

"It means be right back. I'm playing a game. What is it?"

"I just saw that letter you got from those Wackenhut people two weeks ago. I can't believe you haven't gone to get that gun back yet. It's not like you have anything else to do, except leech off me."

Had it really been two weeks?

Lester put the headphones back on and reentered the game. His character stared down the site of hand-held rocket launcher. Game over.

"Quit ignoring me." His mother reached over and grabbed the controller from his hands. "Turn off that stupid TV, and go get the gun."

Surrendering onscreen and in life, he stood up. "Okay. I'll go today. Are you happy?"

"That's a good boy. Be sure and dress nice,

just in case they've changed their minds about rehiring you."

If he only had the gun now. "Yes, Mother." Despondent but obedient, he took off his *Call of Duty: Black Ops* tee shirt and gym shorts and found a clean polo and cargo pants. "Hey, Ma. Can you give me a ride?"

"You're twenty-four. Get a license."

The only way Lester could get to the port was to take his bike on the bus as far as the zoo, then ride five miles to the Wackenhut office in the cruise terminal. He hadn't ridden five miles on a bike since he was a kid in Cub Scouts. In fact, he didn't make the five miles then. But he wanted that gun back, and more, he wanted to show his mom he could take care of things himself.

By the time he panted to a stop at the JaxPort, he was beyond overheated. How long had it been since he'd been out in the sun? Stashing his bike, he headed to the restroom. They'd never give him his gun the way he looked, face crimson, hair dripping, shirt soaked. While his shirt dried on the hand dryer, he splashed water on his face and raked fingers through his hair. At least he didn't look homeless anymore.

In the lobby, a guard (in a uniform just like the one he used to have) gave him directions to the office.

"My name's Lester Nusbaum." He pulled the wrinkled letter from his pants pocket. "I think you have my gun here? I got this letter saying I could come pick it up."

The broad-shouldered woman at the desk— same uniform—took the damp letter between two fingertips and read it. "I see. Do you have your driver's license?"

His mom was right. He had to learn to drive. "No, but I have a passport." His ex-girlfriend took him on a trip to Nassau after high school. Fortunately, the passport had a few years before it expired.

"What about your concealed-carry permit?"

He dug the card from his wallet and slid it across the counter.

The woman reviewed his I.D.s and disappeared through a door behind the counter. Minutes later, she reappeared with his gun. "You'll need to sign these forms."

He signed by the X and took the gun. "Thank you, ma'am. Is Officer Weismueller in? I was hoping to talk to him about giving me another chance."

She looked at him over the top of her readers. "No. Mr. Weismueller is not available. You'll have to call and set up an appointment."

At that very second, the door opened and Officer Weismueller walked through. "Did you need me?"

The now scarlet woman sputtered, "No, um, this young man was asking to see you. I said he needed an appointment."

The officer looked at Lester. "Don't I know you? You look familiar."

Beads of sweat frosted Lester's forehead. "Yes, sir. I used to work here. Lester Nusbaum? I mistakenly carried a gun when I worked at the port?"

"Oh, yes. I remember that. What did you want to see me about?"

"Well, sir, um, I was hoping I could try again. I

promise not to make the same mistake. I really liked working here. It was my dream job." Except for standing all day in the sun.

Officer Weismueller waved Lester over to the edge of the desk. "I'm sorry, son. I would if I could, but we have very strict rules and regulations here. However, you seem like a nice enough guy. I could give you a generic letter verifying your employment here, without mentioning the reason for your dismissal."

"Wow. That'd be great. Thank you, sir."

After a half hour, the snooty lady at the desk handed him a form letter, "To Whom It May Concern," with his own name written on the blank line. Thanking her, he put the gun in one of the many pockets of his pants, carefully held the letter, and headed back out into the blistering heat, reading as he walked along the pavement.

"Heads up, mister!"

Lester looked up to see a large boat alongside the dock lowering a gang plank directly in front of him. As soon as it was secured, several young men and women in matching pants and shirts scurried across it. They quickly set up a canopy-type tent and a small folding table, decorated it with green and gold draping, and arranged cloth bags with a picture of Ponce de Leon on the front. Despite the heat, Lester was curious to find out what they were preparing for. A festival? A promotional event?

"Rita," a man in a captain's uniform strode off the boat and pointed to one of the young women. "Take this flyer and put it on that boarding sign next to the gang plank immediately. We sail again this afternoon, and we need to fill that Security Detail position today."

Lester started to turn away, but stopped himself. This was his chance. Fate dropped this opportunity, literally, at his feet, as he stood holding the key to success. He straightened up, walked over to the captain, and extended the letter. "Excuse me, sir. I don't think you're going to need to advertise that position."

Chapter 10

"Ladies and gentlemen, as we begin our final descent into Tallahassee, please make sure your seatbacks and tray tables are in their upright position and your seatbelt is securely fastened. Place all carry-on items under the seat in front of you or in the overhead bins."

When the plane rolled to a stop, Maggie gathered her things and joined the scrum in the aisle to deboard. After weeks of eating nothing but kale and quinoa and spending more than she could afford on clothes and a Brazilian blow-out, she felt energized. Even though Cheryl would be more gorgeous, there were sure to be enough men left over on the cruise for her. Plus, her fear of being the caretaker for both sisters had waned.

Her attitude had changed the day she talked to the school psych. "I don't think I should go. Having fun is hard."

"What?"

"All those social mixers and activities and excursions. You know how it is with the girls and me. I'll probably just be a huge wallflower while every man is drooling on Cheryl, and Rhoda's off doing God knows what."

"Having fun is hard? Listen to yourself, Maggie. You're awfulizing what should be the trip of a lifetime. And look at you, creamy complexion, big bright eyes, and that adorable nose. If you're a wallflower, it's your own fault, not theirs. You love your sisters, right?"

"Of course."

"And you enjoy being together?"

"Yes."

"Then, stop this nonsense and go. Relax. Enjoy."

She did, and she would. The new Maggie was ready to shine.

After collecting her checked bag, she stepped outside into the three-hundred percent humidity. That ought to put the expensive hair treatment to the test. The salon said her hair would stay straight and shiny for twelve weeks if she used the overpriced products they sold her. She spotted Cheryl standing by her car, holding a sign that said, "Lemon Sisters Adventure Starts Now." Good old Sis. Always so happy and positive. And thin and perfect.

"Yoo-hoo! Maggie. Over here." Cheryl hugged and air-kissed her. "Look at you, you foxy thing. Love the hair and the outfit. Is that GAP?"

"Good eye. You look great, too. Kors?"

"This?" Cheryl struck a pose to show off her sleek, crisp linen jumpsuit. "No. I got this off the rack. But I thought it was so summery. It just screamed cruise."

"It's perfect." Not jealous.

"Uh-oh." Cheryl grabbed Maggie's bag. "Better jump in. That Segway cop's got a bead on us. He's been eyeing me for ten minutes."

Cheryl drove Maggie to the car rental agency near her house. "It's so much cheaper than getting it at the airport. You can follow me home, I'll grab my bags, and we'll be on our way."

"Seems like a lot of extra effort to save a few dollars," Maggie said, "but that's okay. More to spend in the shops on the boat."

Before leaving town, they stopped at the Tally Tearoom for a quick breakfast. Though she really wanted the caramel apple pancakes, Maggie followed Cheryl's lead and ordered the fruit bowl and avocado toast. There would be plenty of rich calories to consume on the boat.

"Here's your Boomers/GenXers' Singles cruise packet." Cheryl pulled a large envelope from her bag and handed it to Maggie. "It has your luggage tags, your ID lanyard, the itinerary, and, get this. There's a dating profile questionnaire we're supposed to hand in tonight. This is such a hoot!"

"Let's see—one conquistador-helmet name badge?" Maggie pulled out the lanyard.

"It's the logo for the Ponce de Leon Cruise Line. See, I have one, too."

"Why is mine green and yours is glittering gold?"

"Because I'm the star attraction, of course." Cheryl flipped her frizz-defiant hair over her shoulder.

Deep breath. Happy for her. "Of course." It is her cruise. "Next, we have the itinerary. Wow, look at all these mixers—cocktail hour every night, speed-date breakfast, scavenger hunt with your best match, and a sock hop the last night of the cruise."

"Don't forget the after-dinner entertainment. Look," Cheryl held up her highlighted itinerary. "I'm the featured singer three of the five nights. I still can't believe I won that contest."

Yes, she sure did. And well-deserved. "It's

about time. You should have won last year, but they couldn't have chosen anyone else this time." Maggie reached across the table and grabbed her hand. "You were spectacular."

Cheryl's eyes teared. "Awww, thanks, Mags. And thanks for all your support over the years." She wiped her eyes and nose with a tissue. "Okay, enough about me — can you believe I'm saying that? Have you heard from Rhoda?"

"Not much. The last I talked to her was after my disastrous date with Lawrence Welk. Other than that, we've only texted. She said she sold her old trailer and bought some new clothes for the trip."

"Can you believe someone bought that heap? Good for her, though. I talked to her about a week ago. She's sounded a little wacky since Ben left. I hope she's not using again."

"Me, too. We'll have a better idea when we see her. If she is, what do we do?"

"I guess we could have an intervention. It's not like she can get too far away from us on a boat."

"I hope she's okay. Nothing like a drug intervention to really perk up a vacation."

Cheryl touched her cross necklace. "We'll just have to pray extra hard on that."

◆◆◆

Marvin would never tell the girls, but he was pretty excited about the cruise. He had a brief stab of guilt that he'd never taken Ann on one. He would have, eventually. But that's not how things worked out. Now, here he was, packing for a singles' cruise. The girls had to explain to him that a GenXer was between

70

forty and fifty-five, hardworking, tech savvy, but still not afraid to read a book or newspaper. His youngest daughter had forced him to open a Facebook account because "all the GenXers use it." It would be a way to keep in touch if he met anyone interesting. Wouldn't that be something? A companion, a friend?

A good first impression was critical. He looked in the mirror. Not bad. His silver hair was full and wavy. It had been chestnut brown once, but he knew a headful of any color hair was a turn on for women over fifty. His dark brown eyes were untinged by cataracts, and he preferred to call his crow's feet laugh lines. He was definitely dateable.

Marvin surveyed the clothes on his bed: a blazer, a gray flannel, and a Madras sport coat. That ought to do it for jackets. He could get two or three nights out of the blazer. They would all go with pants or even his jeans. He added some shirts, including his favorite guayabera, shorts, and of course, the Brooks Brothers pajamas. Satisfied he'd cut a dashing figure, he was ready to pack up.

He got out his biggest suitcase and put a carton of cigarettes, the condoms, and a pint of Heaven Hill inside his shoes underneath all the clothes.

"Hey. Anybody home? Dad?"

He zipped up the bag, grabbed his dopp kit, put on his Panama fedora, and walked into the living room. "What do you think?"

"Very dapper. Are you excited?"

"Actually, I am. It'll be nice to get away from the store and this house for a while. Thanks again."

"Our pleasure. Ready to go?"

Marvin tipped his hat and gave a sly wink. "I

was born ready."

♦♦♦

Rhoda heard honking and walked outside. At the bottom of the steps stood Cheryl holding a Lemon-Sisters'-Adventure-Starts-Now sign and Maggie with three cartoon-character balloons. "Spongebob, Mags?"

"He's yellow, at least. They didn't have any lemon-shaped ones. And just like his motto, this is going to be 'The Best Day Ever'!"

Rhoda's eye twitched. Could she stand a whole week with these two, straight? "Well, then, let's get started. Come on in while I grab my stuff."

Both girls remarked how much better the place looked than it did a year ago.

"I've been cleaning the hell out of it. But I got it sold and put a down payment on that double wide. It's supposed to be delivered the day I get back."

"Good for you, Rho. A whole new start," Maggie said.

"Speaking of new starts," Rhoda set down her suitcases and did a small twirl. "Do you like my outfit? I splurged and went shopping in Gainesville. They had a Ross's and a Burlington Factory Outlet. Starke doesn't have anything that nice."

Cheryl clapped. "Fabulous, darling. A wrap-dress with a flutter sleeve is so slenderizing. And look at your hair."

Maggie agreed. "Love the spiky pixie cut on you. Did you get highlights?"

Rhoda scrunched her hair. "I did. I always thought I was too broad-shouldered for a pixie, but I love it. And it's so cool. I don't sweat so much when

I'm getting ready."

"Gorge. In fact, we all look marvelous. We'll be fighting men off with a stick," Cheryl said, "if we make it to the boat on time. Let's go because the ..." she held up the sign.

"... Lemon Sisters' Adventure Starts Now," they shouted in unison.

Rhoda took the back seat. She needed a little space before the three of them were crammed in a stateroom for six days. As the scrub pine and live oaks whizzed by, she tried to envision what the Year of Rhoda would look like. A new start wasn't very likely in Eugenia. Without Ben, the town was just a boring crossroads between the Oolehatchee Swamp and the St. Johns River. The most exciting events in the area were usually executions at the Florida State prison, notorious for its population of the violent and criminally insane. The proximity of so many dangerous criminals never worried Rhoda before, but now, alone in a tin can on the edge of a swamp, she felt vulnerable in a way she never had before. Her nerves were raw, and the happy banter in the front seat didn't help. Nor did the balloons, which of course, ended up in the back seat with her. She lit a cigarette and rolled down the window.

The three Spongebob's immediately pummeled Maggie as she drove. "Jesus, Rho. I'm going to wreck. And look at my hair. I don't think the Brazilian Blow Out people ever considered the effect of mylar-induced static." She looked in the rearview mirror. "I look like I stuck my finger in an outlet."

"Sorry, sorry. I just cracked the window. I didn't think it would cause that much wind." She took a long drag off the cigarette and flicked it outside. "I'll roll it back up." Not used to automatic windows, she pushed the button the wrong way. The three balloons were instantly sucked out.

"There they go," Cheryl said. "The brothers-Spongebob are going to beat us to the boat."

Maggie honked goodbye to the balloons. "Speaking of—what are we going to do when we get onboard? I mean, I know we have to fill out our dating profiles, but I'd like to relax by the pool while it's still daylight. I'm coming from cold weather, remember. Has anybody seen any pictures of the ship? I tried to find it online once but then got too busy."

"I've just seen a picture of the outside. I'm sure it'll be really nice, though. I want to check out the lounge, see how the stage is set up where I'll be performing." Cheryl pulled a list from her purse and handed it to Rhoda. "These are the songs I want to do. What do you think?"

Rhoda studied the list. "These are good, if you get a choice. I can play piano for you if I have to, but I'd rather not. I thought I'd go to the spa to get a massage and a pedicure. These big feet need some attention if I'm going to wear all my new sandals."

While the girls in front discussed going to the casino, working out in the gym, and taking yoga classes, Rhoda wondered if there was a clinic or at least a dispensary on the ship. If not, there should be plenty of bars and lounges around. Thinking about it made her even more edgy. She rolled down the window and inhaled another cigarette. Nicotine was going to have to work for a while.

Chapter 11

"Hey, Ma. Can you give me a ride to the port?"

"Where do you think you're going? On one of those casino boats? I'm not gonna lift a finger to help you lose money you don't have. The only ride I'll give you is to a job interview."

Ha. "I wish I'd known that earlier," Lester reached in his pocket and took out his name badge. "I already went to the interview and got the job." He loved watching her mouth drop open.

"You got a job? Doing what? What's this, a real name tag?" She put on her glasses and read. "Ponce de Leon Cruise Lines, Lester Nusbaum, Security. Oh my God. That's my boy." She grabbed him in a blubbering bear hug. "I knew you could do it. Is it permanent? When does it start?"

He pried her off and picked up his bag. "I'm the security guard on a river cruise. For now, it's provisional, but if I do a good job, they said they'd hire me on a permanent basis. The pay isn't great, but I get room and board, and I get to travel. All the crew members are about my age, except for the captain."

"What's with the bag? Are you going to be gone overnight?"

"I'll be gone for a week. And if things go well, I could be gone for a few weeks at a time, depending on the cruise."

"It's like I'm getting a raise, not having to feed you all the time. Good for you, Les. You start today?"

"Yep. They were so impressed with my skills, they hired me on the spot." She didn't need to know they were desperate for a replacement.

"I hope you don't have that stupid gun in that bag. Remember what happened last time."

"I remember, Ma. My gun's in the safe. Let's go. I have to be on the boat by 3:00 p.m."

◆◆◆

"Hit it, girls," Cheryl said as they pulled off I95 toward the cruise terminal. "One more round of 'Cruising Down the River.'"

Rhoda squeezed the oh-shit handle above the door even harder. Cheryl had been singing that old song for the last twenty minutes, laughing and slapping Maggie on the arm every time she got to the line about the accordion playing. "I think ten rounds are enough, Cher."

Maggie winked at Rhoda in the rearview mirror. "Agreed. We have to start looking for the car rental return anyway. Let me know where to turn."

Cheryl's bottom lip stuck out. "You guys are no fun. As soon as we get on the boat, we'll get everybody going on 'Proud Mary' as we roll down the river."

"Sure, Cher." Rhoda had to find the bar first thing.

After the girls got their luggage and tipped the driver, they turned toward the dock. "Wow," the three said at once. A sparkling monster of a cruise ship towered before them.

Cheryl's eyes grew wide. "It's amazing. I bet it holds a thousand people. I'll be performing before hundreds at a time."

Maggie read from her itinerary. "I don't think this is ours. Ours only holds about a hundred and fifty. Maybe there's another ship behind it."

"Oh, you're right," Cheryl said. "This one says *Ecstasy*." She dragged her luggage past the mammoth ship. The next boat, clearly labeled *Forever Young,* looked like a dingy by comparison. "Oh, my. It's a lot smaller than I thought."

Maggie looked at the vessel before them. "Looks more like a yacht than a cruise ship."

"Or a fishing trawler," Rhoda said as she limped behind them. Walking across the parking lot and the dock aggravated the leg she broke last year. She hurt, she was hot, and she was stunned as she stared at their home for the week. Green and gold paint barely hid rusty stains that rimmed the waterline. Cloudy portholes reflected little light. Was she destined to spend her life in subpar accommodations? Only a few of the four decks had full-length windows.

"I don't see any balconies." Cheryl frowned. Seconds later, she inhaled deeply and flashed a brilliant smile. "For the Glad List, there's a nice sun deck on top. And those long, sleek windows must be where I'll be singing. This is going to be great."

Maggie nodded. "It is. Very intimate. I've heard those big ships have wild twenty-somethings slamming shots and puking on the decks. This will be much better."

Rhoda's mouth formed a straight line. "Yeah. Much better."

Reaching into her Coach carryall, Cheryl extracted her selfie stick. "Rust bucket or not, ladies, we are going to rock this boat! Everybody lean in, hand on hip, right leg in front, body angled, head tilted slightly, and say…"

Rhoda staggered, laughing. "What kind of contortionist do you think I am? I can't remember all that."

Also trying to maintain her balance, Maggie snorted. "Say COUGARS."

The three collapsed on each other after Cheryl snapped the picture. "That's going to be a keeper."

Before they reached the gangplank, a uniformed man rushed to meet them. "Welcome, ladies. I see you've already drunk from the fountain of youth. What a delight it will be to have beauty and vitality aboard. Your names, please?"

"We're the Lennon sisters," Cheryl said. "And one Mason."

He snapped his fingers and a similarly clad minion rushed up and took their bags. "Jackson here will put your belongings in your state room. You'll need to find and wear your nametag lanyards at all times, especially when you leave the boat. You will not be allowed to reenter without it. There are drinks and hors d'oeuvres at the end of this hall, so help yourself. And don't forget, bring your dating profiles to the muster this afternoon."

The girls opened their cruise packets and donned their lanyards.

At the word drinks, Rhoda was halfway across the gangplank. "Let's go find those refreshments." Sweat dripped from her pixie bangs down her face, causing mascara to raccoon her eyes. So much for the new, hip Rhoda.

As soon as their eyes adjusted from the bright sun to the boat's interior, they looked up and down the halls. Polished brass rails lined the walls and stairwells. Clean, tropical-flowered carpet brightened the floors, and sparkling chandeliers hung in the dining room. Coral-colored silk upholstered dining chairs gave the room a warm yet cheery look.

"This is beautiful," Cheryl said. "Much more like I envisioned. In fact, I'm glad we're not on that big ship. This looks so elegant and refined. Classy, just like us. And look. Here're the food and beverages he mentioned." She inspected the selections. "Elixir of Youth cocktails, Shrimp Puff Doubloons, and La Florida Petit Fours. How fun."

Rhoda slammed back two Elixers and turned to the girls. "Classy and fun would be nice for a change. We don't get a lot of that in Eugenia. Maybe we'll meet some rich bachelors on this thing."

"It really is gorgeous. We're going to have a great time," Maggie said. "Do you want to go straight to our room or explore the ship?"

Exploring the ship was definitely on Rhoda's to-do list, but she'd rather go alone. First, she wanted to find the clinic or dispensary, and then, find all the bars on this thing. "I vote for checking the place out. In fact, why don't we split up, each take a different floor, then meet up at the room?"

"I'll take the sun deck on top," Maggie said. "I want to see the pool and recreation areas."

Cheryl flipped her hair over her shoulder. "I have to see the lounge where I'll be performing. I want to check the acoustics and the stage configuration. Hopefully, it's accessible to the audience. I love to walk around and interact with people while I'm singing."

Perfect. They both had places to go. "If you see anybody there, Cheryl, ask them about your accompaniment," Rhoda said. "I'll play if I have to, but they probably have a real professional on staff."

Cheryl nodded. "Will do. Let's all meet back in the room in about a half hour. That'll give us time to fill out our profiles and get gussied up before we meet all these hot guys."

♦♦♦

"Now, remember, Dad. Relax and have fun. Be sure and take that medicine the doctor gave you. Every day."

"I hate that stuff. It makes me feel funny."

"Take it anyway," Lisa said. "In a few weeks, you'll feel like a new person."

Marvin didn't want to be a new person. He was okay. It was everybody else that had a problem.

"Here we are." Lisa pulled up to the loading zone. "*Forever Young*. I love it. It looks like a nice boat."

Marvin got out and stood, taking in the ship. It looked sea-worthy; had all the essentials. Could use a little spit and polish, though. Must be a lazy captain. If Captain Whitcomb were in charge, this baby would shine. He'd whip that crew into shape in no time.

"Here, put your lanyard on." Lisa hung the name tag around his neck. "Have a great time, Dad. I love you."

"Love you, too, Punkin."

"Mr. Whitcomb, I see." A young kid in a Ponce

de Leon polo came and grabbed his bags. "Welcome to *Forever Young.* I'll take these and put them in your room. Do you need any assistance getting on board?"

"No, thanks. I'm fine." Assistance? Weasely little upstart.

"Great. Help yourself to the hors d'oeuvres and the Elixir of Youth cocktails in the main lounge."

Lisa frowned.

"We leave port at 5:15. You probably have time for a nap, if you'd like." The kid scampered off with his bags.

A nap? Jesus.

Lisa grabbed him in a hug. "I'm going to go now, but you have a good time. And, Dad? Remember, there's an AA meeting every morning."

Pssshaw. "Sure, baby. Thanks, again." Marvin waved goodbye and walked, quite ably, onto the boat. "Where's the main lounge?" he asked one of the dozens of polo-shirted staff.

"Straight down this hall, sir."

"Thanks." He found the room where waiters were frantically setting up for dinner. A bar in the back held said appetizers and drinks. He grabbed one of each and headed for his room. The Elixir of Youth had no more than a thimble full of booze, if that. Should have grabbed two. No problem. He could goose it up with some of his Heaven Hill.

His room was on the lower deck. No window. Not even a porthole. A NO SMOKING sign the size of his head hung on the wall. This is what you get when your kids pay for your vacation. Never mind. There were plenty of open decks. He only planned to be in the room to sleep and, hopefully...

81

♦♦♦

"All right, Nusbaum. Suck in that gut, tuck in your shirt and follow me." The ship's cruise director, who sounded like Glenda the Good Witch when greeting customers, bellowed like an army sergeant. "Since you just got hired this morning, I'm going to have to give you a crash course on keeping the boat and its passengers secure. Remember, passengers are the first priority."

He glanced at her badge. "Yes, ma'am, Miss Reinhart."

"Ms. Reinhart, and smile when you say that. Always smile when you address another human being."

Lester stretched his lips over his teeth. "Yes, ma'am." She sounded like his mother.

"The security office is here on the lower deck. Being the only deck that provides access to land or other watercraft, it's the first line of defense against outside intruders." At the end of the hall, they reached a door labeled STAFF ONLY. "Here's one of three key cards that open this door. Don't lose it. Keep it on your lanyard at all times, and do not, I repeat, do not let anyone else use it."

Finally, a position with a little respect, some authority. Lester puffed out his chest, swiped the card across the key pad, and heard the click.

The cruise director opened the door. "In here, we have monitors linked to security cameras on each floor. Only the public spaces, halls, lounges, libraries, and so forth, have cameras. You and the assistant hotel manager will review these monitors during the overnight and early morning hours when most of the guests are sleeping. Otherwise, when the ship is in port, I expect you to be on the gangway, checking passengers' IDs. If a person tries to board without proper identification, escort them back to the dock. You will also need to check vendors' IDs against the cargo manifest and personally accompany them to the correct location, usually the kitchen. Any questions?"

"Where's the manifest?"

"You'll be given a copy each morning that will list the vendors expected that day."

"Is that all I'll be doing?"

"God no, man. That's the easy part. The rest of the time you should patrol every area of the ship. If you see any suspicious behavior by a passenger or other crew member, report it to me immediately. Obviously, a tipsy passenger isn't cause for alarm, and don't interfere if two passengers decide they want to play a little slap-and-tickle. That's expected on a singles' cruise. But if one person is resisting the pursuer, break them up, and escort the resister back to his or her room."

"Does that happen a lot?"

"No, but I'm required to alert you to the possibility," Reinhart said as she moved toward a closet in the back of the room and opened the door with her key card. "No one else, except the three key holders and the captain, knows about the contents of this closet."

Lester looked on as she opened a large case. In it were two standard-issue nine millimeter subcompact Glocks, two canisters of pepper spray, and two batons.

"While we rarely encounter any problems

requiring a firearm, we do keep them on board. We suggest you holster one when the ship is in port when our passengers and their belongings are the most vulnerable. Since you've been trained by the esteemed Wackenhut Corporation, I'm sure you know how to deescalate a challenging situation by the least confrontational means possible. Always begin with polite interference, then move up to bodily resistance. These devices are only to be used in the case of an extreme emergency."

Lester's heart raced as adrenaline flooded his system. They were asking him to carry a weapon. Daily. This was a hundred times better than playing *Call of Duty*. "Yes, ma'am. I understand." He would not mess this up.

Ms. Reinhart handed him a canister, a baton, and one of the Glocks. "We're in port now, so head to the gang plank. This is the time to be most vigilant. The crew doesn't know the passengers yet, so it's a prime opportunity for some nefarious type to come aboard. Don't be fooled by some old geezer. Anybody could be looking to cause trouble. Keep your mouth shut and your eyes open."

"Yes, ma'am." Lester buckled the holster, grabbed the gun, and looked for the best place to stash the baton and spray.

"Move it!"

Chapter 12

Maggie studied the map of the ship. Their room was on the second-highest deck and looked bigger than the others. Score one for Cheryl. Above that was the upper deck. Hopefully, that little kidney-shaped drawing was a pool or hot tub. She scanned the other deck plans for the spa, shops, and gym, but could only find rooms labeled lounges. Hmmm. Climbing the stairs until she reached the top level, she opened the door to a sea of neon-green AstroTurf covering the entire surface of the open-air deck. Cushioned wicker chairs and chaise lounges were artfully arranged on one side, and on the other was a striped canopy shading one rusted exercise bike. Next to it was a kidney-shaped putting green. One hole. No pool.

She grabbed her cruise book from her purse. "The *Forever Young* features gracious hospitality, luxurious staterooms, lively entertainment, and state of the art fitness equipment and recreational facilities ..." Really. On the bright side, gym rats and rail-thin Yoga-Barbies probably didn't sign up for this cruise. It was peaceful up here, despite the sounds of the workers loading the ship below. She peered down at the dock and was pleased to see some pretty fine looking deck hands. Plenty of beefcake to go around. The breeze was cool, the sun was warm, and the sky was blue. Not a bad start to the Lemon Sisters' Adventure.

♦♦♦

Rhoda explored the bottom deck which held the gangway, reception area, dining room, and a hall of rooms. If there was an infirmary, it would be there. She looked in every direction. Plenty of staff were scurrying about, but no one seemed to notice her. There was one very old man, chin on his chest, being wheeled in by a member of the crew. She let them pass, then headed for the back of the hall where she assumed the offices were. Sure enough, there were four doors in a row marked "Staff Only." She tried the knobs on the first three. Locked. Finally, the fourth door gave way.

"Excuse me, Ma'am. May I help you?"

Rhoda turned to see a corpulent young man in a green, tightly stretched polo with the ship's logo and a name tag that read Lester Nusbaum, Security. His right hand rested on a gun at his hip.

Blood drained from her face, but she quickly recovered. "Oh, thank God you showed up. Officer Nusbaum, is it?"

"Just Lester, Ma'am."

Creepy smile. "Nice to meet you, Lester." She batted her eyes and covered her name badge with her purse. "I'm so turned around. Is there a doctor on board? I forgot to bring one of those seasick patches, and I'm feeling woozy just sitting at the dock. In fact, I feel faint." She noticed his eyes widen, as he looked up and down the hall.

"I, um, I'm not sure. I'm pretty new here. Let me help you to a chair."

His palms were clammy as he grabbed her elbow and steered her toward the dining room at the

86

other end of the hall.

"Can I get you something to drink, Ma'am," Lester asked as he mopped his brow.

Rhoda noticed the Elixir of Youth cocktails on a table nearby. "One of those might help. They look cool and refreshing."

Lester grabbed her a drink and a cookie and handed them to her. "Do you need help getting to your room?"

"Oh, bless your heart. I think I'll be fine. I'll just have this little snack and sit here until I recover. Thank you so much." She touched his sleeve. "If all the staff on this ship are as helpful as you, it's going to be a great trip."

Lester blushed.

"You go on, now. I'm sure you have more important business to attend to than me." She waved as he turned to leave. Newbie Nusbaum Security was not going to be a problem. She'd get in that unlocked room when he was otherwise engaged.

Chapter 13

As the boat started to move, Cheryl took the elevator to the third floor, the highest level before the sun deck. Finding their room was easy; there were only ten. Maybe it was a penthouse; she was famous, after all. Dragging her key card across the lock pad, she opened the door. The room was dark. Good. She was alone. She wanted to pick out the best bed and drawers for herself. Flipping on the lights, she took in the space. Huh. Cozy? Claustrophobic? Dark green carpet and curtains shrunk the small room, and gold, shiny bedspreads covered the beds. Make that bed. A bunk bed, double on the bottom, single on top. There was no way clumsy Rhoda could make it to the top bunk. That left Maggie or herself to climb the ladder every night. She was claiming it. Rhoda cuddled and Maggie snored. They could fight it out on the bottom. She threw her purse on top and found their suitcases stacked in the tiny closet. Just as she grabbed hers, someone knocked on the door. She pivoted and opened it. "Welcome to Versailles."

Maggie squeezed around her and broke out laughing. "My walk-in closet is bigger than this thing. Bunks? I feel like we're at church camp."

Rhoda edged in the room. "It's bigger than the master in my old trailer."

Tears glittered in Cheryl's eyes. "I'm sorry, girls. I thought it would be one of those deluxe staterooms."

Rhoda hugged her. "It's perfect. We've stayed

in tighter spaces than this. Remember our room when we were kids? Three twins smashed together in an eight by ten foot room? This is great. At least we have a private bathroom." She opened its door. "And look at that. You just sit right on the john while you shower."

Cheryl sobbed.

"It's all right. I don't shower every day. I'll just take a dip in the pool."

"No pool." Maggie held her finger to her lips, shushing Rhoda. "But look. Here's a nice chair and dresser."

Cheryl sobbed harder.

"For your glad list, at least the balloons didn't make it. Three Spongebobs would have run us out of here. By rolling down that window, I saved the day," Rhoda said. "I think it's a great room. We're not going to be in here much, anyway."

Cheryl wiped her eyes. "You're right. It'll make for a great story someday."

"That's the spirit." Maggie held up the Sisters sign. "We just have to turn lemons into Lemon Drops or a Tom Collins. Now, down to business. I'll set up a schedule to coordinate when we get dressed and showered. You always go first, Cheryl. You are the star of the show."

"Thanks. I guess it'll be okay," Cheryl sighed. "A Lemon Drop sounds pretty good. Maybe they'll serve drinks at that muster."

Rhoda dug in her bag. "And don't forget, we have to fill out these dating profiles before we go. Let me open these heavy curtains and get some light in here." Behind the curtain was a small sliding door revealing a French balcony.

"Nice." Cheryl's smile broadened. "Things are looking up. Let's get ready to find the perfect partners."

As the three started on their profiles, a voice came over a speaker in the ceiling. "This is your cruise director, Renee Reinhart. Welcome aboard the *Forever Young*. As you probably noticed, we have left the port and are on our way to the adventure of a lifetime. Over the next six days, you will be treated like royalty by our professional cruise staff, dine on exquisite gourmet fare, and enjoy the beauty of Florida coastlines that you never knew existed. But most importantly, you will leave here with new friends and maybe a lover or two! After all, this is the Boomers/GenXers Singles cruise, and it looks like we have a prime group ready to party. And speaking of parties, let's get this one started in one hour in the Peacock Lounge on Deck Two. There's an elevator for those who have trouble with stairs. And if you can't make it to the lounge, we will carry the entire muster and social hour over the loud speakers in your rooms. While reviewing all safety procedures, we will host a full cocktail hour, complete with hot hors d'oeuvres and party favors. So fill out those dating profiles, preen those feathers, and head for the Peacock Lounge. See you soon!"

"Oh, she sounds like a hoot," Cheryl said, as she sat on the only chair in the room. "I'm dying to get a look at this dating questionnaire. This'll be fun."

Rhoda dropped to the edge of the lower bunk and used her cruise packet as a writing surface. "All right, let the bullshitting begin. Should we do these together or fill them out separately and compare notes?"

Maggie squeezed in on the bed, grabbed her form and started in. "Let's do them individually, otherwise we'd be cheating ourselves. We want to attract the best possible match."

"Oh, Mags," Rhoda said. "You are honest and ethical to a fault. Let's have fun with this. It's not like some scientific computer program. What are there, a hundred or so on this boat? All I've seen so far are a fat security guard, a few staffers, and a nearly comatose man in a wheelchair."

"You do it your way, we'll do it ours," Cheryl said.

They all bent over their surveys, brows furrowed, casting pensive looks toward the ceiling, scribbling answers. Finally, Rhoda called time. "Okay. We'll round-robin this thing. First question. I hate this one. 'What are your hobbies and interests?' I put reading, cooking, and quilting. I wanted to put spending someone else's money, having wild sex, and smoking, but, well, you know …"

Maggie raised an eyebrow. "I put biking, reading, and traveling. That sounds okay, doesn't it? I've been on a bike a few times."

Cheryl launched in. "I put 'singing and performing, volunteering in the community, and spending time with my precious dog, Chief Osceola. Oh, yes, and attending sporting events at FSU.'"

"There go all the men," Maggie said. "On to the next one. 'What are you looking for in a partner?' I have 'single male, thirties to fifties, kind-hearted but adventurous.' Cheryl?"

"Good heavens do we have to state gender preference? I just wrote 'accomplished in his field, independent—I don't want any loafers—and loves singing, dancing and sports.' What do you have, Rho?"

Rhoda jerked her head up, hitting it on the upper bunk. "Damn. This place is going to take some getting used to. I put 'looking for a rich, impotent, nonagenarian in poor health with no other living relatives.' You know, one foot on the banana peel."

After two seconds of silence, Maggie exploded with laughter. "That's what we all should have said!"

Cheryl also laughed but then regained composure. "Come on, now. Let's be serious. We might really have a shot at romance here. Maybe not long term, but at least someone to make the week fun."

"That's a good point. We should have some kind of signal worked out, so, if one of us gets lucky, we can let the others know not to come in the room," Maggie said. "Oh, don't look so shocked, Cheryl. We're long past losing our flower. What if you meet a real hottie? What do you say? Do Not Disturb sign on the door? And a text if we're staying out?"

"Sounds like a plan," Rhoda said. "If you do score, take a little advice from your oldest sister; never get on top after forty."

Cheryl gasped.

"Oh, come on, Pollyanna. Gravity is not kind after forty, even for you." Rhoda then finished her profile, though finding a mate was not the first item on her agenda.

♦♦♦

Marvin cursed the tiny room as he tried to look at himself in the mirror. He couldn't get far enough away to see head to toe. He needed to get it right this time. There probably wouldn't be any uptight church ladies like his last date. Everybody who signed up would be after the same thing. He patted the pocket of his chinos. Condom—check. Cigarettes and lighter in his shirt pocket—check. Armed with his dating profile, he slapped on some Old Spice, grabbed his lanyard, and headed for the lounge. He hoped there was at least one forty-something, active woman with a sense of humor and adventure who was looking for a virile, thrill-seeking man who loves to cuddle.

Chapter 14

After much discussion in the room, the girls decided more casual wear was appropriate for the muster. Cheryl, of course, chose a fancier red sundress with a topstitched bodice, in case she was asked to sing. Rhoda wore a pair of turquoise Bermuda shorts and a gauzy peasant top she had picked up at the Dress Shed.

"That's a bit too casual," Maggie said. "Maybe a little jewelry? Try this shell-and-sea-glass bib necklace and matching cuff." She fastened them on. "Perfect. Now fix those eyes, fluff that hair, and knock 'em dead."

Maggie chose a cotton seersucker shirtwaist and gold-braided espadrilles. She re-tamed her hair after the balloon incident and walked through a puff of perfume before heading to the lounge.

A woman, name-tagged Cruise Director, greeted her at the door wearing a peacock-feathered headband and a ruff of leis. Beside her stood a tall, broad-shouldered man with dark, glittering eyes and thick, black hair gelled into a helmet. "Welcome to the Love Boat." He flashed an over-whitened smile that sparkled like the sequins on his tuxedo jacket. "Wanna get lei'd?"

"What?" Maggie had been so fixated on his teeth and his smarmy leer that she hadn't noticed the plastic leis hanging from his forearm. She recovered some composure as he slipped three of the kitschy necklaces over her head. "Thanks, I think."

"Ha! Scare you, did I? Sorry about that. Just a little singles cruise joke." Exaggerated wink. He grabbed her hand and gave it a good squeeze. "My name's Lyle Broadmoor, and I'll be your host, entertainer, activity director, cruise historian, and chief cook and bottle washer."

He had to have been a radio or game show announcer at some point in his life. Plus, he was a close talker. She stepped back, tripping into the cruise director. "Sorry. It's kind of tight here in the doorway, isn't it?"

"Yes, but we want to make sure we greet every single guest and, most importantly, collect the dating profiles." The woman shoved a peacock headband in Maggie's hair. "My name's Renee. Welcome! Come on in, grab some refreshments, and get to know your fellow passengers. We're all about being relaxed and friendly here. By the end of the week, we'll be one big, happy family."

Maggie looked around hopefully as she entered the lounge. Silver hair, bald heads, and heavy toupees dominated the room. She had to be the youngest by at least ten years. But that was okay. Ten more years for them to make their millions. At the bar she ordered a double Lemon Drop and a plate of assorted appetizers. The food did look good, and the drink was delicious. After a few more, she wouldn't care about hair or lack thereof. She couldn't abide men with rugs, though. Definitely off the table.

Where were Rhoda and Cheryl? She looked at the crowd and her insecurity took over. Standing in front of a class of thirty kids didn't faze her, but a group of adults made her want to run to a corner and disappear. Not this week, though. She grabbed another martini and marched toward a coffee table in the front of the room. Taking a seat on the couch, not alone in a chair, she would be forced to socialize. Soon, three women, one on a walker, came and joined her. Finally, two elderly gentlemen also sat down. One wore a tee shirt and overalls; the other sported a polyester leisure suit. Did they even sell those anymore? Mr. Greenjeans had real hair. She took a deep breath. "Hi, everybody. I'm Maggie."

The woman with the walker held up her name tag. "Dot. Nice to meet you. Are you here with your parents?"

Odd question. Who would take their parents on a singles cruise?

"I'm Florence and this is my friend, Eleanor. Nice to meet you, Maggie. Have you sailed with Ponce de Leon before?"

Maggie shook her head. "Nope. This is my first time."

"I'm Earl," the man in overalls said. "Never been on one either, but I sold my big tobacco farm in North Carolina and decided to treat myself."

The other man stood, reached across the table and took Maggie's hand, raising her knuckles to his lips. "Nice to meet you, Maggie. My name's Roberto. I'm a singles' cruise virgin, myself."

Upon closer inspection, Maggie noticed the line between the sideburns and the wig. "Well, it's a pleasure to meet you all. I guess we'll be seeing a lot of each other over the next few days."

A deafening squeal shrieked through the room. "Sorry, ladies and gents," Lyle said into a microphone.

"Nothing like a little audio feedback to get everybody's attention. I hope nobody's pacemaker skipped a beat, ha ha. We're going to start the official muster announcement, so listen carefully. Happy hour will be open until six-thirty, so belly-up everybody."

The recorded safety drill droned above the crowd noise, informing everyone where life vests were placed in each room, which exit path each hall and floor were to use in case an evacuation was necessary, and of course, the location of the life rafts. A series of bleeps, honks, and blatts were sounded to indicate different types of notifications and emergencies. Maggie paid close attention rather than subject herself to Roberto's constant chatter. As if the toupee wasn't bad enough, he was a spitter. Probably loose dentures. She excused herself and trolled the room. There had to be some younger men on this boat somewhere.

◆◆◆

"I'll take a bourbon and branch water, easy on the water. In fact, make it a double." Marvin had been watching the bartenders barely fill the jigger for each drink. Cheap asses.

"Yes, sir. The hors d'oeuvres are at the end of the bar. Please help yourself."

The jury was still out on his chances of scoring on this cruise. The women he'd seen so far looked well-dressed, but no one looked to be under sixty.

Upending his glass, he grabbed a plate of shrimp and circled back to the queue at the bar. One more and he'd head up to the sundeck for a smoke. This could turn into a tedious trip. Just as he got his drink, a shrill screech sounded in the room. He turned and noticed the sequined lounge lizard who greeted him at the door standing at a microphone. That guy was a real piece of work. Turning back toward the bar, he felt a tap on his shoulder.

"Hi. My name's Dot." She leaned toward him on her lei-festooned walker. "Why don't we take our drinks over and sit by the window? It's so romantic looking out at the river flowing by." Lipstick spotted her teeth, and her orange hair was thinly combed over a bald spot.

Typical. Another old woman looking for a caretaker. Been there, done that. "I don't think so, Dot." Marvin bugged his eyes and leaned in close. "I just got out of the insane asylum last week. Doctor said red hair is one of my triggers."

"Oh, my," she gasped and clanked off toward the appetizers.

♦♦♦

Waiting for her turn at the bar, Rhoda overheard an interesting exchange between the woman and a man in front of her. Did she hear him right? Released from an insane asylum? As the woman moved away, Rhoda stepped closer. If he was telling the truth, he probably had some pretty good head meds. She sidled up next to him. "Excuse me. Have you tried the drinks yet? Are they any good?"

He turned toward her and smiled. He looked normal enough.

"You gotta ask for a double. They're pretty chintzy on the pour."

"Good tip. Thanks." Rhoda ordered a double scotch on the rocks and headed for the table where

Cheryl sat. Of course, it was right in front, in case Cheryl got introduced as the star. By the time she got there, Maggie had joined them. "Hey, Mags. Glad you found us. We wondered where you went."

"I tried to be bold and go sit with a group of strangers."

"Good for you. Did you meet anyone?"

"Yeah. Farmer John and a badly toupeed Ricardo Montalban." Maggie sighed. "There were also three women there. They were nice enough, but nobody dateable. Most of the people look pretty old. Do you think they're hiding the hot guys until dinner?"

Rhoda felt a presence behind her.

"Excuse me, ladies. Is that seat reserved?"

She turned. The man from the bar pointed next to Maggie. He didn't look crazy, a little older, but not crazy. Whatever he was taking must be pretty good stuff. "No, no one's sitting there. Please, join us."

"I'm Marvin. Marvin Whitcomb." He sat down. "And you are?"

"I'm Rhoda Mason and these are my sisters, Maggie and Cheryl Lennon." He seemed like a friendly guy. He shook each of their hands, but she noticed he lingered a bit longer with Maggie. Good. Mags needed some positive male attention.

"IS EVERYBODY HAVING FUN?" Lyle screamed into the mike. The crowd murmured yes. "Come on. You can do better than that!"

"YES!" screamed the group, causing the sound system to squeal again.

"That's more like it. If I haven't told you already, I'm Lyle Broadmoor, your host, entertainer, activity director, cruise historian, and chief cook and bottle washer. The only thing I don't do around here is steer the ship. It's my job to make sure we all have a great time this week, but before I begin the entertainment, I have to get a few housekeeping things out of the way. You've no doubt met our cruise director, Renee. Wave, Renee."

She waved.

"The number one rule is to wear your name badges at all times on and off the ship. Well, you don't have to wear them to bed, unless you don't know who you're sleeping with, wink, wink. Each table should have a list of all the excursions offered during the cruise. We ask that you please complete this tonight and hand it in at dinner. Speaking of meals, tonight's dining is open seating. Meal times are listed in your cruise packet. Each morning we ask you to complete your preferred menu choices for the day and leave it with our wait staff. And, most importantly, every night after dinner, there will be cocktails, snacks, and entertainment here in this lounge."

Rhoda noticed Cheryl rise slightly from her chair, anticipating an introduction.

Lyle caught her eye, smirked, then continued. "And that's about it for housekeeping. Does anyone have any questions?"

Dot raised her hand. "Do you have any charging stations on the ship?"

"Good one," he squinted at her name tag, "Dot. Each room is equipped with a charging station for both wheelchairs and oxygen machines."

"What?" Rhoda whispered when she saw Maggie's mouth drop open.

"I thought she meant for laptops and cell

phones. Wheelchairs? Oxygen machines? What kind of a cruise is this?"

Cheryl leaned in and whispered, "I'm sure he's required to say that by law. ADA enforces a lot of regulations."

Lyle continued. "We're almost finished here. For tonight's social mixer, you'll notice a colored dot on your nametag. Find a table that has that color centerpiece, and that's where you'll sit tonight. In fact, we'll mix up the seating throughout the week, so you can get to know everyone on the ship. Who knows? Maybe you'll meet that special someone tonight!"

Rhoda noticed Dot clap her hands, but no one else seemed to be paying attention. This guy was a real sleaze. Poor Cheryl had to work with him all week. She looked over at Maggie and Marvin. He tried to engage her in conversation, but Maggie had adopted an aloof posture. Too bad. He was actually kind of handsome. His clothes looked expensive. She wouldn't mind getting to know him a little better, maybe get into his room and check out the medicine cabinet.

Lyle walked behind a massive KORG keyboard, complete with stands holding a sax and cymbals, and a base drum by his feet. He switched a button and the keyboard started in with the theme to *The Love Boat*. He crooned the first few lines, blatted out some notes on the sax, and ended the song brushing the cymbals into a fade. What a cornball. She felt the giggles start just as he looked at her. She smiled to try and hold hysteria at bay, which he obviously misread. Finishing the song, he looked directly in her eyes, raised his hand and cocked his index finger toward her. Dear God.

"Does anybody else have a green dot?" Rhoda asked.

"Mine's yellow," Cheryl said.

"I have red." Maggie held hers up.

"Great. I'm red, too," Marvin said.

Rhoda noticed Maggie roll her eyes. Good. If she didn't want him, Rhoda could cozy up. She looked at the room number on his lanyard. 120. Must be on the same floor as the offices.

As the lounge lizard stepped away from the still playing keyboard to dance with the cruise director, Marvin stood. "Ladies, it's been nice to meet you. If you'll excuse me, I'm going to get ready for dinner. I'll see you there."

"Nice to meet you, Marvin." Rhoda said. Not a bad looking guy at all. And polite. He didn't seem near as crazy as her missing husband.

♦♦♦

Maggie also rose. She'd had enough of Get-Lei'd-Lyle, Farmer John, and the rest of them. "Are either of you going to change for dinner? Rhoda?" She couldn't help it. Everyone else was in a dress, skirt or at least long pants. Rhoda looked like she was ready to go to the grocery.

"Very subtle, Mags," Rhoda said. "Okay. Let's all go back to the room, and you can tell me what to wear."

"Sorry, but shorts are a bit too casual for dinner, I think. Maybe that pretty tiger-print caftan you showed us. By the way, I have a little something for all of us. A petite cadeau, if you will."

Cheryl brightened. "Oh, I love a good present.

How fun. Come, girls. Off to the Penthouse."

Maggie was glad Cheryl could joke about the tiny room. When Pollyanna lost her glow, things could get ugly. They climbed the stairs to the third floor while the party continued in the Peacock Lounge. She opened the door to their room, and they all filed inside. The setting sun cast an orange glow through the French balcony, bathing the room in soft light. "You know, it really is a nice room, Cheryl."

"You're right. I just had a different picture in my head. But it's fine. I love the big open slider." She took her seat on the only chair. "Now, what about those presents?"

Maggie mined the tiny closet from which she extracted three Victoria's Secret bags. "Here you go, ladies."

Rhoda held it up. "Isn't that a porn shop?"

Cheryl straightened in her chair. "No, silly. It's a high-end lingerie store, although, it is losing its appeal among the Me-Too crowd."

Maggie laughed. "Enough about the bag. They're all the same."

"What's a Kinoki pad?" asked Rhoda, holding the object like it was a dead mouse.

"It's a detoxifying pad you put on the soles of your feet at night. By morning, it will have pulled all the impurities out of your system. I figure since we're probably going to be drinking more than usual, we could use a little help."

Cheryl raised an eyebrow. "Condoms, Mags? Really?"

Rhoda pulled a tube out of the bag. "Lube?"

"Just a joke. Unless you get lucky. Then it's

your best friend. But look, there are some exfoliating face cloths, anti-wrinkle cream, cooling gel facial masks, a tin of Altoids, and the big one, a black satin kimono for each of us."

"Oooh, these are nice," Cheryl rubbed the soft fabric across her cheek. "Very sexy, yet classy."

"I'm glad you like it. Now, unless one of gets lucky tonight, we'll plan on detoxifying, de-wrinkling, and de-puffing our eyes, so we can hit the road running tomorrow."

Chapter 15

Captain Whitcomb took a long drag off the unfiltered Camel. Clouds and mist shrouded the quarter-moon obscuring the horizon. The sea was calm. Nearly perfect conditions for the USS Cushing. They'd been tracking the U-boat for hours.

"Excuse me, sir," a young cadet materialized beside him. "Sonar indicates the enemy is two nautical miles off port, sir."

"Good work. Load the Y-guns, increase speed to eleven knots."

"Aye, sir."

Lighting another cigarette off the butt of the first, Whitcomb waved the cadet back over. "Location?"

"Just off the port bow, sir."

"Fire."

"Aye, sir."

Whitcomb braced for the percussion when a tinkling bell sounded over the intercom.

"Hi everybody. This is Renee, your cruise director. We hope you had fun at our cocktail hour. Now's your chance to sample our world-famous cuisine in the dining room located on the first floor. Don't forget, find the table with the colored centerpiece that corresponds with the dot on your lanyard. Let the matching begin."

Captain Whitcomb flicked the butt over the side of the ship, smiling at the ever-widening oil slick from the destroyed submarine.

Turning on his heel, he headed down the stairs for dinner.

♦♦♦

From behind the exercise bike on the upper deck, Lester watched a man leaning on the railing. Smoking was allowed up here, but he wanted to make sure nothing fishy was going on. Sure enough, the old guy flicked the butt right into the water. Lester longed to prove himself by catching a rule-breaker, but he didn't want to make any mistakes like he had on the Wackenhut job. He pulled the list of infractions from his back pocket. Damn. Nothing about cigarettes off the deck.

♦♦♦

Maggie lingered behind Rhoda and Cheryl as they entered the dining room. She knew Cheryl, with her golden hair cascading from waterfall braids, sparkling chandelier earrings, and shimmering organza wrap would command everyone's attention. Sure enough, the clatter of plates and glasses stopped and conversation ebbed when she entered the room. Deep breath. It's her cruise. Happy for her.

Rather than walk in her sister's shadow, she made a detour to the nearest restroom and waited for more diners to show up. Unfortunately for Cheryl, her grand entrance was to a nearly empty room. When Maggie heard enough conversation out in the reception area, she freshened her lipstick, brushed her hair, and waited until the noise died down a bit. Maybe someone would notice her.

Opening the door, she found herself stuck behind a line of walkers, wheelchairs, and a variety of Hurrycanes slowly advancing from the elevator. The sight of the mobility-assisted army broke her spirit. Singles cruise, her ass. This place was nothing but a floating nursing home. Unless she wanted to employ Rhoda's scheme of snagging the rich and frail, her hopes for romance evaporated. She plodded behind the group to the table with the red rose centerpiece.

She spotted Rhoda at the green table, greeting everyone, jumping up to make room for the wheelchairs and position walkers and canes near their owners. Cheryl, luminescent at the table in the front of the room, chatted with what appeared to be an officer of the ship, possibly the captain. There he was. The only man under eighty on the boat, and Cher had already snagged him. Tears threatened until she felt a tap on her shoulder.

"Hey. Nice to see a familiar face. Maggie, isn't it?" He pulled out the chair to her right and sat. "Marvin Whitcomb. We met at the cocktail hour."

Truth be told, he wasn't bad. Definitely closer to her age than most of the others, but still probably thirty years her senior. "Yes, Marvin. Nice to see you again." There was one younger man, mid-sixties, sitting across from her. Beside him was a tiny, very old woman who, despite her age, had bright apple cheeks, and eyes that sparkled with mischief. The rest of the six-top held two slumping men, deflated in their vintage sport coats. Maggie glanced back at Rhoda, who was laughing and talking with everyone. Might as well follow her lead. Rhoda always made the best of a bad situation. Usually.

"So, why don't we go around the table and introduce ourselves. I'll start. I'm Maggie Lennon from Greenville, South Carolina." She turned to the man on her left. "And you are?"

"WHAT?"

"Your name?" Maggie shouted.

"Oh. Sorry, hearing aid's acting up." On cue, a high-pitched whistle drowned him out. He stuck a finger in his ear until it stopped. "I'm Maynard Scott. Cedar Rapids, Iowa."

They proceeded around the table until they got to the energetic granny. "I'm Hilda Schneider, and this is my son, Fredrick." She patted the younger man's hand. "He's my constant companion. In fact, this is our fifth Ponce de Leon cruise. We're members of the Conquistador Club, isn't that right, Freddie?"

Freddie looked toward his lap. "Yes, Mother."

Mama's boy. Definitely not going to be a love interest. God knows what kind of issues he had. A vision of Norman Bates danced through her mind.

Someone clanged on a glass and got the room's attention. The officer stood next to Cheryl, flanked by Renee Cruise Director and Lyle Entertainer. "Ladies and Gentlemen, welcome to the *Forever Young*. I'm Captain Tyler Cabot. In case you're worried, First Mate Gregory Tuttle is steering the ship."

Renee and Lyle flashed white smiles and laughed.

"It's my pleasure to have all of you aboard this week, and we promise you the trip of a lifetime. We know there are lots of vacation options out there, and we truly appreciate that you have chosen Ponce de Leon. By the end of the cruise, it's my goal to be on a first name basis with all of you."

Amid the applause, Maggie clapped louder than everyone at her table. The captain was gorgeous. A full head of sandy-blond hair, piercing blue eyes, chiseled jaw, and physique. He belonged on the cover of a romance novel, especially in his dress whites.

"At this time, I'd like to introduce you to our very special guest. We are excited to have on board with us the winner of the hit TV show, *Florida's Hidden Treasures Tournament of Treasures*, Ms. Cheryl Lennon. Stand up, Cheryl." He offered his hand and helped her from her chair. She rose with the grace of the Duchess of Cornwall. "As a special treat for all of you, Ms. Lennon will be performing throughout the week alongside our own Lyle Broadmoor."

Wild applause filled the room. Rhoda whistled through her fingers.

"Cheryl, do you have any words for our friends?" He had not yet let go of her hand.

"Thank you, Captain Cabot. I'm so honored to be here. And thank those of you," her arm swept the room, "who watched the show and voted. I will do everything I can to live up to your expectations."

Cheers and more whistles, though it might have been the hearing aids again.

"I hope to see everyone in the Peacock Lounge for my first performance tomorrow night. If you have any special requests, just leave them on the keyboard. I'm sure Mr. Broadmoor and I can accommodate them. Isn't that right?"

Throughout Cheryl's speech, Maggie watched

Get-Lei'd-Lyle. He glared through narrowed eyes and clenched his jaw. He gripped his arms across his chest. Didn't look like he wanted to share the spotlight. She'd have to warn Cheryl when they got back to the room.

"Thank you, Cheryl. We're all looking forward to it." The captain faced the group. "I've kept you from your delicious meal long enough. Please, eat, drink, and be merry. And let us know if we can do anything to make this your best vacation ever."

He could strut his lovely self over to Maggie's table. That would help. But the likelihood of that seemed slim, as he bent down and whispered something in Cheryl's ear, causing her to toss her flaxen hair back and laugh.

"Good evening, ladies and gentlemen. My name's Raul, and I'll be your server tonight." Instead of the ubiquitous green polo shirt, the waiter wore a white button-down and black pants. The shirt stretched tight across his chest and biceps. "What can I get you to drink?" He turned to Maggie.

"I'll have a light beer now and then red wine with dinner." She looked around the table. "Lots of red wine with dinner." She gave him her best rescue-me look and smiled.

He wrote down her order, leaned over and whispered in her ear, "You got it, dear. We aim to please."

"I'll have a bourbon and branch water," interrupted Marvin. "Make it a double."

Maggie didn't hear the rest of the table order as she watched the perfect ass in the black pants move away from her. Things were looking up.

♦♦♦

This was better than Rhoda could have dreamed. After a round of introductions, the conversation quickly turned to illnesses, surgeries, and the medications needed to treat them. Who needed an infirmary? The number of prescriptions on this boat had to be in the thousands.

First, there was Glenda, an eighty-something widow suffering from crippling anxiety. Next to her, Elmer, sitting so low in his wheelchair his chin barely cleared the table, complained of insomnia. Dot had Type II diabetes—no help there—and Joseph, whose head now rested on his chest, had revealed his battle with narcolepsy.

"Good evening, ladies and gentlemen. My name is Jeffrey. I'll be your server tonight. Can I start anyone off with a drink?"

The word drink must have brought Joseph out of his coma. His head snapped up. "I'll take a martini."

"Yes sir. Did you want that dirty?"

"You bet your ass, son. Dirty as you can make it."

"You got it." Jeffrey turned to Elmer. "And for you, sir?"

"Just water. Don't want to dull my reflexes. But you wouldn't know about that would you, son? I bet you don't have any trouble getting a hard-on."

Jeffrey smiled and turned to Rhoda. "And you, ma'am?"

"Well, I'm not worried about a hard-on, so I'll take a scotch and soda, please."

"Yes, ma'am." Unfazed by the bizarre chatter, the waiter took the rest of the orders and left the table.

Elmer reached over and grabbed Rhoda's leg. "I was just teasing the waiter, honey. There's a benefit to insomnia; I'm up all night." He broke into a phlegmy cackle ending in a frightened gasp. "Can't breathe."

Rhoda jumped up and slapped him on the back until he finally relaxed.

He took her hand. "You're a real angel. Thank you. If you could just do one more thing for me."

"Sure, Elmer. What's that?"

"I'm worn out. Could you take me back to my room? It's right on this floor."

"Don't you want your dinner?"

"I'll have them bring me something later. I just need to lie down for a while."

He seemed harmless enough. Rhoda unlocked the wheels and steered him across the dining room and into the hall. "Which room is it?"

"Second one on the left."

She opened the door with his key card eased him into the tiny room.

"If you could just help me onto the bed, I'd appreciate it. Oh yeah, and one more thing. Could you get my sleep pills out of the bathroom? They're on the counter. Look for the Ativan."

One of her favorites. "No problem, Elmer," she said, guiding him to the bed. "You just get settled, and I'll be right back." In the bathroom, she found a tackle-box pill caddy, each section labeled with the name of the medication and time of day. She grabbed a handful of Ativan from the bottom row, filled a glass of water from the faucet, and carried it into the bedroom.

Elmer, splayed naked on the bed, laughed

maniacally. "Bring it on over here, sweet thing."

Pills flew from her hand. "Really, Elmer? That's your idea of foreplay?" She wound up and pitched the glass of water across the room, hitting his decidedly erect penis. "Strike three, you asshole. Stay away from me for the rest of the cruise, or I'll report you to security." Slamming the door as she left, she shook her head. There was no unseeing that. Ever.

Chapter 16

While the passengers ate dinner, Lester leaned back in the office desk chair and watched the monitors. The halls were empty except for a staffer now and then. So far, this had been a pretty cake job. Besides the cigarette-butt flipper and the seasick lady, he'd seen nothing amiss. Maybe things would pick up when they stopped in port in the morning. Renee had said that's when he had to be the most vigilant. He'd re-holster the gun then. She'd made him put it back in storage once the boat left the dock, but he was able to hold on to the pepper spray and the baton.

Something on the screen caught his eye. He focused on Deck One. It looked like that woman from earlier, running from a room. Was she okay? No one seemed to be after her. He leaned in for a closer look. Was she crying or laughing? Kind of looked like laughing.

Someone else came out of another room. That guy in the sequined jacket. Who was that, Lyle? Yeah. Lyle somebody. Why would he be in a guest room? Who knew? Maybe he also did maintenance or something. They all had multiple jobs. Lyle stopped and talked to the woman. She slowed her pace and grabbed his offered arm as they headed toward the dining room. No excitement there.

Lester's stomach started growling, so he checked the kitchen camera to see what was cooking. The staff didn't get to eat until after they closed the dining room. It looked like meat, some kind of

114

seafood, and potatoes. Maybe he'd stroll down there and have a look.

◆◆◆

Maggie had to admit, the meal was delicious, spiny lobster tail on a bed of pink shrimp in Key Lime butter, crusty bread, and crisp asparagus. If all the meals were this good, she'd have to go scrape the rust off the ship's exercise bike and saddle up. Her hot waiter had been true to his word and kept her wine glass full. When he brought her a huge helping of caramel flan with mango topping for dessert, she knew he was flirting. Maybe it was the wine talking, but she could definitely cozy up to Raul.

Otherwise, the prospects were slim. Frederick the mama's boy was beyond timid, the two ancient gentlemen were definitely out, and then there was Marvin. Nice Marvin. He was interesting, handsome for his age, and certainly attentive. In fact, he had asked her to join him on the top deck for a night cap. She just couldn't see it. He was old enough to be her father. Some people didn't mind that much of an age difference, but it made her skin crawl. It was obvious he wanted to be more than friends. She'd begged off on the drink, saying she had to help her sister get ready to perform after dinner.

"Hey, Cheryl. Wait up," she called as she hurried away from Marvin. There was actually no need to rush, as Cheryl was still deep in conversation with the captain. Didn't he have a job to do somewhere?

"Hey, Sis." Cheryl didn't even look up.

"Hi," Maggie said, extending her hand toward Mr. Gorgeous. "I'm Maggie Lennon, Cheryl's younger sister."

He immediately jumped to his feet and shook her hand. "How nice to meet you, Ms. Lennon. I'm Tyler Cabot. Cheryl didn't tell me she had a sister on the cruise with her."

Of course she didn't. "Actually, she has two sisters here." Maggie leveled the stink eye at Cheryl.

"We're glad to have you all aboard. I hope you're enjoying the cruise so far." He looked at his watch. "Speaking of which, I'd better go relieve my Mate. I've stayed down here longer than I planned. Good to meet you both." He turned to go, then looked back at Cheryl. "I can't wait to hear you perform."

Maggie might as well have been invisible. "Good to meet you, too," she said to his back as he strode down the hall.

Cheryl stood and faced Maggie. "I call dibs."

Damn. Why didn't she think of that? Calling dibs was as sacred as calling shotgun among the three sisters. "All right. You win. He is gorgeous. I wonder what the Mate looks like?"

"I don't think it matters. It's a she."

"Of course. The one time you hope that glass ceiling hasn't been shattered. Oh well. There are some pretty hot waiters, but that's about it. I'm definitely going to concentrate on the crew." She started climbing the stairs to their room. "Have you seen Rhoda anywhere? She was just a few tables away from me, but after they served the drinks, I didn't see her anymore."

"I saw her take some guy in a wheelchair out of the room, but she returned a little later. I lost track after that. Too busy staring into those gorgeous blue eyes,"

Cheryl said.

"Yeah, I kind of got distracted, too. Raul, our waiter, filled my wine glass so often, I'm a little drunk. He was definitely hot for me. Are we going to the lounge for the entertainment later? If not, I may troll the floor where the staff hangs out."

"Oh, come to the lounge with me. I'm hoping I'll get to sing," Cheryl said as she opened the door to their room.

"Okay. I'll check it out for a while," Maggie said. "Rhoda seems to be doing pretty well, don't you think? She doesn't seem all spaced out or anything."

"Let's check her bag."

"Cheryl! I'm surprised at you. That seems much more like something I would do."

They looked through the luggage and found nothing but a bottle of mouthwash.

"Wow," Maggie said. "There's a pretty hefty percentage of alcohol in this—twenty-six percent."

"Yeah, but she seems to be able to handle a drink or two. Usually when she's messed up, it's on pills. I don't see any of those in here. Not even a vitamin. I think you're right, Mags. She's doing okay."

"Thank God. I was not looking forward to a confrontation."

"Me either," Cheryl said. "Ready to go? I'm just going to brush my teeth and use some mouthwash."

"Cheers." Maggie toasted with the bottle, before putting it back in Rhoda's luggage.

◆◆◆

Marvin was pissed. Maggie obviously didn't

want anything to do with him. Sure, she was cordial, but she turned down his offer for a drink on the deck and practically ran from him. Maybe she was a little too young, but he had to give it a shot. She had a tight little body and creamy smooth skin. He didn't see much of that anymore, except on his daughters. Ugh. She was probably about their age. Shit. He grabbed his drink off the table and headed upstairs for a smoke.

The night air was refreshing after the overpowering smell of rich foods, perfumes, and aftershaves in the dining room. He tamped the cigarette on the box and lit up. That little old woman at the table seemed pretty spry and ornery. If she were ten or twenty years younger, he might consider it, but that pasty-faced son probably lived with her. Nope. He squinted through the smoke as he exhaled. There had to be more possibilities on the ship somewhere.

"Excuse me. Mind if I join you?"

He turned to see one of Maggie's sisters pull a cigarette out of her pocket.

He flicked his lighter. "Allow me." Her face was pretty in the glow of the flame. Large dark eyes caught the light.

"God bless you," Rhoda said as she tilted her head back and exhaled a perfect smoke ring. "I've been having a nic fit for about a half hour now. What a night. You're Marvin, right?"

Nice that she was a fellow smoker. There were so few of them left. People looked at you like you were a bed-wetter if you lit up anywhere. "I'm sorry. And you are? I've met too many people tonight. Plus, I'm no good with names."

"Rhoda. Rhoda Mason. I'm traveling with my

two sisters. We met at the cocktail hour."

"Rhoda. Of course. Nice to see you. Did you enjoy dinner?"

"Not really. Some old geezer at my table asked me to wheel him back to his room and get his pills. By the time I got them, he'd stripped down and had a hand on the throttle, if you know what I mean."

"What'd you do?" Stupid old dolt. You couldn't flash somebody and expect anything. You had to woo a woman. Show some interest. Show her you cared.

"I threw the water glass right at his pecker. Knocked his hand clean against the wall." She laughed. "Horny old coot."

"That's quite a kick-off to a singles cruise."

"They certainly didn't advertise that in the brochure," Rhoda agreed. "Of course, I'm not here to find the perfect mate."

"Really? Why are you on the cruise, then?"

"My sister won some singing contest and got this as a prize. She wanted Maggie and me to come with her. Plus, things have been kind of rough lately, so I thought a little break might be just what the doctor ordered."

"I'm sorry to hear that. The doctor, huh? Have you been sick?"

She laughed. "Just an expression. No. Physically, I'm fine. Emotionally, not so much. My good-for-nothing husband disappeared last year, which is okay. But then my boyfriend, a really great guy, I thought, took off out of the blue. Gave me the old 'it's not you, it's me' routine. I've been pretty depressed ever since."

"Ouch. That must have hurt."

Eyes glistening, she waved off the thought. "What about you, Marvin? Do you go on a lot of singles cruises?"

"Nope. First one, though I wouldn't mind finding someone. Not to marry or anything, just someone to do things with. A companion."

"Are you divorced?"

He flipped his cigarette over the rail, took a sip of his drink, and stared out over the water. "No. Widowed. My wife died a few years ago, though she'd been bed-ridden so long, it seems like I've been alone forever. Plus, she was pretty cranky and needy toward the end. Kind of takes the romance out of a marriage, you know?"

"I do. I'm sorry for your loss." Rhoda briefly placed her hand on his arm.

"I guess you could say I've had a rough time, too. Trying to figure out what to do with myself after caretaking for years. I haven't been real successful getting back out there." He turned and looked at Rhoda. Tears still glimmered in her eyes. "They tell me I'm depressed, though I don't really believe in all that hogwash."

"They who?"

"The doctors at the nut house. I got drunk one day and pushed some bitchy customer, and she called the cops on me. They hauled me off to some drug/alcohol rehab place. I didn't need it, though. It's not like I get drunk a lot. I'd just had a rough night."

"Did it help?"

"Naw. I just needed to sober up. But I've had to put on a big show for the psychiatrist and my

120

daughters. I've gone to their stupid group sessions and met with the doctor. I even filled the prescription for their zombie pills, but they can't make me take them."

Rhoda finished her cigarette and tossed it over the side. "Pills can be helpful."

"You want 'em?"

Rhoda drew her head back. "Me? You'd do that?"

"Sure. I'm not going to take them. Plus, if my daughters see the empty bottle, they'll think I've been following doctor's orders."

"I guess it wouldn't hurt to try them, but you might need them."

"Not me. The only reason I filled the script was to keep my kids and that psych off my back. They're all yours."

"Won't your kids notice?"

"Probably." He paused, eyebrows knitted together. "How about this? I'll bring you one every night at the cocktail hour. It says you're not supposed to drink with them, but that's just more of their bullshit." He finished the rest of his drink.

"That's very generous of you. Thanks, Marvin. You let me know if I can ever return the favor."

"If I think of something, you'll be my first call. I'm heading to the lounge for another drink. Care to join me?"

"Sure. I'll meet you there. I have to touch base with my sisters first—see if they met their one true love at dinner."

Marvin's face fell. Rejected again. "Right."

Rhoda patted him on the back. "I promise. I'll meet you down there in a few minutes. I've really enjoyed our talk. You're a great listener." She turned toward the stairs. "Come on. Walk with me."

He smiled. Maybe she was sincere. "My lady?" He offered his arm.

Her eyes brightened as she gave a small curtsey and wrapped her arm through his. "Lead the way, sir."

Chapter 17

As the elevator doors opened, Cheryl heard a Beatles song coming from the direction of the Peacock Lounge. Not her favorite music to sing, but certainly a crowd favorite among the Boomer set. She wasn't supposed to entertain tonight anyway, unless the crowd insisted.

Maggie, lips pursed and eyes rolling, stepped back into the elevator. "I can't do it, Cher. I cannot go listen to Lyle almost hitting the notes to 'Good Day Sunshine' and watch all those old farts shuffle around the dance floor. I'm going back to the room."

"No, you're not." Cheryl grabbed her by the arm and pulled her forward. "Quit being such a killjoy. So most of the folks are older. So we don't have the Chippendales on this cruise. We can still have fun. Everyone I've met seems very nice. You don't have to marry one of them or even go out with them. Why can't you just cut loose and enjoy the moment?"

"I think you got all the positivity in the family."

"Enough with the pity party. Come on. Just take it for what it is."

"You mean grab a geezer and join in the fun?" Maggie pouted.

"Yes. No. I mean enjoy a first class river cruise with good food, free drinks, and beautiful views." Cheryl waved to Rhoda as she came down the stairs. "Not to mention a week with your two most favorite people in the world."

Rhoda joined them. "What's going on? Did I

miss anything?"

"No. Just Maggie being a stick-in-the-mud."

Maggie closed her eyes and drew in a deep breath. "Okay. Okay. You're right. I can have fun with you guys. The rest of this bunch, I'm not so sure."

"Good. It's settled. Let's go in the lounge and get this party started."

The staff had cleared the middle of the room for a dance floor. Dot was front and center doing donuts with her walker while, beside her, Farmer John jiggled to "She Loves You." Lining sides of the room were rows of chairs and wheelchairs.

"See there, Mags? You ought to be more like Dot."

"I might be able to manage that after a bottle or two of tequila, but I don't think it's worth the hangover. I promise, I'll try to lighten up."

Lyle, belting out the last line while hammering away on his snare drum, opened his eyes as the song ended. "All right, dudes and dudettes. Next up, we have a popular instrumental version of 'Something.' It's a great song for a slow dance, fellows. So grab a gal and snuggle up." He flipped a few switches and a full orchestra began playing the song. Fitting the microphone back in its stand, Lyle started making small talk with a group of women.

"Cheryl, you ought to go and properly introduce yourself to Lyle. Maybe he'll let you sing along with the music machine tonight," Rhoda said.

Cheryl's eyes brightened. "Really? Do you think he would? I bet people would much rather listen to live music than some computer-generated stuff."

Maggie slumped into a chair. "I know I would.

Especially these slow songs. Am I invisible enough to avoid being asked to dance?"

Cheryl raised an eyebrow. "Maggie. Go with the flow, remember?"

"Right. Why don't you flow on up there and put some life in this party? Look over there. Half of those people in the chairs look like they're asleep."

Sure enough, two out of five had their heads propped against the back of their seats, mouths open, eyes closed. Cheryl shimmied a little, tugged at her dress, and fluffed her hair. "I think I will."

As she made her way across the dance floor, someone in the crowd yelled, "Woo-hoo! It's the *Tournament of Treasures* Champ! Sing us a song!" The group started clapping and cheering.

Grabbing the mike, she turned and radiated toward the audience. "Oh, my goodness. Aren't you all just lovely. Thank you so much."

Just as she started singing along with the keyboard, Lyle, face beet red and eyes bulging, marched across the room and snatched at the microphone, knocking it to the floor. He leaned in close and hissed, "Now look what you've done. You've ruined the show. That's what happens when amateurs try to compete with professionals."

Cheryl, heart pounding in terror, leaned away from him as he continued his rant. "I'm going to have find another mike."

He turned on his heel and stopped. The room was still and silent, as everyone stared in disbelief. "Oh. Excuse me, ladies and gentlemen." He forced a smile. "Just a little misunderstanding. No real casualties, except the equipment, ha ha." He held up the pieces of the mike. "But don't you worry. The fun will continue. Renee? Leave that bar open for another hour while I prepare to put a little magic in the night."

He turned off the KORG, and cued up a number on the boom box in the corner. "Enjoy this beautiful rendition of 'Hey Jude' by none other than the great crooner, Bing Crosby, and his orchestra. I'll be right back."

Cheryl still stood, stunned, in the front of the room while Bing and his band butchered the McCartney classic.

Rhoda and Maggie rushed to her side. "Are you all right? Did he hurt you?" They talked over each other.

Tears filled Cheryl's eyes. "Wow. I did not see that coming. He seemed so nice last night." She sighed. "I didn't give him any reason to hate me, did I? I try to be nice to everyone."

"You know, I noticed him glaring at you when the captain introduced you at dinner. I think he's jealous," Maggie said.

"I think he's fucking crazy," Rhoda said. "And I know crazy."

"Jealous? Of me? He must know I'm here to perform."

"Just be careful around him." Rhoda looked toward the door. "At least he's gone now."

"Maybe I should apologize to the group. I didn't mean to ruin the party."

"It wasn't your fault, but it wouldn't hurt, either," Maggie said.

Cheryl took a deep breath, flipped back her hair and stepped into the middle of the dance floor. "Hey, everybody!" She projected her best stage voice over the slogging tune on the boom box. "I'm so sorry if I spoiled your fun. But the night's young, right?"

All eyes turned toward her, as Bing slid through a tortured vocal riff of the final refrain. When the recording ended, the crowd began to chant her name. "Cher-yl! Cher-yl! Cher-yl!"

Beaming, Cheryl inhaled, stood straight, and in perfect pitch, sang her prize-winning rendition of "Crazy" without accompaniment. The crowd went wild.

◆◆◆

For the next hour, while the bar remained open, Rhoda played the keyboard while Cheryl thrilled the audience. In keeping with the Beatles theme, they got the crowd moving with a rousing rendition of "Twist and Shout." The normally sedentary group moved every body part they could as they laughed and sang along, making for a lively evening.

For their next number, Rhoda chose "All You Need is Love," and Marvin materialized beside her and began to play the sax. He was actually pretty good. Cheryl, of course, lavished in the attention and joyfulness of her audience. Even Maggie got up and grabbed a tambourine and played along, though Rhoda suspected she was really escaping the tottering line of octogenarians who kept asking her to dance.

Finally, at the prompting of the cruise director, Rhoda switched the keyboard to auto and turned down the volume. It definitely had a calming effect on the group. Some began to trickle out while others lined up for last call.

Marvin cleared the reed, replaced it on the sax, and turned to Rhoda. "Nice work on the ivories there, Rhoda. I'm impressed."

He was a nice guy. "Thanks. I've played as long as I can remember. I love it. It transports me." She wiped her damp forehead with a cocktail napkin. "You're not so bad yourself."

"I played in the Air Force Band back in the sixties, but I'm pretty rusty now."

"Oh, were you in Vietnam?"

"I'd rather forget about those days, if it's all the same to you." Just then, the keyboard began a smooth-jazz version of the "Fool on the Hill." He held out his hand to Rhoda. "Care to dance?"

"Sure." She rose from the bench. "I meant to ask you, did you mean it about bringing me some of your Celexa?"

"Damn. I knew I was forgetting something. Do you want me to go get it?"

Not just one little pill. She didn't want to come off as needy, but she was sick of drinking, and all the festivities were making her a little edgy. "Oh, no. That's okay. Maybe tomorrow, if you remember."

Finally, the song ended. Marvin asked her to join him for a smoke upstairs, but she declined. As she tidied up the keyboard area, she noticed Glenda, the anxious dinner companion, stagger into the room sobbing. "Help," she slurred as she ran into a pillar and fell against the back of a chair. "Pleezh."

"Glenda, right? Are you okay?" Rhoda watched the woman sway and stagger as she attempted to stand. "Let me help you."

"Thanks, shweetie." Reaching for Rhoda's

128

hand and missing, Glenda pitched forward until they were nose to nose. "I've had a li'l assident, and I can't find my room."

Rhoda, arms wrapped around the woman to keep them both from crashing to the floor, felt mid-region wetness begin to seep into her own clothes. Good god. "Let me look at your name tag."

"Wha' name tag?"

"The one around your neck." She had thought the crew was making too big a deal about the whole lanyard-at-all-times business, but she was starting to get it. "It says here you're in room 204. Let me help you find it." If this gal was diagnosed with GAD, she was bound to have a pretty good stash of Xanax, Prozac, or some other scheduled drug. And she was shit-faced enough not to notice if some went missing.

In the room, Rhoda sat Glenda on the desk chair and found her a nightgown. "Do you think you can sit here and get yourself changed? Let me bring you a washcloth so you can clean up." In the bathroom, she ran the water and began rifling through the makeup bag on the counter. Sure enough, there was a ninety-count bottle of Klonopin, another of Prozac, and one called Trandate. She'd never heard of it, but it had "tran" in it, so maybe it was a tranquilizer.

Just as she won the war of the child-proof cap and began to pour out the contents, the door burst open. Glenda shoved Rhoda aside and vomited all over the sink. Rhoda slipped out and raced upstairs. She pitied the room steward who had to clean up that mess.

♦♦♦

Lester leaned back in the office chair, a plate

full of food balanced on his stomach, and watched the monitors. His trip to the kitchen had been richly rewarded—filet mignon, scallops, mashed potatoes, and rolls. He'd passed on the broccoli. Mom always made him eat it, but he hated the stuff. This was the dream job he'd been looking for. If he could just keep it.

After poking the last of the rolls in his mouth, he set the plate aside, stood, and stretched his arms. Maybe he needed to walk around a little to keep the threatening food coma at bay. There was hardly ever anyone in the halls, except right before and after an event. When he'd gone to the kitchen, the only person he'd run into was Lyle leaving a guest room.

Lester had straightened his shoulders, put his hand on the baton, and asked if there was any trouble. Did Lyle need assistance?

Apparently, some old person had fallen asleep in the lounge, so the entertainment director escorted him back to his room. Said this kind of thing happened a lot on these cruises. "It's all part of the job, you know," Lyle had said.

Lester vowed to be more alert to passengers having problems. He wanted to be sure and go the extra mile.

Refreshed, Lester focused again on the monitors. Two women staggered down the hall on Deck 2. Were they both drunk? He zoomed in. There was the seasick lady again. It looked like she was practically carrying an older woman toward a room. Was she sick? Drunk? She opened the door and they both went inside. Minutes later, the younger one edged out of the room and walked briskly toward the elevators. That was the third time he'd seen her in different hallways, twice with different people. She couldn't have buddied up with these people in one afternoon. Troublemaker or good Samaritan?

The kitchen monitor showed the place clean and empty, except for two staffers huddled over a countertop in the corner. Were they supposed to be in there?

Then, he noticed the time stamp on the screen. 11:45 p.m. His workday was officially over. Logging all of the activity he had witnessed so far to share with Renee in the morning, he put the baton and spray back where they belonged and headed for his bunk.

◆◆◆

"Well, that was an interesting night," Cheryl said as the three women jostled for space to unpack their bags.

"You don't know the half of it," said Rhoda, pulling a faded nightshirt over her head. "Not only did I get flashed by a geezer, I got puked and peed on by an extremely drunk grandmother. They may be old, but there are some wild ones in this crowd."

Maggie's mouth dropped open. "You're kidding? You did all that and had time to play the keyboard?"

"Fortunately, I'm faster than they are, and that's not saying much, so I was able to make a quick getaway."

Cheryl hummed while she removed her makeup. "Thanks for playing for me, Rho. I think everybody enjoyed my singing, don't you?"

"Everyone except Lyle," said Maggie. "He was

131

practically foaming at the mouth when he stormed out of there."

Rhoda nodded. "What a prima donna. All that fuss about you picking up the mike? I thought he was going to hit you with it."

"Me, too," said Cheryl. "But, I guess if the tables were turned and somebody took over my performance, I would be upset, though I think I'd be a little more gracious, at least in front of the crowd. He never did come back to the lounge. I'll have to apologize to him tomorrow. I'm sure they keep to a tight schedule, and I messed it up for him. Other than his little temper tantrum, he seems like a nice man. He's certainly good looking and young enough, don't you think, Maggie?"

"Mr. Sparkle Coat? I don't know if I could get into that."

"You never know until you try," said Cheryl.

"We'll see," said Maggie as she opened her gift bag. "Okay, ladies. It's time to detoxify. Everyone kindly remove the Kinoki pads and apply them to the soles of your feet. Mine will probably turn neon green after all that wine and rich food tonight."

Rhoda opened the packet like it contained live snakes. "Are you sure about this? It kind of creeps me out that all this poison is going to ooze out of my feet."

Cheryl opened hers. "Well, I'm not worried. I've hardly had anything to drink, and I ordered the vegan option at dinner. I have to be careful if I'm going to fit in my performance gowns all week."

After the girls completed their beauty routines, Cheryl found a schedule for the next day's excursions and activities on the table. "Oh, they must give us a new list every night." She looked over at the beds. "And I just noticed, we must have turn down service. With chocolates and everything. This cruise keeps getting better all the time."

Maggie popped the candy in her mouth. "Delicious, though I should probably just smear it right on the poison pad. So what's up for tomorrow?"

The main excursion was a walking tour of historic Fernandina Beach, promising boutique shopping and gourmet dining. There was also a guided boat tour around Cumberland Island, highlighting lush vegetation, wild horses, hundreds of bird species, and some glimpses of the historic mansions built by the Carnegies.

"I'd love to go on both tours," said Cheryl. "Who's in?"

Maggie raised her hand. "It sounds interesting. Especially Cumberland Island. Plus, I don't think I can stand hanging around on this boat all day. What are the other activities?"

"There's canasta in the second floor library, ballroom dancing lessons in the Peacock Lounge, and a watercolor class in the Hibiscus Salon. Oh, and there's a contract bridge sign-up sheet in the dining room."

"Canasta? Do people even play that anymore? I'm definitely going on the excursions. What about you, Rho?"

"I think I'll stay on the boat. My ankle never has been right after I broke it last year."

"You mean after Lute broke it," said Maggie. Was it only a year ago that Maggie had spent her summer break helping Rhoda after she fell? Lute, her good-for-nothing husband had tripped her, causing the injury, then refused to drive her to the hospital. Maggie still fumed about it, even though the SOB had disappeared without a trace shortly after that.

"Whatever. I don't think I can handle a walking tour. But the watercolor class sounds fun. I always have liked sketching."

Cheryl edged her way into the bathroom to brush her teeth. "Sounds like a plan. Ready or not, it's time for bed. I need to get my beauty rest."

Chapter 18

Maggie did not sleep well. Crammed against the wall, she nearly sweat to death next to Rhoda. What a hot box. Plus, she was a kicker. Cheryl didn't help either. She tossed, turned, and moaned all night on the top bunk. Finally, as the sky began to brighten, Maggie drifted off.

"HELP ME!"

Maggie bolted upright, smacking her head on the bed above her. "Jesus Christ, Cher. What is it?"

"I don't know. I can't move my feet. I can feel them, but I can't move them."

"Hold on. Let me see what's going on." Maggie shoved the still snoring Rhoda off the edge of the bed and climbed over her.

"What'd you do that for?"

"Something's wrong with Cheryl." Maggie panicked. Maybe there was a poisonous tropical spider or something that paralyzed Cheryl's feet. They had left the sliding door open all night. She grabbed Cheryl's covers and threw them back, revealing two feet, glued to the sheets with an oozing, black, tarry substance. "What the hell is that?"

Rhoda got up off the floor, grabbed one of Cheryl's toes and pulled the foot from the sheet. They all stared in horror.

Maggie was the first to make the connection. "It's the Kinoki pad. What the hell did you eat and drink yesterday? Are you taking any medications?"

Pale and eyes glittering with tears, Cheryl

135

looked at her feet. "Nothing. I mean I had a lemon drop during the cocktail hour and a white wine spritzer with dinner, but that was it. And no, I don't take any medications." She glanced down at their feet. "What do yours look like?"

Rhoda sat on the edge of the bed and lifted her foot. "Mine's still white, except for a little smudge of brown in the middle."

"Mine, too," said Maggie.

"And you two drank like sailors last night." Cheryl's bottom lip stuck out.

Rhoda laughed out loud. "I've been telling you guys, clean living and honesty don't pay."

Cheryl's pout increased. "That's the end of the damn Kinoki pads for me. I felt like I was possessed all night and now this. Help me into the bathroom, so I can shower this gunk off. Our tour leaves in ninety minutes."

While Cheryl showered, Maggie and Rhoda made their way to the dining room for breakfast.

Renee welcomed them at the door. "Open seating this morning, ladies. Tonight, we'll seat you at a table with your best matches from the dating profiles." She winked.

Maggie scanned the room. "I don't see that hot waiter I had last night, but he was stationed toward the back. Let's sit there." Just as they sat down, Raul emerged at the door to the kitchen, along with another extremely handsome staffer. Maggie caught his eye and fluttered her fingers in a little wave. He looked past her, his mouth set in a line, his eyes narrowed. "Well, that's just rude. He was so friendly last night."

Just then, Raul and another man were pushed

forward by two uniformed police officers. The fat security guard from the ship raced behind them, his hand on a holstered gun at his hip. The clank of forks and dishes ceased at once, as if cued by a conductor, and the room fell silent. Momentarily.

After the men were paraded through the room and off the boat, the crowd began to buzz in whispered tones.

"Oh my!"

"What do you suppose…"

Maggie's jaw dropped.

"Was that him?" Rhoda asked.

Maggie still did not speak.

"I'll go see what I can find out." Rhoda left the table and cornered one of the other wait staff. Minutes later, she returned. "Rumor has it they were both spotted on the security camera snorting coke in the kitchen after hours. One was your waiter and the other was a maintenance man."

Maggie's face turned from white to red. "Goddammit. The one cute guy on this fucking tub who paid attention to me gets arrested the second day out. I'm such a loser."

"No. He's the loser. Don't give up yet, Sis. Maybe your tour guide will be a hottie." She looked toward the kitchen. "I wonder where they got cocaine?"

Maggie pushed her plate of lobster benedict away and slammed back her mimosa, while Rhoda stared very intently toward the ceiling. "What're you looking at?"

"Nothing. Just noticed how many security cameras there are in here."

♦♦♦

Marvin watched from the top deck as those going on the excursion boarded the bus. He'd thought about it. The nature tour sounded good, but he'd been on one. With Ann. Before she got sick. A lifetime ago. Instead, he decided to try the ballroom dancing. At least he'd get a chance to hold a woman in his arms. Surely, he could find a willing partner. Maybe even one who could walk and dance without assistance. He'd almost given up on a younger woman. Those three sisters were the youngest he'd seen, but Maggie acted like he had leprosy, and the pretty blond didn't even notice him. Rhoda had potential, though she disappeared from the lounge after their dance last night. The jury was still out on her.

The ding-dong of the PA system sounded, signaling an announcement. "Good morning. This is Renee, your cruise director. For those of you who decided not to take an excursion, the onboard activities will begin in five minutes. All locations are printed in today's itinerary. We will remained docked until midnight, if you'd like to do some exploring on your own later. Have a good day!"

The cruise director was way too chipper for his taste. That sing-songy voice made him want to shake her and scream, "SHUT UP." But he wouldn't. Hostile behavior like that is what got him thrown in the nut house. He'd just avoid her whenever possible.

The chairs in the Peacock Lounge had all been moved to the edges of the room, leaving a large dance floor. Marvin, apparently, was first to arrive, even though he stopped by his room for a quick bracer from the bottle of Heaven Hill. He'd wait five minutes, and if no one showed up, he'd leave.

"Oh, goody! We have our first dancer."

Renee. Dear God, he was going to have to listen to that fake cheer for the next hour. He checked his watch. "You can go on and do something else. Doesn't look like anyone else is coming."

"Oh, no. I have nothing else to do, except make sure you have the best dancing experience ever. If no one else shows, it'll just be you and me cutting the rug."

There was that damned wink. She must have a tic or something.

"Let me just get the music set up. I'm sure the others will be here soon."

Sure enough, Dot and that little ninety-something woman came through the door followed by a few other men. Marvin grabbed the granny to avoid getting stuck with Dot or Renee. "My name's Marvin. Care to dance?"

"Sure, honey. I'm Hilda." She threw her arms around his neck. "I'd love to bump and grind with you."

He had to admit, she had plenty of energy and was light on her feet. He just didn't think he could get past the sagging neck folds and age-spotted hands.

After a waltz, a cha-cha, and a foxtrot, Renee announced they were ready for the rumba. "This one can get pretty steamy, folks. Lots of hip action, so let 'er rip. I promise, what happens in the ballroom stays in the ballroom."

The thought of slinking around with Hilda made bile rise in the back of his throat. After the first few moves, he gasped, and limped toward the door. "Sorry, just a little trouble with my hip replacement. I'd better call it a day." He dragged his leg down the hall until he was out of site, then sprinted to the elevator. He needed another snort of the bourbon in his suitcase after that.

As he approached his room, he noticed the door ajar. Probably forgot to lock it. Plus, he really hadn't gotten the hang of the key card system. Every time he swiped it, he got a red light and a beep. Twice already, the maid had to let him in. Unconcerned, he swung open the door, which immediately banged into the bathroom door, leaving little room for him to enter. He knew he hadn't left that door open. It was too hard to maneuver around it. Squeezing through the narrow opening, he stopped short. "Rhoda?"

Rhoda's head snapped up as she pulled her hands from his dopp kit. Her startled expression quickly gave way to a smile. "Oh, Marvin, you scared me."

He raised an eyebrow. "I see that." Why was she in his bathroom, and what was she looking for? "Can I help you?" He looked toward the bag on the counter.

"Need? Um. No, not really. I didn't see your name on the list for the excursion, so I figured you might be around somewhere. I went to the watercolor class, which was really good by the way, but it's over now. I was a little bored, but didn't want to play canasta, and I have a bad ankle which eliminated ballroom dancing, so I came to look for you and noticed your door was open. I thought I'd just come in and wait. I wanted to apologize for taking off after our dance last night, but some drunk woman about passed out on me, so I helped her back to her room."

Her words tatted like machine gun fire, and her voice was higher than before. He'd caught her. Doing what, he wasn't sure, but he'd caught her. A smile curved his lips. Maybe Miss Rhoda wasn't the little do-gooder she'd made herself out to be. This situation might work in his favor. He had a little power over her, plus, he liked that she was a bit of a rogue. "Did you need something out of my dopp kit?"

She looked at it like she'd never seen it before. "What? This? No. No, no. I came in to use the toilet, and my big clumsy hand hit it and knocked it over. I was just putting it back when you came in." She stepped from the bathroom. "How are you?"

He laughed. She was smooth. "I'm good. Ballroom dancing was a bust, by the way. You didn't miss much. And how are you? You seem a little high strung."

"I do?" She took a deep breath. "Actually, I guess I am. I struggle with anxiety. Ever since my husband disappeared, well, actually, long before he left, I've been jumpy. He was kind of a loose cannon, happy and sweet one day, then crazy-bug-eyed screaming and punching the next. Even though he's been gone a year, I'm still scared he's going to jump out of the bushes at me or something."

He noticed she rubbed her thumb and forefinger together the whole time she talked. "I'm sorry to hear that. No one deserves to be treated that way." The pills. That's what she was after. He'd almost forgotten he offered them to her. He softened his voice. "Were you looking for the pills, Rhoda?"

She lowered her head. "Yes. I'm sorry. I should have just waited until you got back."

"I'm surprised your doctor hasn't prescribed something, since you've been suffering with this for so long."

"I don't have any health insurance. I thought I could handle it on my own, but it just seems to be getting worse."

"Is that why you're helping all the old folks on the ship? Looking for meds?"

She raised her head and stared at him with bovine eyes glimmering with tears. "No. I mean, I haven't…" She turned and headed for the door. "I've gotta go."

Marvin grabbed her arm. "Hey, slow down. It's okay. I said you could have the pills."

Her shoulders dropped as she sighed. "Really?"

"Sure. I'm not going to take them. In fact," he leaned toward her and whispered. "I'll tell you what. If, during your room-escort adventures, you happen to come across any Viagra, grab me a few. It'll be our little secret."

Rhoda threw her arms around him and kissed him on the cheek. She leaned back and took his face in her hands. "You're a real sweetheart, you know that?" Again, she gave him a fierce hug.

Ample bosom, nice ass, long legs. He savored the moment.

"I don't know, Marvin," she laughed. "I'm not sure you need Viagra."

Chapter 19

Behind mirrored aviator sunglasses, Lester's eyes darted side to side, up, down, and straight ahead. He stood at full attention, adrenaline still coursing through his system from the arrest of the two staffers this morning. Renee and the captain had credited his keen observation skills and detailed notetaking from his time on the monitors for the evidence the police had needed. All his *World of Warcraft* training finally paid off. Take that, Mom.

Today, he was assigned to supervise the delivery and loading of pallets of food and beverages to resupply the kitchen. As the vendors arrived, he checked their credentials against the order forms. For the less vigilant, it would be easy for someone to pose as a supplier to gain access for nefarious purposes. Not under his watch. Once he verified the vendor against his list, the staff could inspect the pallets and load them on the ship.

"Hey, Lester," shouted Renee. "When you're done here, I'm going to need you to put this job posting out by the gang plank. We're down one wait and one maintenance staffer, and we need them today, if possible. If someone expresses interest, write down their driver's license number, their name, address, and phone number, and then escort them up to my office. I'll be in there all day, God willing."

"Yes, ma'am," he said. "Um, since I'll be interacting with strangers, don't you think I ought to carry the gun?" You never knew what kind of riff-raff

143

might show up.

"I don't think that'll be necessary. The baton and pepper spray will be enough. And make sure you have your walkie-talkie tuned to channel seven."

"Yes, ma'am." Shoulders slumped, he returned his attention to the last of the food trucks. When the cargo was processed, he took his clipboard and the job advertisements to the other side of the ship. As directed, he posted the sign at the end of the gangplank, found a folding chair and waited.

After an hour, a man stopped and read the notice. He turned toward Lester. "Do you know anything about this?"

"Yeah. We had a few people leave the ship unexpectedly this morning, so we're a little short staffed. We need to fill the jobs immediately." Lester looked him up and down. Probably late-thirties? His hands were calloused and muscles bulged underneath his tee shirt. Obviously, the guy was no stranger to hard work. "You got any experience?"

"Not as a waiter, but I've worked on a fishing boat before, had to repair it and then keep it running. Plus, I've had a lot of experience in a machine shop."

"Can you start today?"

"I don't see why not. I'm in between jobs right now."

Again, Lester looked him over. He was clean. His hair was longer but well-kept. "If you'd like to apply, I'll just need to get some information from you. Then I can take you to my boss. What's your name?"

"Buddy. Buddy Crapps."

♦♦♦

Hearing aids whistled as the sightseers on the bus struggled to understand the tour guide. The only words that came through the speaker system were numbers. "On your left is the famous…thirty-six-thousand… of…by…Carneg…eighteen-eighty-four…"

"Oh, for God's sake," said Maggie. "You think they'd double check the P.A. system before the tour."

Cheryl nodded. "I know. It seems no matter how prepared you are or how great your information is, it's always ruined by a glitch in the technology."

"Doesn't matter. I think every word he's saying is printed on the brochure. It even tells you approximately how many steps it is to the sites. And they have golf carts for those who have mobility problems. Boy, they sure know their audience."

"It certainly is an older crowd than I expected on a singles cruise."

"False advertising. I have yet to see someone on that boat I'd be interested in."

"What about Lyle? He's really handsome, and he can walk unassisted." Cheryl winked.

"The entertainment director? The guy who almost attacked you last night?"

"I think he was just nervous. It was the first show of the cruise, after all, and I disrupted his program. I probably would have gone a little bonkers myself. He seemed pleasant enough when I saw him in the hall this morning."

"I don't know if I can lower the bar that far," Maggie said. "I mean, yeah, he's good looking, but that super white smile and the one-man band routine. That's way past my comfort zone."

"Says the woman who dated an accordion player."

"One time!"

"I'm teasing, Mags. You don't have to marry him, maybe dance a few times, or have lunch or drinks or something. I bet he's got some funny stories to tell about this place. You could use a few laughs. He seems popular with everybody else."

"We'll see," Maggie said as the bus rolled to a stop.

The tour guide had abandoned the PA system. Instead, he shouted, "All of those who signed up for the Cumberland Island boat tour, please assemble on the dock to the left of the bus. If you need assistance, just let me or the driver know."

After the island trip and lunching and shopping in Fernandina Beach, the girls re-boarded the bus. Cheryl looked at her Apple Watch. "I hope we get back soon. I have to practice for tonight. What do you think I should wear? I want to look nice for the captain."

"I saw you talking to him forever last night at dinner. What's he like?"

Cheryl smiled as color rose to her cheeks. "Oh, he's so nice. He told me how long he's been with the cruise line and how he started out in the Navy. He said he'd seen me on TV and was excited to learn I was going to be on his ship. He's going to try to make it to the cocktail hour tonight and to my performance after dinner. I think he likes me."

"Of course he likes you. All the handsome men

with good jobs like you. Me, on the other hand? I've had maybe two dates in the last year."

"Two? I thought you'd only gone out with that coach." Cheryl sipped from the complimentary bottle of water they handed out on the bus.

"Don't remind me. I guess, technically, you're right. My other date was more of a fling when I was at Rhoda's last summer."

Cheryl choked and spit water on the seatback in front of her. "What? You had a fling? With who?"

"Whom."

"Whatever. When did you have time at Rhoda's? Between my tryouts for Choir Wars, Rhoda's broken ankle, and Lute going berserk and almost killing me, how did you squeeze in a fling?"

Maggie blushed this time. "It doesn't matter. I met some guy, really hot by the way, down at that scrungy bar on the water. We sat there forever, drinking and eating and drinking and drinking. Anyway, I saw him a few more times just by chance, and we, well, we kind of got together."

Cheryl's eyebrows hit her hairline. "Didn't you lecture me about not going too fast with that producer? And you were out shagging some guy from a bar?"

"I'm sorry I brought it up."

"No." Cheryl exhaled. "I'm sorry. It's your business. You obviously liked him. Do you still hear from him?"

Maggie looked out the bus window. "No."

Cheryl patted her on the knee. "He probably lost your number."

"Yeah, probably."

"What was his name?"

"Buddy."

"Did you even know his last name?" Cheryl arched a brow.

"Yes. He had a last name."

"Well?"

Maggie buried her face in her hands. "Crapps. His last name was Crapps."

♦♦♦

"Well, that was bizarre," Rhoda said, "even for me. I've heard of speed dating, but pairing us up with a different person for each course? What did they call it?"

"Progressive dinner date," Maggie said.

"Did you meet anyone with possibilities?"

"Uh, no. For the appetizer, I had pasty little Frederick, the mama's boy. He kept wrenching around in his seat looking for her. I think the tightly stretched umbilical cord must have been pulling at him. How about you?"

"My first course wasn't too bad. Ricardo with the toupee. He was nice, but he threw his arm around me and kept rubbing circles on my shoulder with his finger. I think he wore off the top layer of skin. And you were right the other night. He is a spitter."

"I know. He was my dessert course. Ruined my appetite."

"Too bad Cheryl missed it. She would have found some way to make it fun."

"Good old Pollyanna. I hope her rehearsal went well. I can't wait to hear her sing tonight. I wonder what she's wearing?"

"I'm not sure," Rhoda said, "but we only have

148

about a half hour till show time. I'm going up on the top deck for a smoke. Wanna join me?"

"No, thanks. I think I'll head back to the room and freshen up." Not that there was anybody to impress. "I'll just meet you in the lounge. Whoever gets there first, save a seat."

Back in their state room, Maggie squeezed in the shit-and-shower toilet to touch up her makeup, though why she bothered, she didn't know. Most people on the ship probably had cataracts and couldn't see anyway. But, she promised Cheryl she would make the best of it, and so she would. False eyelashes, red lipstick, and an extra swipe of glow-blush would have to do. If she was going to dance with that crazy emcee, she might as well look like a stage performer.

The lounge was mostly dark, with ambient lighting from battery-operated candles and small spotlights on the keyboard and microphone stand. Cheryl would be in her element. Maggie found two seats near the front, which was not difficult. All the wheelchairs were in the back row, and everyone else was seated on couches and comfy chairs ready for their pre-bedtime naps.

"Hey," whispered Rhoda from behind. "I guess saving a seat was a little unnecessary." As she made her way toward Maggie, she stubbed her toe, stumbled, and landed with a thud on the edge of the chair.

Maggie grabbed her arm to steady her. "You okay?" Rhoda's pupils looked dilated, but then again, the room was pretty dark.

"Yeah, I'm fine. I drank a martini up on the top deck. It must have been a strong one."

"Drink water for a while."

"Yes, ma'am," she giggled.

Surely Rhoda wasn't using again. There weren't any pills in the room, and Maggie doubted she could get any from the ship's doctor, if there even was one. No. It must have been the drink. She closed her eyes. Deep, cleansing breath. Stop worrying about everyone else. Relax. Have fun.

Just as she exhaled, a loud screech from the microphone echoed throughout the room. Her eyes popped open. Before her stood Lyle, aglitter in a red tux with silver sequined lapels.

"Good evening, ladies and gentlemen! Welcome to tonight's onboard entertainment. As you know, if you've read your daily itinerary, we have a special guest who's going to do her best to outperform me—ha ha. Please give a big hand for our visiting star, Ms. Cheryl Lennon."

As Cheryl took her place at the microphone, Maggie watched Lyle closely. No evil looks tonight. In fact, he seemed euphoric at the sight of his guest performer, his eyes twinkling, his smile revealing every perfect tooth in his mouth.

"Thanks, Lyle. Hello everybody!" Cheryl waved as she approached the mike. "Because I know I can't outdo Lyle," she turned toward him, smiled like an angel, and extended her hand, "I decided our first song will be a duet." Removing the mike from its stand, she walked over to the keyboard. "How about a little Sonny and Cher? What do you say, everyone." She turned to the crowd. "Who wants to hear 'I Got You, Babe'?"

Everyone clapped, and Rhoda whistled through her fingers. Lyle started the music and hammed it up imitating Sonny with a nasal croon. The two singers fell into a natural rhythm and sounded better than the original. Before the last line, Cheryl paused and said, "Everybody now!" Those who were still awake sang along as Lyle brushed the cymbals into a fade.

As Cheryl resumed her spot in the center of the room and began her next selection, Maggie noticed red and blue lights flashing through the window. She tapped Rhoda on the shoulder and pointed. "Do you think those are the cops? I wonder if someone else is getting arrested."

"I don't know. They're not using any sirens. Want me to ask someone?"

Maggie squinted toward the flashing lights and noticed people wheeling out a stretcher. She moved toward the window where she could see the person being transported. They seemed to be moving their head and hands. Must not be life or death. No surprise that someone needed medical attention on this boat. Over half of the passengers were in frail health.

After a few more numbers, Cheryl and Lyle cued up the boom box and took a break while waiters circulated through the room offering snacks and drinks.

"What was going on out there?" asked Rhoda.

"Looked like someone must have gotten sick or hurt. Oh, here comes a waiter. Ask him."

Rhoda waved her hand. "Excuse me, sir? We saw an ambulance outside. Is everything okay?"

"I think so. Just as I was coming in here, I saw them taking Ms. Glenda out. She was shrieking about chest pains. Said all her medicine was missing."

"Oh, my. That's unfortunate," Maggie said.

"Let's hope she gets straightened out before the boat leaves, right, Rho?" She turned to see Rhoda, head lowered, moving quickly toward the door. Odd. Oh, well. She looked toward Cheryl, but before she could get her attention, the captain materialized at Cheryl's side. The two walked, arm in arm, toward the outside deck.

Damn. Alone again. Might as well get some wine to take back to the room. Standing at the bar, she felt a tap on her shoulder.

Teeth. "Hello there," Lyle bent to look at the name badge that dangled between her breasts, "Maggie. Care to dance?"

A shiver went down her spine and not in a good way. But she had promised Cheryl she would give him a chance. Just one innocent dance. What harm could it do? Maybe this slimy, lounge lizard act was just that—an act. "That would be nice, Lyle. Thanks."

He pulled a remote control from his pocket and pointed it toward the boom box, took her hand, and spun her into his arms. The disco hit, "Can't Get Enough of Your Love," filled the room with Barry White, and Lyle, panting about making love and not getting enough. Maggie tried to put some space between them, but as the song picked up tempo, he held her tight around the waist and ground his pelvis into hers.

"Oooh, Babe," he whispered into her ear canal, "You're just what I need. Wanna come up to my suite for a nightcap? I think your sister has the entertainment under control." His eyes were glassy; his lips curled in a leer.

Leaning as far away from him as she could, she

struggled in his grasp. "That, Lyle, would be a hard no."

"Come on, baby. Don't fight it. You know you want me." In a last attempt to keep her close, he stomped his foot on hers.

She pushed away from him with considerable force, kicked her foot free and left him, his hips thrust forward, arms in an empty embrace, and grabbed a bottle of wine from the bar before racing upstairs to her room.

Chapter 20

Rhoda's first conscious sensation was the sound of a vacuum cleaner running nearby. Without opening her eyes, she reached for a pillow to put over her head. No pillow. She patted the area around her. No sheets. No Maggie. What the…?

The vacuum droned. "Is everything okay, Ma'am?"

Her eyes popped open to one of the room stewards leaning over her.

"Can I get you anything? Help you find your room?"

How the hell did she end up here? She bolted upright. She was on an overstuffed, brocade couch in one of the many lounges on the ship.

"Ma'am?"

"Uh, hi. Yes, good morning. I mean no. I don't need any help." Her brain hurt trying to recall last night. How many people had she escorted back to their rooms searching for good drugs? "I was sitting up late reading and must have drifted off." She only remembered taking two pills. She'd dropped Elmer's Ativans when she'd caught him in flagrante delicto, the horny old bastard. And Glenda had puked all over her meds. Then she'd gotten some of Marvin's Celexas. She checked her pocket. There was still one in there. So, yeah, she'd probably only taken two. Usually, she could handle that, but she'd been clean for almost a month. Her tolerance must be low.

The steward finally turned off the infernal sweeper. "Sorry to wake you. Are you sure I can't I help you to your room?"

"No, I'm good. What time is it?"

"It's almost eight-thirty. You still have time to make it to breakfast, if you want."

Breakfast? Questionable. Coffee, though, was a must. "Thank you. I'll just scoot on down to the dining room. Have a nice day." Rhoda hoisted herself from the couch, back and knees cracking. She had a crick in her neck from sleeping without a pillow. Must be more careful.

After stopping in the room to wash her face and brush her teeth, Rhoda scanned the dining room for the girls.

"Yoo-hoo, Rhoda, over here." Cheryl waved from a table by the window.

She sat down to two sisters, leaning toward her, eyes wide.

"Okay, spill it," Maggie said. "Where were you last night?"

Cheryl chimed in. "Or who were you with?"

She needed time to figure out how to spin this. "Good god, girls. What is this, high school? Let me get some coffee first."

Cheryl flagged down the waiter with the refills, waited until Rhoda stirred in her three sugars and cream, and started in. "And?"

After a slurp of good, strong brew, she was ready. "Nothing nearly as exciting as you two have conjured up. I walked by the room and saw the magnet on the door, so I went to the lounge and fell asleep on the couch. See, sleep lines to prove it." She pointed to the indentations on her face from the corded edges of the sofa cushion. "The bigger question is, who got lucky last night?"

"What magnet?" Cheryl said. "I came back about one thirty after a marvelous evening with the captain, and Maggie was already asleep. With a half-empty bottle of wine next to the bed, I might add."

"Hey. Don't judge. If you'd gotten the groin-grind I got from Lyle, you would have finished the whole bottle. Ick." Maggie shivered.

Relieved to have the attention diverted from her, Rhoda pressed for details. "Groin-grind? Gotta hear that one first. Then, Cher, we want to know what you were doing with the captain so late."

Maggie relayed her misadventure with Lyle. "The one time I decide to follow Cheryl's advice and be nice, I get slimed by some pervert. That guy gives me the creeps. He'll be okay one minute and then, bam, it's like he's possessed. We were dancing, normally for a few seconds, then the next thing I know, he's got his tongue in my ear, and he's rubbing his…never mind." She buried her face in her hands. "I can't even say it. He even tried to keep me there by stepping on my foot!"

Cheryl placed her hand on Maggie's shoulder. "I'm sorry. It was my idea you dance with him. I should have known, after his little fit about the microphone the other night."

"That's not the worst of it. When I got back to the room, guess what I found on the top of my shoe?"

Both sisters leaned in.

"Your nasty old Kinoki pad. Do you know what that means?"

Mouths agape, they shook their heads no.

"He's been in our room! That slimy bastard has

been in our room. Check your underwear drawer, ladies. He probably stole them all to make soup."

Cheryl gasped. "Oh God. That does kind of give me the willies. But, in his defense, he said he has multiple jobs around here. Maybe he does the turn-down service."

"God. He touched my bed? That's even worse. You can believe that if you want since you have to work with him. But me? I'm going to give him, and every other male on this cruise, a wide berth."

Rhoda finished her coffee and signaled for a refill. "I gotta say, Mags, you might be as unlucky with men as I…"

"Well," Cheryl interrupted. "I've had my share of losers, too, you know. But so far, I think the captain might be a keeper."

"Do tell," sighed Maggie.

"Well, first we danced, and then he took me out on the front deck. He knows so much history about the river and the area. It was fascinating."

"Did he kiss you?"

"Rhoda! I just met him."

"So? Did he?"

"No. But he linked arms with me as he gave me a tour of the bridge. He showed me the GPS navigation, radars, the depth finder-thingy—that's very important on a river cruise—and all the communications systems."

"And that's it?"

"Yes, that's it. Although he did ask me to join him at the captain's table for dinner tonight." Cheryl wiggled in her seat. "I can't wait."

Rhoda, despite her throbbing head, was glad for

Cheryl. At least somebody on this cruise might get lucky. "So, what's on the agenda today?"

Cheryl pulled the itinerary out of her pocket. "It says here we're on the boat all day cruising down the Intracoastal Waterway to the Tolomato River. There's going to be a naturalist and a river historian on the top deck. Then lunch is supposed to be a speed dating exercise."

"Sounds like a real barn-burner," Maggie said. "We'd have to wheel most of them around. I think I'll pass on the lunch, find a book in one of the libraries, hide myself, and read."

"What are you going to do, Cheryl?" Rhoda asked. She hoped she could get away on her own for a while. So far, she hadn't had much luck getting her hands on meds. Plus, she wanted to score some Viagra for Marvin.

"I'll probably go up on the deck for a while. But then I have to rehearse. The evening show is called 'Western Hoedown.' That ought to be a real hoot."

"Watch out for Lyle. He's a loose cannon," Maggie said.

"Here's hoping he won't try anything with me. Last night, he was downright gracious, letting me finish the show by myself. Even if he does act up, I can take care of myself."

Good. They both had plans. "I may go to the lecture on deck," Rhoda said, "but then I want to go back to watercolor class. I really enjoyed it yesterday. And, who knows, I might try my hand at canasta." That would give her several hours on her own.

♦♦♦

After they all returned to the room, Cheryl insisted Maggie "put her game face on," and proceeded to give her a full makeover. "Well? What do you think?" Cheryl stood back waving a cosmetic brush like a magic wand. "Is that a 'bibbidi-bobbidi-boo' transformation or not?"

Maggie had to admit, she looked pretty good. Really good. Obviously, there was a difference in the quality of designer makeup versus the stuff she bought at the grocery store. "Thanks, Cher. Too bad I'll be wasting it on this tub."

"Attitude, Mags. Attitude. Maybe this pumpkin will turn in to a royal carriage for you today. Always expect a blessing just around the next corner," she said as she turned to put her beauty gear away. "I can feel you rolling your eyes at me. Stop being such a dud."

"Yes, ma'am." Maggie smiled. If she only had an ounce of her sister's indomitable spirit. Deep breath. New attitude. She looked outside. The sun danced off the water; trees draped in Spanish moss whispered on the shore of the Tolomato River. She should be enjoying this. When she checked her weather app this morning, it had been thirty-four degrees back home. "You're right. It's beautiful outside. I think I'll find a good book, a quiet place on one of the decks, relax, and get a tan. I have to have something to show for a week in Florida, and it's obviously not going to be a new boyfriend."

"You sure you guys don't want to join me for a bit of the lecture upstairs?"

Rhoda shook her head. "Watercolor class starts soon. I'm working on a river landscape. The interplay of light and shadow in the trees is so beautiful. I hope I can capture it. Maybe I'll see you at lunch."

"Sorry, Cher. I'm sure it'll be interesting, but I like my plan for the day better. Have fun." After both girls left the room, Maggie pulled on a swim suit and slid the gauzy cover up and sunhat off her one allotted hanger in the closet. As she stepped into flip-flops, she noticed the pricey pedicure she'd gotten already had a chip in the paint. Rummaging through her drawer, she found the polish. That would be something else to occupy her time in the sun.

In the library on their floor, Maggie scanned the titles and authors on the dusty book shelves. *The Ais, Original Settlers of Florida*. No. *A Comprehensive Maritime History of the World, Volumes One through Ten*. Big no. *Cross Creek* by Marjorie Kinnan Rawlings. Wow. Very possible. After reading *The Yearling* as a kid, Maggie would hide behind the hedges in their yard and pretend she battled the untamed wilds of Florida during simpler times. A memoir of the author's life in rural Florida during the thirties was sure to entertain. Maybe it would give her a real sense of the place. She grabbed the book, a bottle of water, and headed for a remote sun deck at the opposite end of the boat.

The halls were dark, made more so by the blinding sunlight shining through the portholes in doors at either end. Seeing the silhouette of a man coming out of a guest room at the far end, she stopped and waited for him to pass since the halls were rather narrow. Instead of coming toward her, he swiped a key card and entered another room, so she headed on toward the sundeck, head bent toward her book as she walked.

"Whoa there, little lady. I almost got you with the door. Better watch where you're going."

Dear God. Lyle. Hopefully, this was not his room. She feared a repeat of last night's amorous advances. "Lyle, you scared me." She skirted to the other side of the door. "Are these staff rooms?"

"No." He looked up and down the hall. "I'm just helping out the housekeeping staff. Like I said, entertainer, historian, chief cook and bottle washer. I do a little bit of everything around here." He scanned the hall again. "Nice to see you. Enjoy your day." He closed the door behind him, trotted toward midship, and took the stairs two at a time.

Odd fellow. At least he didn't try to hit on her again.

Settled in comfy lounge chair, Maggie alternated between watching the wake vee out behind the boat and immersing herself in the woodsy hummock of Cross Creek. Okay. This part of the trip was nice, as was yesterday's tour. She just needed to adjust her expectations. Not going to find the love of her life here, but she could relax. From now on, she'd enjoy the beautiful scenery, the serenity that came from not standing in front of a classroom of adolescents, and the chance to spend time with her two favorite people. She closed her eyes, tilted the brim of her sun hat over her face and drifted off.

ZZZZzzzzzttttt. ZZZzzzzttttt.

She bolted upright. What the hell was that?

ZZZZzzzzzztttt. ZZZZzzzzzztttt.

Sitting on the edge of the chaise, she looked around the deck. Empty except for her.

ZZZZZzzzztttt.

It sounded so close, but she was alone out here. She stood, opened the door to the interior hallway and let her eyes adjust to the darkness. No one there.

ZZZZZzzzttt.

Back outside she noticed a hook and a strap attached to one of the railings along the side of the boat. That must be it. She walked to the edge and leaned forward. Below, a worker sat on a small scaffold suspended from safety harnesses. She peered down to see broad shoulders and biceps straining the fabric of one of the ubiquitous Ponce de Leon Cruise polo shirts. Golden brown hair ruffled in the breeze. Muscular legs braced his body against the hull. An electric zing shot through her. Unless he had a face like a troll, he was the most promising thing she'd seen on this cruise.

She lost track of time staring down at him. He glowed in the reflection of the water. There was something familiar in the way his head tilted forward, the broad expanse of his upper back, his hair shimmering in the sun. She was transported to that pivotal scene in a romance novel, the rough and tumble hero catching her eyes, the magnetic pull between them irresistible as they fell into each other's arms.

ZZZZZzzzttt.

She jerked at the noise, sending her sunhat drifting over the edge, landing on the scaffold. He looked up. She squinted through her sunglasses. Couldn't be. Couldn't possibly be. "Buddy?"

◆◆◆

Lester reluctantly returned the baton and

pepper spray to the office. No gun today, either, despite his protests to Renee.

"We're going to be on the water all day, so there's no threat from outside troublemakers," she'd said.

"What do you want me to do?"

"Continue to watch the monitors and walk the halls making sure there are no distressed or disorderly passengers. Keep your walkie-talkie with you at all times."

He settled in front of the monitors. Breakfast was over, and most of the passengers were attending one of the activities for the morning. Several people crowded the top deck to hear the lecture by the naturalist. Nothing amiss there. The housekeeping crew should have been done with the third deck by now, but he noticed a few people in the hall. Was that a stray housekeeper coming out of the far end room? He zoomed in. He couldn't quite make out the face, but the build and the hair definitely looked like Lyle.

Lester switched to the mid-ship camera. Nothing down that way. He turned the lens back to the first hall. Wow. Hot chick in a bathing suit. He couldn't see her face since her head was down but she sure looked good from the back. Watch out for that open door, lady! Man, that was close. Who left that open? As he zoomed in again, Lyle stepped from another room. That guy was incredible, singing, lecturing, doing magic tricks all night in the lounge and then helping the cleaning staff all day. That was two rooms in less than ten minutes. Amazing.

A quick glance at the other decks revealed little activity except housekeepers and their carts and vacuums. Might as well grab a couple of pastries left over from breakfast and go patrol the place.

Chapter 21

"Good morning, fellow aquarellists!" The squat woman waddled from table to table, squirting blobs of paint on paper plates, arranging brushes and cups of water. "My name is Hermione, and I guess you could call this my magic wand." She flourished a paint brush. "I'm so happy to see some familiar faces from yesterday and a few new ones, too. Don't you newbies worry. Everyone works at their own pace in my class. Please, take a seat wherever you like."

Rhoda scanned the room looking for the oldest or most infirmed and walked toward a table with Elmer, the horny insomniac. He was bound to have Viagra in that tackle box of pills. She wasn't sure yet how to get her hands on them, but she was determined to fulfill her promise to score some for Marvin.

"I knew you'd be back, Sweet Thing." Elmer winked and slapped her on the behind.

She stifled a gag. This had better be worth it. Marvin was nice and all, and he did say she could have his Celexa, but pretending to want the big nasty from this geezer was almost enough to make her clean up her act. Deep breath. It was show time. She widened her eyes, pressed her lips into a coy smile, and sat beside him. "You devil, you. Are you enjoying the cruise so far?"

"It's a lot better now that you're here," he waggled his eyebrows as he leaned toward her. "You've been thinking about me since the other night, haven't you?"

With supernatural control, she held the smile

on her face and batted her lashes. To avoid looking him in the eye, she focused on his nose. Silver hairs curled from the cavern of his nostrils toward the scraggly brows. "I must confess, you're hard to forget."

"I knew you were hooked when you threw that glass at me. I like me a feisty one."

This might not be worth it. Just as she started to rise from her seat, Hermione swooped toward them. "Ahh, Rhoda. So glad you decided to come back. I have the background piece you were working on yesterday." She slid it on the table. "Such nice muted colors. Were you planning a landscape?"

Thank God for the distraction. "Why yes. I'd love to try to capture the riverbank at dusk. It has such a ghostly quality."

"That would be lovely. I think you have some real talent." Hermione turned to Elmer. "And you, this is your first day with us. Let me get you all set up. Here are some paper and brushes, and this paper plate will be your palate. Have you ever painted before?"

"No. Can't even draw a stick figure. I'm just here to check out the chicks."

"Now, now, an able man like yourself ought to be able to do both. Like I said before, everyone is an artist in my class. Let me help you get started. Just dip your brush in the water and either drip it or swipe it across the paper. Don't be afraid to get it too wet."

"It can never be too wet." So tickled by his own joke, Elmer cackled until he choked.

Obviously a veteran of working with geriatrics, Hermione whacked him on the back and continued her lesson.

Rhoda concentrated on her work, the gauzy reflection of the mossy trees on the water both eerie and soothing. She'd have to try this at home. Very relaxing.

A phone alarm tinkled. "Oh, dear, fellow artistes. I'm afraid our time is up for today, but we'll be here again tomorrow and the next day. Remember, all your work will be exhibited in the Peacock Lounge the last night of the cruise."

Rhoda looked up. Back to reality. "What a nice start, Elmer." She stared at the puddle of brown water collected in the center of his painting. "Do you need help getting back to your room?"

"I thought you'd never ask."

◆◆◆

After visiting the kitchen, a chocolate croissant in one hand and a bear claw in the other, Lester positioned himself just underneath the stairs on the first deck. He could keep an eye on things here while finishing his snack in private. The ding of the elevator made him tuck further back out of view.

"Now, Elmer. Don't get yourself too worked up. I'm just helping you to your room."

"Don't kid a kidder, Little Miss Mason. I know what you're after. This is the second time you've thrown yourself at me. I know you got a little spooked last time you laid eyes on the Elmer-Monster, but you haven't stopped thinking about it, have you?"

Lester recognized the woman pushing a wheelchair down the hall. He'd seen her help more than a few people to their rooms. Odd that she'd pair up with such an older man. What had Renee called it, a little slap and tickle? The man had called her Miss Mason. A little investigating wouldn't hurt. He'd look her up when he got back to the office.

So far, things had been pretty slow, and it wasn't noon yet. The days in port were more exciting, and tomorrow might be the best day yet. Renee was going to lead a tour group through St. Augustine for the whole day. No one would know if he was carrying the gun.

Chapter 22

Glad to see the Peacock Lounge empty, Cheryl walked to the keyboard and reviewed the list of country selections preprogrammed into the machine. Not bad. Some very old folk tunes, songs by classic country artists like Tammy Wynette, Loretta Lynn, Waylon Jennings and Buck Owens. Personally, the hard-hitting, tear-jerking songs from this era were among her favorites. She liked the more modern stuff, too. For mass appeal, she'd pick the most upbeat songs from every period to keep the mood light and the audience awake.

She circled fifteen selections to clear with Lyle, trying to split them evenly between men's and women's songs, though, truthfully, as the guest star, she should sing more. Too bad Rhoda wasn't here to fire up this complicated key board. It looked more like the flight deck on a rocket than a musical instrument. She couldn't even find the ON switch.

"WHAT THE HELL DO YOU THINK YOU'RE DOING?" Lyle glowered from the doorway. "That's a very expensive piece of equipment." He strode across the room in three steps, mumbling to himself. "I keep telling them not to bring in these stupid, novice karaoke singers."

Maggie was right. He was a loose cannon. Better appeal to his ego. "Oh, Lyle. I'm so glad you're here. I'd love to hear some of these arrangements, but I'm afraid to touch this thing. It's way too complicated for me, but you play it so well!" She took a step back and watched as her ploy had the desired effect.

His breathing slowed as he unclenched his fists. "Oh. Well. It is a professional piece of equipment, only for those of us who've had lots of training." He squeezed in front of her and commandeered control.

"I thought we might look at some of these songs for tonight. You'd be great at 'Cryin' Time' and 'Good Hearted Woman', and I could maybe try 'Stand by Your Man' and 'Don't Come Home A'Drinkin'. Those are all crowd favorites. What do you think?"

Lyle stared at the keyboard in a trance.

"Lyle?"

He jerked his head up.

"What do you think of those songs?"

Lyle turned and looked at her, his eyes slightly glazed. "What songs?"

"Oh, sorry," Cheryl said. "You must have been concentrating on the equipment. I just wanted to run some possible selections by you."

"Well, hello, my two favorite performers," Renee came into the room, arms laden with straw hats and paisley bandanas. "Are we getting ready for the big Hoe Down? Don't mind me. You go on and rehearse. I'm just going to put up a few decorations and party favors."

Lyle looked over the choices Cheryl had made. "I don't like Buck Owens. Jennings is okay. Why don't we start with a duet. Maybe 'Jackson'?"

"Sure," Cheryl said. "I like that one. You're right. It's very upbeat. Let's try it."

"We'll sing the first verse together, then alternate until joining together on the last three." Lyle found the music, fired up the machine and started playing.

Cheryl took the mike from its stand and held it so they could both reach it easily. They started the song together on key. It sounded pretty good for a first try. She leaned in a little closer and accidentally bumped the mike against her lips.

Lyle slammed both hands on the keys. "Godammit."

"What?"

"What? You don't know? You're off-key, off-tempo, and you just got lipstick all over the mike. Now it's ruined." He grabbed it and marched toward the door.

Renee stepped in his path. "Everything all right, Lyle? I thought it sounded pretty good. Just needs a little tweaking. That's what rehearsal's all about."

"Screw you, Renee," he said as he pushed past her and out the door.

Renee turned and looked at Cheryl. "I'm so sorry, Ms. Lennon. He's been getting upset a lot lately. I'm sure it's not you, but I'll have a talk with him. He must be having some personal problems. You go ahead and practice. I'll make sure he's calmed down for tonight." She headed into the hall, then turned. "You sounded great. Really."

♦♦♦

Marvin walked to the other end of the upper deck. Damn onboard naturalist didn't know his ass from a hole in the ground about the Tolomato River. First off, it wasn't called just the Tolomato; it was called the Guana-Tolomato-Matanzas Preserve. And it

171

wasn't actually a river; it was part of an estuary. Stupid twit. Called cord grass corn grass, for chrissakes, and all those idiot passengers believed it like gospel…

Captain Marvin Whitcomb led the small group of explorers on a kayak tour of the GTM Preserve. It was his job to protect these tourists from their own stupidity. They wanted adventure but were ignorant of what lay beneath the saltmeadow hay and marsh elder. Sure there were diamond terrapin, soft shell turtles, harmless birds and geckos, but underneath, the place teemed with coral snakes, cottonmouths, rattlers, and of course, the stealthy Florida alligator. He looked back at his motley crew, trailing their hands in the water, throwing out bread crumbs.

He spotted the monster behind the last kayak, swamp algae camouflaging it perfectly. Only a seasoned professional would spot the horny ridges and those yellow eyes just above the waterline. It glided in silence toward them. With no notice or fanfare, he dragged his paddle and turned a one-eighty, signaling the others to move forward. Just as the beast approached the rear craft, Marvin swept in and swung the broadside of the paddle toward its snout…

"There you are. Guess what I have for you?"

He turned to find Rhoda smiling like the Cheshire Cat. He lit a cigarette. "You look like you've been up to no good. Whatcha got?"

She stepped closer, looked around, and pulled a Ponce-de-Leon-Cruise-Lines envelope from her bag. "Ask and ye shall receive." Her voice dropped to a whisper. "It's your Viagra."

He took the envelope and pocketed it. He never

dreamed she'd really get some for him. Not that he needed it. But who knew? A little extra boost might be fun. "Where'd you find this?"

"I got it from some horny old coot in my watercolor class. I took him back to his room and pretended like I was ready for the taking. I went in the john, grabbed a handful of these, and bolted. He probably thinks I'm still in the bathroom."

The way her eyes twinkled, he could tell she very much enjoyed getting away with something. Certainly a change from Ann. Ann followed every rule and law, never lied, and raised that left eyebrow at him when he pushed the boundaries. A little troublemaker might be fun for a change. "Thanks, Rhoda. The rest of my Celexa is yours. I'll bring it to you at lunch."

"Did anybody ever tell you you're one hell of a guy, Marvin? Thanks." She leaned in and kissed him on the cheek.

She smelled good, like a woman. Not a prissy one, though. No heavy perfumes, lacquered hair or caked-on makeup. A little on the plump side, but not fat. Comfortable. Plus, she had those big, bedroom eyes.

"What are you doing back here? Don't you want to hear the lecture?"

"Naw. The guy's an idiot. I know more about this area than he does. Back in the day, Ann and I used to take the kids canoeing all through here. Then the kids grew up, and Ann got sick."

"I'm sorry. Sounds like a fun family. Are you from this area?"

"St. Augustine. What about you?"

"I'm from a town near Starke called Eugenia.

One crossroad kind of place. And no, I was not part of a happy, little family."

"Starke—isn't that where the state prison is?" God that was a depressed area. Last time he drove through there, every other house had piles of junk and rusted cars everywhere. "I remember you mentioning your husband. No kids?"

"No. No kids. Thank God. I mean I love kids, but Lute would have screwed them up royally. Truthfully, neither of us were good parent material."

"Didn't you say he just disappeared, and you don't know if he's dead or alive?"

"You got it. Somehow, I doubt that he's dead. Too mean to die. He was so spooked about a government conspiracy, he's probably living in some Central American country by now. The only thing he took with him was his 'bug-out' bag with money, guns, and a passport. I just hope he doesn't come back any time soon." Rhoda paused to light a cigarette. "Now, my boyfriend, Ben. That's a different story. He was a doctor. Smart, classy. I still don't know why he took off. No warning, no signs of dissatisfaction. He just sold his house, left his business, and disappeared. Son of a bitch."

Marvin looked at her. She might be a bit of a renegade, but she didn't deserve to be treated that way. What kind of man abandons a woman? "I'm sorry that happened to you. Not all men are like that."

"Maybe all the bad ones live in Eugenia. I'd probably be better off somewhere else, but I wouldn't know where to go. Plus, I just bought a new doublewide."

Marvin shook his head. It didn't seem right.

She seemed smart enough, carried on a good conversation. She was incredible on the keyboard and sang beautifully. Too bad she got stuck in some crazy, redneck town. "Maybe we could ignore all the singles-matching bullshit and sit together at dinner tonight."

"That'd be nice, Marvin." She threw out her cigarette and turned to go. "See you then."

He watched her leave, her hair dancing in the breeze, hips swaying seductively. Viagra, schmiagra. He leaned on the railing, and watched the wildlife that dotted the estuary.

"Help, help, Captain Whitcomb!" The paddle-to-the-gator snout had only enraged the beast. It swung its muscular tail toward one of the kayaks causing it to flip. In a flash, Marvin grabbed the woman from the water and dragged her out of harm's way. She threw her arms around his neck, planted her lips on his and gave him the most searing kiss he'd ever experienced. As she trembled in his arms, he glanced at her nametag. Rhoda Mason.

Chapter 23

Maggie squinted for a closer look. "Is that you?" It was hard to tell with his sunglasses, but he sure looked like Buddy.

"Who do you think I am?" The man below stared up.

The voice sounded familiar but it had been almost a year. "Buddy? Buddy Crapps?"

His brow furrowed and the corners of his mouth dipped into a frown. "Who wants to know."

"Don't you recognize me?" Maggie's heart plunged.

"I can't even see you. That sun is like a laser in my eyes."

That made sense. "It's me. Maggie Lennon. We met last summer in Eugenia?"

He lowered his head. For a long time.

"We had drinks a couple of times at that bar and bait shop? Then we met again in the hospital? I stayed with your brother while you went and cleaned up in my hotel room?"

His head tilted back a fraction. "Oh yeah. Now I remember. Sure. Mattie, was it?"

Tears threatened. "Maggie." Surely he hadn't forgotten their steamy romp in the front seat of that old Buick.

"I remember all that, but you don't look like the same…wait a minute." He untied a rope, pulled the scaffolding upward, tied off, and climbed over the rail. He took off his sunglasses. His eyes, starting at her

176

face, traveled down her body slowly. He let out a soft whistle. "I definitely remember the face, but," he checked her body again, a slow smile forming on his lips, "wow. You look really different."

The heat started south and spread north, turning her crimson from bikini bottom to hairline. "Oh, that. I've been working out a little."

"I'll say. So Maggie, huh. Sorry about the Mattie." He stepped closer. Those gray eyes stared into hers as his smile deepened. "How could I forget you? You were the only good thing about that shithole town. Yeah. Smart, sassy, and correct me if I'm wrong, a hell of a kisser."

Her face burned. "I'll have to take your word for that. But yeah, I remember a pleasant experience." They stood close, her looking up into his crystal gray eyes for minutes. She started to feel dizzy and stepped back a bit. "How's your brother, by the way? He was in a coma for a while, right?"

Buddy laughed. "Delbert? He's good. That kid can bounce back from just about anything. He's doing real good. In fact, he's engaged."

"Awww. That's great. I'm glad he's okay. What about you? I'm guessing you've been pretty busy, since you never called." Her left eyebrow raised.

"Well, yeah. I've been busy." He looked at his feet. "Listen, I meant to call you, but you remember how hard it was raining in that parking lot when I last saw you? By the time I made it into the hospital, I was soaked. I dried off with paper towels in the bathroom, and the ink smeared." He looked at her. There was that stern school-teacher look. "I swear."

"Right." She crossed her arms. "Very

convenient."

The crystal gray eyes turned steely. "You can dismount from that high horse. Just exactly how much time did you spend trying to find me?"

The blood that seconds ago turned her face crimson drained to her toes. She lowered her eyes. "You're right. Sorry."

"Forget it. We're both here now. It really is good to see you. I've thought about you a lot. How you stayed with Delbert while I got cleaned up, and how you gave me money for laundry. I was in a hell of a state after that boating accident, and suddenly, there you were, ready to help, no questions asked. I can't say anybody's ever been that nice to me before."

She thought back to their steamy romp in Rhoda's old Bonneville. Damned right she was nice to him. But it was pretty sad if he meant it. She'd never been known to be sweet and kind. She was more the get-it-done type who stepped in during a crisis and fixed things. "Thanks, but it was nothing. You helped me out too. Gave me some much needed respite from my family's craziness." She looked up at him again. Neither of them spoke for what seemed forever.

Uncomfortable with the silence, she grabbed her book off the chaise. "It was great running into you. Kind of a bizarre coincidence, but great. I guess I'll see you around?"

"Yeah, sure." He cleared his throat. "Are you here with anyone? A boyfriend or somebody like that?"

She stifled a laugh. "I'm traveling with my sisters."

"What about your crazy brother-in-law? Is he

here too?"

"No, thank God. He disappeared right after I last saw you. No one's seen or heard from him since. So, it's just us girls." She turned to leave when he grabbed her arm.

"Good. That's good. Maybe we could get together later. It really is good to see you again."

Maggie tried to be aloof and calm, but her grin gave her away. She was past pretending. Every pulse point in her body was pounding. "I'd like that."

"Great. My shift's over at 9:00 tonight. The boat's going to stay docked until late tomorrow evening. Maybe we could go in town for some drinks or something."

Drinks or something was what got her in trouble with him last year. "I'd love that."

"I'll meet you on the dock. If they caught me leaving the ship with you, I'd lose my job. Not supposed to fraternize with the passengers, you know."

"Got it. I'll see you at 9:00."

Buddy pulled a cell phone from his pocket. "Why don't you give me your number again?"

"Better yet, let me call you and you can just add me to your contacts. That way neither of us will have an excuse for losing contact." After exchanging numbers, she turned and walked back toward her room.

Things were looking up.

♦♦♦

"Good afternoon, Cruisers!" Renee's voice blasted through the loud speakers. "We hope you enjoyed your peaceful day on the river. Tonight we have lots of options. In a few moments, we'll be docking in St. Augustine, the oldest city in the U.S. We'll be moored here all night and tomorrow, so everyone should have the chance to see the sights and take a big slurp from the famous Fountain of Youth. Tonight you can dine on the ship and enjoy our Country Hoedown in the Peacock Lounge, or you can eat at one of the fine restaurants on shore. One note of interest, because of damage to the docks at the St. Augustine Marina, we'll be tying off just south of the port near the River House Event venue. Don't worry, though. It's less than a mile to all the main attractions. There will be shuttle buses running on a fifteen minute loop until two a.m. and all day tomorrow. If you have any questions or need assistance, ask a staff member."

The announcement jolted Maggie from her reverie as she leaned on the French balcony replaying every word, look and gesture from her conversation with Buddy. Just the thought of him had her heart pounding and her skin tingling. She hoped they could recapture some of the attraction they'd had before. Obviously no problem for her, but she wasn't sure about him. Just in case it was a bust, she decided to keep their rendezvous from Rhoda and Cheryl, at least for now. She could sneak out during the show, and if things went well, she could give them the scoop later.

While thinking about what to wear—sexy but not slutty, stylish but not flashy—she watched as the boat glided against the edge of the river and stopped. There was no dock. Only a wide swampy-looking area with a large building and parking lot on the other side. Her hopes fell. What if she couldn't get off the boat tonight?

Soon, though, the crew below began to float a long, metal walkway toward the shore just as a flatbed truck arrived with another metal walkway. Within ten minutes, a long gangway was extended all the way to the parking lot. Problem solved, she began to rummage through her things for the perfect outfit.

♦♦♦

Lester stood back as the temporary dock was secured. Renee called on the walkie-talkie to inform him that two separate passengers had requested an ambulance, and he should be ready to assist the paramedics. The life squad arrived in spectacular fashion, two ambulances, a firetruck and two police cars, all with sirens blaring, against the cruise line's request. A squadron of EMTs jumped from their vehicles, unloaded gurneys and bags of lifesaving equipment, and boarded the ship. Lester led them to the appropriate rooms where they attended both patients, determining their conditions acute enough to warrant a trip to the hospital.

As the excitement coincided with the beginning of cocktail hour, a large crowd had gathered to watch patients being hauled out and across the gangway. "Please return to your rooms," Lester shouted, as he physically held people back to let the paramedics do their job.

"But it's time for cocktails," someone yelled.

"What's going on here? Was it food poisoning?"

"Legionnaires? COVID?"

"COVID? We're all going to die!"

181

"It's not COVID. We couldn't get on the boat unless we were vaccinated, remember?"

"Oh my God! Are they dead?"

Just as panic began to fully escalate, Renee arrived, holding a platter of hors d'oeuvres in one hand and a tray of champagne in the other. "You guys are late for happy hour. Let's get this party started!" The crowd turned from the excitement and fell in step behind her.

Lester watched the herd follow the refreshments to the lounge. He had to give it to Renee. She was a master at diversion. The EMTs loaded the patients into the ambulances and left with considerably less fanfare than when they arrived.

After a few minutes, Lester noticed the sounds from the cocktail lounge had shifted to laughter and normal conversation. He could hear Lyle crooning "Do You Believe in Magic," a precursor to a corny but impressive magic show. With the crowd well under control, Renee and the captain approached Lester.

"Good job handling the passengers, Renee," the captain nodded in her direction.

"Thank you, sir, but Lester was doing a fine job holding them back so the emergency crews could do their jobs."

Lester stood a little straighter.

"Give me a full report. I'll need to file the appropriate paperwork with the local authorities and the cruise company." The captain took a notepad from his pocket and poised to write.

Renee told them both how she'd received calls from the two cabins within minutes of each other. Apparently, one of the victims had severe COPD and couldn't find her pills or inhaler. The other, according to her husband, was hallucinating about giant bears stalking her, and he'd been unable to find her psychotropic medications. "You know," she whispered, "that's three people who've been taken off the ship due to missing medications."

The captain's brow furrowed. "I don't recall that happening before. I mean, we've had to have sick passengers transported in the past, but I don't remember missing pills being the culprit. I think we should do a little investigating. It could be nothing, but just in case, I'd appreciate you two checking into it. But keep this among the three of us. I don't want to alarm anyone. It's probably just a coincidence. Let me know what you find out."

"Yes sir," Renee said.

"I'm on it, sir. Is that all?" Lester had some ideas. He'd seen that one woman, Mason, coming in and out of a lot of rooms over the last few days. It seemed like she'd been helping some of the older passengers, but maybe there was more to it. "I'd like to check the rooms in question, sir, if that's okay."

"Certainly. Just make sure you don't go in alone and remember to leave the door open. We don't want to arouse undue suspicion. Housekeeping staff can go with you, just don't let on what you're looking for."

After getting the room numbers from Renee, Lester enlisted the help of a buxom room steward named Isabella. As far as he could tell, her English was limited to perfunctory phrases like "cleaning service," "more towels" and "thank you very much." Chances were good she wouldn't ask many questions. He flashed his ID badge, pointed to one of the rooms, pantomimed the turning of the knob, pointing from himself to her, then walking his fingers toward the door.

Her eyes grew wide as she pointed to herself.

He nodded yes.

"Tu y yo?" She batted her lashes. "Ches." She giggled as she stepped in front of him, slid the key card across the lock twerking him as she opened the door. Inside the room, she crooked a beckoning finger toward him as she sat and patted the bed.

Holy shit. Did she think he wanted to…did that kind of thing really happen on this ship? Where had he been? Jesus. He needed to search the room, but did he want to pass this up? He looked at her name badge and reluctantly shook his head no. "Um, Isabella. I think you misunderstood me."

"Que? No te gusto?" She unbuttoned the top of her uniform.

Wishing he had paid more attention in high school Spanish class, he held up his hands indicating he didn't understand.

She flattened out on the bed and held her arms toward him.

What the hell. As he climbed on top and tried to keep up with her frenetic embrace, he looked at the floor beside the bed. Several pills of multiple colors covered the carpet next to the nightstand.

Unfortunately, the tryst was over quickly. "Ees okay." Isabella patted him on the shoulder. "You like, si?"

He remembered yes. "Si. Very nice."

"Hasta luego, chico amante." She sashayed

down the hallway, her uniform stretched tightly over those ample hips.

Lester waved. He'd have to try that again. Soon. Now, however, he needed to look in the other rooms and report back to Renee and the captain.

"You're saying each of the rooms had a number of pills on the floor?"

"Yes, ma'am."

"What did the housekeeper say?"

Lester blushed. "She didn't speak much English."

The captain pulled out his walkie talkie and summoned the head of housekeeping. She confirmed that, particularly in the rooms of older passengers, pills were often scattered all over the place. She had instructed her staff to collect them and put them in a pile on the night table. As she left, the captain whispered to Renee and Lester, "That could be your answer."

"It might, sir. But I've seen a few people who frequently accompany the more infirmed passengers back to their cabins. With your permission, I'd like to check into that a more thoroughly."

"Interesting," Renee said. "Keep an eye on it. If you see anything suspicious, let us know. Good work, Lester."

"Thanks." The praise helped him refocus after Isabella. With renewed commitment to being the best security guard ever, he vowed to be extra vigilant, starting with watching Ms. Mason more closely. He'd been suspicious of her from the start.

He headed for the office to double check the

monitors and equip himself properly for the job. After all, they were in port, so he had to be at the ready at all times. This called for the gun.

Chapter 24

Maggie wanted to steer clear of her sisters for the evening. The upcoming rendezvous with Buddy had her nerves buzzing. She really didn't want to tell them anything until she knew if things were going to work out. Deliberately choosing a table with only one seat left, she scanned the room to see where they were. It was easy to find Cheryl who radiated from her guest-of-honor seat at the captain's table. It took a little longer to find Rhoda at a table with several frail passengers and that man they'd met, Marvin.

Maggie squinted for a better view. Rhoda and Marvin seemed pretty chummy, laughing and joking, whispering to each other on occasion. Wouldn't that be nice? Big sis with a normal, polite man for a change. Apparently, Rhoda's lover, the doctor who also disappeared on her, had seemed like a good guy, too. Maybe this one would be different. He had seemed too old for Maggie, but he was closer to Rhoda's age. Fingers crossed for them.

When she felt certain that both sisters would be busy with their respective beaus, she ate quickly, slipped out of the dining room, and headed back to the cabin to get ready for her hopefully hot date.

♦♦♦

Despite having a delightful time at dinner with Rhoda, Marvin felt uneasy. He'd spotted the security guard, who usually walked the halls playing with his phone while stuffing food in his mouth, propped against a post near their table. What a turd the guy was, standing at parade rest, wearing mirrored sunglasses in the dim dining room. You'd think he was guarding a prison yard rather than a luxury cruise. While Marvin couldn't tell for sure, Barney Fife seemed to have his sights set on their table.

Rhoda leaned toward him. "Marvin, I don't think you've met everyone at the table. This is Jackie from Idaho, Bob from Miami, Mitzi from…wait a minute…Texas?"

Mitzi nodded yes.

"And Penny from Georgia."

"Nice to meet you all," Marvin looked over the group. Rhoda had managed to pick a table with the ugliest women on the boat. But that was okay. She was cute enough, and she seemed to be warming up to him. He wouldn't mind giving her a spin. She might be a little broken, but vulnerability didn't bother him. Speaking of broken, one of the gals at the table, was it Mitzi or Jackie, had a full arm cast on. The kind that was propped out from her side. That had to hurt. "How'd you break your arm?" He knew he'd be sorry he asked. Old women loved to go on and on about their health issues.

Mitzi-or-Jackie heaved a great sigh. "Nothing very exciting. I should say I broke it skydiving, but the truth is, I missed the top step coming out of church last Sunday and landed on the sidewalk. Broke it in three places. I have pins and plates and screws everywhere. Plus, I bruised my hip."

Marvin lowered his eyes in false concern.

"That's terrible," Rhoda said. "Just last

Sunday? You must be in a lot of pain."

Mitzi-Jackie rubbed the cast with her good hand. "I am. But I figured I might as well be in pain here than back at home. That reminds me," she grabbed her purse and started digging through the contents. "I'm supposed to take a pill with meals." She rummaged in the bag some more. "Oh, dear. I seem to have forgotten them. I hate to go all the way back to the room."

Marvin watched as Rhoda alerted like a coonhound.

"Let me help. I can get them for you in no time."

"Would you, dear? That would be so helpful."

"No problem at all. I'm happy to help." Rhoda rose from her seat. "Which room is it? Is it locked?"

The woman pulled the key-card lanyard off and handed it to Rhoda. "The room number's on there. On the table by the bed there should be a bottle of Vikingdon or whatever they call it."

"Vicodin. Or hydrocodone." Rhoda grabbed the lanyard and headed out of the dining room.

On the edge of his peripheral vision, Marvin noticed Barney Fife come to life. The mirrored sunglasses followed Rhoda from the room, then he turned and started following her slowly. When the idiot reached around and patted the side of his waistband, Marvin realized he carried a weapon. Damn. "Excuse me, folks," he said to the table. "I'll be right back."

Marvin sprinted down the hall, past Barney and caught up with Rhoda, just as she was opening the room. "Don't say anything," he whispered in her ear, as he threw his arm around her shoulder and nuzzled her neck, "You stay here by the door—leave it open—I'll get the pills and take them to the table."

"Why? What are you doing?"

He shushed her. "That security guard was listening to our table, and he followed you out. I think he's lurking in the hall. He must suspect you of something, so let's do exactly what you said you were doing."

Rhoda's eyes grew wide. "Really?"

"Really," he said as he grabbed the pills. "Let's go. Act like we're a couple." He held the pills in full view of anyone watching and said in a loud voice. "How about we get these pills back to Mitzi, and then head to the top deck, Sweetheart?" Arm around her shoulder again, they returned to the dining room, heads together like love birds.

◆◆◆

It took two Cosmopolitans at the after-dinner show for Maggie to quell her nerves, but then she turned to seltzer and lime. She didn't want to pass out before it was time to meet Buddy. Sipping her mocktail, she watched Cheryl and Lyle ham it up *YeeHaw* style at the hoedown. The ambulatory guests were loving it. Bedecked in straw hats and bandanas, they square danced, sang along, and shouted out requests. Even the overalled farmer got in on the performance grabbing an empty half-gallon bottle from the bar, pursing his lips and bleating out some surprisingly good jug band music.

Maggie scanned the raucous crowd from the back of the room. Everyone's attention was on the show, making her practically invisible to the partygoers. Perfect. It was almost nine o'clock. She slipped out the door and speed-walked toward the gangway and her date with destiny.

"Leaving the boat for a while, Ma'am?"

Startled, she turned to find the fat security guard, wearing ridiculous mirrored sunglasses at night, gun on his hip, standing to the side of the doorway. "Hi. Yes. I thought I'd take the shuttle into town and see what's going on."

The guard picked up a clipboard. "I'll need your name and room number. We have to account for passengers' whereabouts at all times. And you'll need to show your ID badge to come back on board."

"Sure, sure." She gave him the information and hurried ashore. There really wasn't a dock. The gangway terminated onto the edge of a large, empty parking lot, next to a building of some kind. The place looked deserted. Why hadn't she pressed Buddy for more specific details on where they were to meet? Maybe she'd missed him. Maybe he never intended to come at all. No. Think positive. He'd be there. It was just a few minutes after nine.

As she walked past the building, she spotted a bench with a makeshift sign. "Cruise Ship Shuttle Stop." Might as well wait there. After a few more minutes, she became uneasy. The place was kind of creepy. No one else around, no other businesses. Plus, the parking lot and building sat on the edge grassy swamp land. God only knew what kind of critter might crawl out there. She closed her eyes and took a deep breath. She was probably safe; after all, there was an armed security guard nearby.

Something brushed up against her back

prompting her to whirl around, swinging her purse as hard as she could. Her bag caught Buddy across the nose.

"Jesus Christ!" He grabbed her arm and looked into her eyes. A small, red bump rose on his upper lip. A smile started at his eyes and made it to the corners of his mouth. "A little jumpy, there, aren't you?"

Her blood drained to her feet, and her knees went weak as fear turned to mortification. "Oh, Buddy. I'm so sorry." She noticed the swelling lip and reached into her purse for a tissue.

He flinched. "You gonna hit me again?" The sly grin deepened.

"No. God, I'm so embarrassed. I was just sitting here freaking out about how deserted this place is when I felt something brush against me. I'm so sorry." She dabbed at lip. "Do you want me to go get some ice off the boat?"

He laughed. "I'm fine. Didn't mean to sneak up on you. You seemed so peaceful sitting there with your eyes closed, I hated to startle you. Sorry." He slid his hand down her arm and locked fingers with hers. "How about we start over?"

Her arm tingled at his touch. The whole time since she clubbed him, his eyes never left hers. Slowly her blood pressure stabilized, and her knees stopped shaking. She got lost in his gaze. Pull yourself together, woman. "Good idea. Sorry again."

Deciding to forgo the shuttle and walk into town, they found several bars less than a mile up the road.

"Is one of these okay?" Buddy asked.

Maggie looked around. "Well, I can smell the

'Blow Me Down Pub' from here, so that's out, and the Matanzas Tea Room looks a little prissy."

"What about this Ale House? They have live music. Or, speaking of prissy, does it flunk your smell test?"

Those eyes. Twinkling with mischief while lasering straight to her libido. She throbbed with desire. Could he see it? "This place looks fine, smart ass."

She didn't know how many hours passed in a blur of beer flights, slow dances, and easy conversation, but her head spun for a number of reasons as he led her back toward the boat.

◆◆◆

Once again, Rhoda ended up at the keyboard and, using the banjo simulator, played a rousing version of "The Crawdad Song" ably accompanied by the jug-puffer Farmer John and Lyle on the harmonica. Cheryl yodeled into the mike, "You get a line, I'll get a pole, honey. You get a line, I'll get a pole, babe. You get a line, I'll get a pole, we'll all go down to the crawdad hole, honey, my sugar baby mine..." a shocking number of people knew the words to all four verses.

At the last "Yee Haw!" the lights flickered and Lyle, beet red and sweat soaked, panted into the microphone, "All right, ladies and gents, you have officially worn me out. Thanks to all for a great Hoe Down. If you need assistance back to your room, please let one of our staff know."

Marvin, joining Rhoda at the keyboard, squeezed her shoulder and whispered, "Don't volunteer."

"All right all ready. Jesus, Marvin. You're kind of turning into a nag."

"I don't mean to be. I overheard the staff talking about the two people they hauled off to the hospital tonight. Apparently, they had both misplaced or lost their medications.

Rhoda's eyes grew wide. "What kind of pills?"

"I'm not sure. One of them needed head meds of some kind and the other had trouble breathing. Then that old guy in the wheelchair, Elmer I think, said someone had been stealing his stuff."

"Uh-oh. That's where I got the Viagra."

Marvin lowered his voice. "Whatever. It just seems that, all of a sudden, the security guard has you in his sights, so you need to be careful. Personally, I don't think you need the pills, but that's up to you and your doctors. It's just that I really enjoy your company and don't want you getting in trouble. You're talented, funny and incredibly resourceful. And spunky. I like spunky." Placing a finger under her chin, he raised her head. "I think you're fine just the way you are." As her eyes filled with tears, he leaned in and kissed her forehead.

Rhoda looked at the floor. "Thanks for that. I like you too, Marvin."

"Let's forget about all this for now. How about I take you and your sisters into town tomorrow? After living in St. Augustine for so many years, I can show you lots of great places without all the crowds. What do you say?"

She nodded. "Sure. That'd be fun."

"You going to be okay tonight?"

Mind racing at the prospect of getting caught with other people's meds, Rhoda sighed. "I'm fine. I'm just going to stay here and wait for Cheryl. You've given me a lot to think about." She grabbed his hand. "Thanks again." Who knew she'd be the one to meet a great guy on this trip? She let go and walked toward the stage.

Lyle was expounding his virtues to Cheryl as Rhoda approached. "Man, I nailed it tonight! Better than Johnny Cash and Willie Nelson combined. I ought to drop this gig and go to Nashville. Oh, and you weren't too bad either, ol' gallie gal." He winked and do-si-doed out of the room.

"That guy kind of reminds me of Lute—euphoric one minute and rabid the next," Rhoda said as she helped Cheryl turn off the equipment.

"I know. I'm just glad he was up tonight. I only get to perform one more time on the last night of the cruise. I'll miss singing, but I won't miss him. Speaking of missing people, have you seen Maggie?"

Rhoda looked around. "No. Now that you mention it, I haven't seen her since dinner."

"I saw her back by the bar at the beginning of the show. I wonder where she went?"

"You know Mags. She probably got sick of old men hitting on her and went to the room to sulk. Let's go check on her."

Cheryl hesitated. "I, uh, I'm, um, well, I'm supposed to meet Ty soon."

"Ty?"

"The captain, remember? Tyler Cabot? He told me to call him Ty." Cheryl giggled like a teenager. "He calls me Cher. Get it, Cher because I'm a singer?"

"Clever."

"Anyway, he had a staff member bring me a note, on a sliver tray no less, to meet him up on the bridge for a surprise." Cheryl did a little shimmy. "I wonder what it is?"

Rhoda rolled her eyes. Cheryl could be so naïve. "Oh, I have a pretty good idea."

"Rhoda! He's a gentleman!"

"He's a man."

Cheryl purred. "He's a man all right."

"Go on, then. Get your man. I'm going to look for Maggie. I'll see you later, or in the morning, if Ty gets his way."

Rhoda watched as Cheryl practically skipped toward the bridge. So much for a soul-searching convo with her. Maybe Maggie could help her sort things out.

Chapter 25

The walk back to the ship may have helped Maggie sober up, but burning lust fogged her brain just the same. Buddy was so hot. And funny. And nice. And hot. God he was hot. "What time do you go back on duty?" She had no idea what time it was.

"Four a.m."

"I'd better meet you at the room. Don't want that security guard seeing us together. Give me two minutes."

She checked her phone as she opened the door when he got to the room. Only two hours left. "I think I have a bottle of wine. Interested?"

He pulled her against him and nuzzled her neck. "Not in wine."

Her knees buckled. She managed to free an arm from his roaming embrace, slid the key card and opened the door. To her delight, the room was empty. Without breaking their serious lip lock, she slapped the DO NOT DISTURB magnet on the door and pulled him inside. In two steps they were on the bottom bunk, shedding shoes, clothes and inhibitions. As they locked together, all rational thought vanished as sensations exploded like fireworks.

◆◆◆

Rhoda started to slide her key in the lock when she noticed the DO NOT DISTURB magnet, crooked and upside down, on the door. Somebody must have been in a hurry. Maggie or Cheryl? Hard to tell. She leaned in and listened. The moans were indistinguishable. Of course, all three sisters sounded exactly the same when they talked. Half the time she couldn't tell which sister it was on a voicemail. No matter. At least one of them got their wish tonight.

With the room unavailable, Rhoda headed to the top deck for a smoke. The baggie of Celexa in her pocket weighed heavily on her conscience. As far as she knew, at least three people had gone to the hospital from missing meds—one the night before and then those tonight. But, except for the Viagra, she hadn't really been very lucky scoring pills. She'd dropped Elmer's Ativans when he flashed her, and Glenda had puked all over the ones she tried to grab. But still, she'd messed with them. Was she responsible for the rash of hospitalizations? A wave of guilt washed through her.

She pulled out the baggie and stared at it. He told her she didn't need meds. Nobody, except her sisters, had ever said they liked her the way she was. With Lute, she'd always felt so manipulated, having to play-act happiness, tenderness and joy; anger and fear had been her only true emotions with him. But now, she was actually enjoying herself with very little pharmaceutical help. How long was she clean before the cruise, a month? And since she got here, she'd only taken two of the antidepressants Marvin gave her.

She had accomplished a lot on her own, come to think of it. Cleaned up and sold that old shit box of a trailer she lived in, bought a newer one, and managed to get herself cleaned up and ready for this trip. Marvin was right. She was talented and funny. Standing straighter, shoulders squared, she opened the baggie and dumped the contents in the water. It was the Year of Rhoda.

A slow clap startled her.

"I knew you could do it."

She turned and saw Marvin. "How long have you been standing there?"

"Just walked up. Good for you. If you need any help, I'll do whatever I can. According to my kids and my doctor, I have some addict tendencies. In fact, I'm supposed to be attending AA meetings on the ship."

"Really? You? You seem so calm and level headed."

"Most of the time, I am. But I have struggled lately, though I think my kids make a bigger deal out of it than they should. It's just that, since my wife died, I've been rudderless. My whole being was defined by her illness. I thought when she was gone, I'd travel the world, date lots of women, do whatever I wanted. But it's harder than I thought. So, I drink. Just when I've had a particularly bad day. But getting thrown in the looney bin to sober up scared my kids. I don't want them worrying or upset about me. So I'm trying to be more careful. I want to live again. I just need to figure out how."

Rhoda noticed a glassiness to his eyes. Maybe she wasn't the only one who needed fixing. She wrapped her arms around him. "You help me; I'll help you. Deal?"

"Deal."

He relaxed in her arms and sighed. Without thinking, Rhoda moved her head slightly and kissed him. She'd never encountered such vulnerability and kindness in a man before. A sense of hope warmed her heart.

Marvin, a surprisingly good kisser, stepped back, grabbed her hand, and headed for the stairs. "Come with me."

Cheryl tiptoed out of the Captain's suite after making sure the hallway was deserted. Not that she'd done anything wrong, but she definitely had that walk-of-shame thing going on. Snaps were missing off her bedazzled Reba shirt, her hair was tousled, makeup smudged, and her false eyelashes migrated toward her chin. She smiled. What a night.

Ready to collapse into bed and relive her evening with Ty, she stopped short when she saw the DO NOT DISTURB sign on the door. She whipped out her phone, then put it away. No sense disturbing whoever got lucky. She'd just have to stretch out in the lounge for a while.

◆◆◆

Lester barely woke up in time for the 4:00 a.m. shift. That was the worst thing about this job. There wasn't much down time. At least the place was quiet this early in the morning. The outside doors were all secured, while the geezers and staff slept in their rooms. He and the captain's crew were the only ones working. He stationed himself by the stairway on the bottom deck, scanned the area, settled against the wall and pulled out his phone. A quick round of *Assassin's Creed* would pass the time until people started stirring.

His character in the game, Desmond, had just employed Eagle Vision and was able to see his main opponent, now illuminated a bright green, when a door creaked open down the hall. Damn. The distraction was just enough for the foe to strike Desmond down. Game over, Lester looked toward the source of the noise. He squinted into the darkness.

Ah ha. There she was. The room surfer. He'd seen that Mason woman come out of at least four different cabins over the course of the cruise, though he'd never spotted her this late at night. He flattened against the wall, angled his phone and took a short video of her as she closed the cabin door and hurried down the hall. Gotcha. He couldn't wait to share this with Renee and the Captain.

◆◆◆

Maggie kissed Buddy goodbye at 3:55 a.m. after they finished an acrobatic shower in the toilet/sink/rainhead combo bathroom. She was impressed with her flexibility, though there were bound to be a few bruises from the sink. Her skin tingled from the afterglow. This was certainly one for the books. Beat the hell out of her date with the accordion player.

As she climbed back in the bunk, her phone pinged. Twice. God that's right. The girls must have tried to get back in the room. She looked at the group text.

Rhoda: Luuuuucy, you got a lot of 'splainin to do. LOL

Cheryl: OMG!! Who's in the room? Rhoda? Maggie? Spill, Sister! I want details. Are you STILL at it, or are you sleeping?

She chuckled as she tapped the keyboard. All clear. You can come back now. I am definitely awake!

Cheryl and Rhoda tumbled through the door in a nanosecond.

Chapter 26

"All right, ladies. Are you ready for a super-deluxe tour of the oldest city in America and the home to the Fountain of Youth? I'm going to show you the town the locals enjoy." Marvin stood proud in his white chinos with matching deck shoes, a crisp, light blue linen long-sleeved shirt and a woven hiker hat angled on his head.

Rhoda smiled at the image. He was quite the character, snarling insults at people one minute, then tenderhearted and romantic the next. She didn't regret their lovemaking last night. In fact, it helped her forget about the men in her recent past. She didn't really give a flip that her husband had disappeared. But her lover, Ben, taking off with no warning, had hurt. She'd thought they were going to be together forever. Even though he had started acting distant and distracted right before he left, she never dreamed he'd desert her.

Marvin, though, had shown faith in her inherent goodness, something no one else except her sisters had ever done. Plus, he'd said she was funny, spunky and pretty. Who doesn't like to hear that? And yeah, he was a pretty masterful lover, despite the fact that he was more than a decade her senior. She planted a sun hat on her head, grabbed his arm, and said, "I'm ready when you are. Let the tour begin!"

Cheryl and Maggie fell in step behind them as Marvin laid out the agenda for the day. "I thought we'd take the shuttle into the historic section. We can go to the Fountain of Youth and the Castillo de San Marcos if you'd like, though I think they're over-hyped. What do you think?"

Rhoda considered the options. "I don't really care about touring a fort, and I'm a little late for the Fountain of Youth. What about you girls? Maggie?"

She shook her head. "Nah. I'm more of a drive-by tourist. As long as I can say I've seen the site, I don't really care if I explore it. I'd be up for a good museum or art gallery, and of course, some shopping."

Cheryl raised her eyebrows. "What? No Fountain of Youth? It's never too late to try and hold on to your youth, and I, for one, have plenty of youth to hold on to," she said as she looked in the mirror of her lipstick holder.

Marvin laughed. "Okay. We'll shuttle up to the Fountain and then back to Old Town. From there we'll begin our trek toward the boat on the back streets. It's about a mile walk, but there's lots to see. We can grab a coffee somewhere, and then I want to show you the fabled Love Tree. The legend says that a husband and wife, when first married, wanted to plant a tree as a testament to their love, but they couldn't decide which kind, so they planted both right next to each other. As you'll see, the trees grew into each other and are permanently locked in an embrace."

Rhoda looked at him. "Why, Marvin, you old romantic. You surprise me. I've never heard of that."

Marvin looked off in the distance. "It was one of Ann's favorite sites. Anyway, from there we can go to the Villa Zorayda Museum, a small scale version of Spain's Alhambra."

"When do we get to the shopping?" asked Maggie.

"We can make our way over to Charlotte Street. There are some great little shops there. After you've spent all your money, I'll treat you to lunch at the Floridian."

Cheryl stuck out her bottom lip. "Oh, I wanted to go to the Columbia. I've been to the one in Ybor City and just loved it."

"Achh. You don't want to eat there." Marvin sneered. "Yeah, the food's good and the building's pretty, but the Floridian is where all the natives go. The chef uses regional growers and producers. Being a local businessman, I like to support them whenever I can."

Cheryl blinked and raised a brow. "Well, certainly. As I said, I've already eaten at a Columbia."

"You have a business here? I'd love to see it, Marvin," Maggie said. "What do you say? Let's get this party started!"

◆◆◆

Lester stood at attention as the staff helped the mobility-challenged guests off the ship and onto the tour bus. It promised to be a slow day. Maybe, if things got really boring, he could sneak off and find Isabella making up a room somewhere. But probably not. There were several passengers still aboard the ship, so he'd have to stay at his post.

After an hour in the hot sun, he ducked just inside the doorway and leaned his head against the cool interior wall. No one had been on or off the boat in a while. A quick snooze wouldn't hurt anything. He rested his hand on his holster and closed his eyes.

The creaking of the long metal walkway alerted

him. Someone must be returning. He jumped to the doorway and looked toward the noise. The bright sun blinded him momentarily, but the creaking grew louder. Looking toward the shore, he didn't see anyone approaching, then his eyes dropped to the grated bridge in the direction of the sound. Holy shit. A gator, at least six feet long, was raised up on all fours, marching toward the boat, only occasionally snagging a great claw in the aluminum joints on the bridge. Each snag made it rise higher and move faster.

Lester was paralyzed. The monster had nowhere to go but past him. Finally, as the beast reached the halfway point, he jumped back inside the doorway and fumbled to secure the bulkhead door. The clicking of claws grew louder. There was no time. Standing just inside, he unsnapped his holster, pulled the gun, sighted it as best he could with trembling, sweaty hands and pulled the trigger.

The shot sounded like cannon fire inside the small vestibule. His head ringing, Lester looked at his target, only to see an enraged alligator moving at top speed toward him. As it entered the ship, Lester scrambled backward toward the far wall, finally hitting up against the freight elevator controls and alarm buttons. Just as the beast approached, the doors slid open and the predator wedged inside. Lester pressed the button again and the door closed.

With shaking hands, he screamed into his walkie-talkie, "GATOR ON THE SHIP. Do not open the freight elevator. I repeat, DO NOT OPEN THE FREIGHT ELEVATOR!"

The sound of the alarm brought Renee, the captain and several crew members running into the vestibule, all walkie-talkies screeching and bleating. They found Lester, sunk to the floor by the elevator, one hand on the STOP button, one hand still on his gun.

Renee's voice pierced the chaos. "EVERYBODY QUIET." All noise ceased. "Lester, did I understand you correctly? Did you say there's an alligator on the ship?"

Perspiration beaded on his pale forehead as he nodded yes.

"HOW THE HELL DID IT GET ON THE SHIP?" Her voice, several octaves above commanding, pierced his eyeballs.

"I, uh, I uh…" He recalled his brief nap. "I stepped inside for a second to check the passenger manifest to see how long people had been gone. Then I heard a noise, like someone was coming up the walkway. At first I couldn't see anything because of the sun, but then, there it was. A huge gator halfway to the boat."

The captain placed his hand on Renee's shoulder to silence her. "How big is huge?"

"At least six feet." From the stern looks on his superiors' faces, Lester suspected he was in trouble.

"And what happened next?" asked the captain. Renee's eyebrows were well above her hairline.

"I pulled my weapon and shot at it." He could be fired for this.

"Did you hit it?"

"I think so, but I'm not sure. Whatever happened, it pissed him off, and he came charging onto the ship."

"Then what happened?"

No need to tell them he fell against the elevator's control panel. "He was headed toward the elevator, so I opened the door, and in he went." His finger still pressed the STOP button. "I didn't know what else to do."

The captain barked an order to one of the crew. "Call Fish and Wildlife. No, call 911 and tell them what happened. They can send someone over to remove it. In the meantime, deactivate the elevator and place caution tape and signs on every level."

Lester's arm began to shake. "Sir? Can I let go now?"

"As soon as they shut off the power. Quick thinking, son. I'm impressed. You're heroic actions will be duly noted in your personnel file." The captain nodded to Renee to ensure that was done.

"Thank you, sir." Mom would never believe this, not in a million years.

◆◆◆

Rhoda looked in amazement around the shop. "Marvin, this is incredible. You have such beautiful things in here." Nicer than anything she had. She wandered around checking prices. "And they're pretty reasonable. Maybe I could come up after the cruise and pick out some stuff for my new place."

Marvin gave her a sheet of red stickers. "Tag whatever you like, and I'll make sure you get the best price. Even though it's consignment, I have authority to make deals. A lot of this stuff has been sitting a while, so I'm sure you can get it for next to nothing."

She gave his arm a squeeze. "You're too kind, Mr. Whitcomb." She started picking out some key

208

items. "I'll just have to borrow someone's truck."

"No problem. I have a big van we could fit everything in."

The fabric on the couches and chairs looked like they'd never been sat in, unlike the worn, sweat-stained furniture in her living room. She red-tagged a couch, chair and a recliner—real leather—and some end tables. What a different life she was returning to, an almost new double wide, new furniture. The Year of Rhoda was looking up. She quietly sang "Something's Coming, Something Good," one of her favorites from *West Side Story*, as she waltzed around the store feeling the promise of tomorrow.

Marvin smiled. "Maggie and Cheryl, you two be sure and pick out something you like."

Cheryl smiled through tight lips. "Oh, thank you. But I have too much stuff as it is. It's all lovely, though. Really." She looked out the window. "What's that over there? Is it a music shop?"

Marvin looked where she pointed. "Oh, that's Dan Crandall's recording studio."

"A real recording studio? Oh my gosh! Could I go over there and make a record?"

"Possibly. I don't know how busy he is. It's not like St. Augustine is the hub of the music scene. He might be able to fit you in. Let me give him a call."

Cheryl warmed up by singing along with Rhoda while Marvin placed the call.

"He says to come on over. If you'd like to record something, he'll only charge you for the CDs since you're a friend of mine. Come on, everybody. I'll introduce you, and we can watch the session."

Rhoda tore herself away from all the pretty

things, met Mr. Crandall, then declined to accompany Cheryl. "It would sound too amateurish. Can't you use some canned background music, or sing a cappella? You have such perfect pitch, that might be best."

"What can I say," Cheryl giggled. "When you're right your right!"

It took at least three practice sessions before the actual recording began, so Rhoda stepped outside for a smoke. She wanted to dream more about her future. Would it include Marvin? Very possible. He might be good for her. She hadn't felt any need to medicate when she was with him. That could be a good thing.

She strolled down the block to a bench under a large live oak. Even though it was March, the sun was hot. She liked St. Augustine. Just look at those cute old townhouses across the street with ornate wrought iron and heavy wooden shutters. How rich did you have to be to live in one of those?

As she admired, a car pulled up and parked in front of one. When the door opened, Rhoda went cold. The man dashing from the car to the townhouse was Ben. Her old lover who swore he'd always be there for her.

Blood pounded in her ears and her hand shook as she threw the cigarette on the ground, looked to make sure Marvin and the girls were still occupied, then marched across the street. She had to talk to him. Maybe he had a good excuse for leaving so suddenly. Maybe Lute had threatened to hurt him or even her again. That had to be it. He'd left to protect her. She had to tell him that Lute had disappeared, and they were safe now.

Taking a deep breath, she knocked on the door.

No answer. She knocked again, using the big, brass knocker this time. Still no answer. He had to have heard that. One more time she knocked and stepped back to look up at the windows. A curtain drew to one side, and she saw him. Their eyes locked for a second before the curtain dropped back into place. She waited for several minutes before she realized he had no intention of answering the door.

"Rhoda!" Cheryl's voice penetrated the roaring in her head. "Rhoda! What are you doing over there? We're all done. Don't you want to hear my record?"

Dazed, she turned and walked back across the street. Thank god Cheryl's incessant chatter about having her very own CD allowed her to remain silent on the way back to the boat. When they arrived, there was frantic hubbub in the lobby. Caution tape lay across the floor, people were craning to look inside an elevator, and she heard some mention of an alligator. The chaos was enough to help her disappear into the restroom without anyone noticing.

She stared at herself in the mirror. Was she that undesirable that Ben couldn't even bring himself to speak to her? Nothing had gone wrong between them. After Lute left, they never even argued. Then he just took off. And now that she'd found him, he wanted nothing to do with her. He saw her. She knew he did. And he ignored her. Hid from her. She pounded the bathroom sink. Bastard. Bastard. Bastard.

Tears flowing, she dumped her purse onto the counter frantically searching for a pill of some kind. Anything. But she'd been very thorough, dammit. Splashing her face with water and drying it with paper towels, she peeked out the door. The crowd had cleared the hallway, so she headed back toward the gangway. Thank god that stupid guard was gone. She'd seen a liquor store just a block away. It wasn't the best solution, but a bottle of 190 proof Everclear was better than nothing.

Chapter 27

Marvin kept an eye on the door of the dining room throughout the whole meal. He saw Cheryl and Maggie eating at the Captain's Table, but no Rhoda, not at any table. Maybe she was worn out from the tour today. They had walked quite a ways in the hot sun, and she did seem pretty quiet on the last leg back to the boat. Surely she'd show up for Cheryl's final performance tonight.

He finished his meal quickly and went by her room and knocked. No answer. "Rhoda? You in there?" Nothing.

A young room steward came down the hall. He quickly stashed his ID badge/room key in his shirt. "Can you help me? I seem to have misplaced my key."

"Que?"

He pantomimed opening the door.

"Si." She swiped a card over the lock and it clicked open.

"Thank you, dear." Nice security.

"Si," she smiled and walked on.

Opening the door just a crack, he looked around inside the cabin. Nope. Maybe she was up on deck smoking. That must be it. He made his way up the stairs and out into the fresh air. Clouds had moved in, and the temperature had dropped since this afternoon. Still, no Rhoda. He didn't have her phone number, so he had no choice but to wait until he could talk to Maggie or Cheryl.

As he leaned on the railing, he noticed a lone

213

passenger, arms flailing, lanyard swinging wildly around her neck as she staggered toward the boat. Rhoda. A paper bag stuck out of the top of her purse. Damn. What had she gotten into? He raced down the stairs and met her just before she entered the vestibule.

"Marvy! Where you been?" She squinted at him with one eye closed. "I got one helluva buzz going." She pulled out the bottle of Everclear. "You wanna slug?"

Her skin looked pale and clammy, eyes bloodshot and puffy. Just as he put his arm around her to steer her toward the elevator, an ambulance came screaming up to the gangway, and a phalanx of EMTs stormed toward the ship. He shoved her inside the lift and propped her against the wall.

Hoping the fresh air on the top deck would revive her, he led her to a chaise and sat her down. "Have some water," he said softly as he held a bottle to her lips.

"Naw, I don' need any wa…" She keeled over mid-sentence and passed out. Not being a stranger to the effects of Everclear himself, he grabbed a towel from the exercise area and placed it next to her head. He slid a trash can on the floor beside her. The din of screeching walkie-talkies and shouting voices drew his attention to the dock. Medical personnel had pushed a gurney down the gangway, an inert body in tow as they took turns performing CPR. Their efforts did not seem successful in reviving the person before loading him onto the ambulance. They drove off, lights flashing but, eerily, no siren.

◆◆◆

"Hello, passengers! This is your cruise director, Renee. I see that all of you look ten years younger after drinking from the Fountain of Youth. Are you ready to strut your revitalized stuff? We have a surprise presentation for you in the Peacock Lounge immediately after dinner. Our dynamic duo, Lyle and Cher, are going to perform some of your requests, and then we'll see if you can out-sing them during Cruise-Line Karaoke! So bring your best voices down to the lounge and try to beat the stars! We have lots of prizes, and of course, plenty of refreshments to go around. See you soon!"

Renee had whispered in Cheryl's ear at dinner asking if she would please consider performing an extra night. She wanted to keep the passengers busy, as local law enforcement officers were coming to investigate the alligator incident. It didn't seem to Cheryl that anyone needed distracting. The alligator had been the most exciting thing to happen on the whole cruise, but she didn't mind getting an extra chance to perform. Maybe she and Lyle could take turns, since they hadn't practiced anything, but they could team up for "See You Later, Alligator." Hurrying to get herself stage ready, she was glad she'd bought an elegant off-the-shoulder jumpsuit at one of the boutiques on Charlotte Street earlier.

◆◆◆

Maggie had just finished getting ready when she heard a muffled bump on the door. She brushed her hair one last time and looked through the peep hole.

God he was gorgeous, even in sunglasses and a ball cap.

"Maggie? You in there? Open the door; my hands are full," Buddy said from the other side.

"Wow. Where'd you get all that?"

He stood, arms laden with cheeses, fruit, bread and chocolates. "The chef let me have them. I told him I was meeting up with some old friends during my time off."

Maggie's eyebrow cocked slightly. "Old friend?" Oh, that smile.

"I was afraid if I told him it was for a date, he'd suspect a passenger, and I'd lose my job." He set the food on the small dresser and took off his hat and sunglasses. "That's why I had these on. All the halls have cameras, and I didn't want to be spotted going in your room."

"So," she slid her hands up his chest and around his neck, "this is like an illicit tryst? I like the sound of that. Kind of dangerous, exciting." She nibbled on his earlobe. What was it about this guy? She was usually the shy, reticent type around men, insisting on getting to know their personality, intellect, and drive before even thinking about becoming physical. Yet after, what, five encounters with Buddy, she'd jumped his bones twice and was more than ready to go for the trifecta.

They repeated the same two-step-to-the-bed routine as last night and collapsed on the bottom bunk. Music filtered up from the Peacock Lounge and a cool breeze from the open slider washed over them as they found their rhythm. She felt like she'd known him forever, though she actually knew very little about him. She'd have to investigate that—but not now. Now was the time to get to know every other part of this fantastic specimen.

After her pulse and respiration returned to normal, she propped herself up on an elbow and prepared to learn more about this man. "I'm starved. How about some of that food you brought? I have a bottle of wine I picked up in town today."

The only chair in the room served as their dinner table while they perched on the edge of the bed. Fortunately, the overhead bunk was a single, so they didn't have to hunch over to sit and eat.

Finishing off a cheese cracker, Maggie broke the ice. "So, I know about your brother, Delmont, and I know you used to work on a crabbing boat with my idiot brother-in-law, but what else is there? Do you have any other family? Where do you live?"

He sat a little straighter, a somewhat defensive posture. "I don't know much about you either."

"Ask me anything. I'm an open book. Not a very exciting one, but open."

"I know you live in South Carolina and that you have two sisters. Any other family? Husband? Kids?"

She laughed. "No. No other family. Our parents have passed, leaving just the three of us. We're lucky to get along so well. We always have. I remember when Rhoda turned sixteen and got her license. Even though I was only nine at the time, she always took Cheryl and me with her to ride around town when she could have taken friends her own age. We lived in Miami then, and we'd drive to Matheson Hammock, then cruise through Coconut Grove, Key Biscayne, and

Coral Gables. Music blared from the AM radio station the whole time, the three of us singing our hearts out." She paused in the memory. "Man, I miss those days."

"Sounds nice. Good childhood I take it?"

"Better than most. Like I said, we were, and still are, lucky." She took a sip from her wine. "Your turn."

He squirmed and took a deep breath. "Not so lucky. Great mom, shitty dad. I always felt responsible for Delmont." He drained his glass. "My dad was a hitter. Beat my mom a lot, me pretty often, and took too many swings at Del. Mom and I always tried to step in to protect the little guy."

Maggie grabbed his hand. "I'm so sorry. That's horrible. Where are your parents now?"

"Mom died. Got hit too hard one night. Del got it pretty bad, too. That's why he's kind of slow and practically deaf in one ear." He poured more wine.

"Oh my god. Did your dad go to jail?"

Buddy was quiet for a long time, his jaw tight, his eyes closed. "No." He put his head in his hands. "I did."

Maggie sat very still. Jail? She'd been sleeping with a convict? She weighed the idea with the story he just told. "What happened?"

"The old man ran off the night my mom died. We never heard from him again, so I basically raised Del on my own. The neighbors helped some. But then, about five years ago, I ran into the fucking bastard at a bar. He was slapping some waitress around out in the parking lot. I lost it. Grabbed my tire iron and beat the living hell out of him. Did three-plus for assault with a deadly weapon." He slumped against the side of the bunk, eyes closed, head down.

Stunned into silence, she realized it had been minutes since she'd taken a breath. Criminal or hero?

"I'm sorry. I'm sorry you asked and that I told you. I should go."

She grabbed his arm and pulled herself up as he stood to leave. She turned him to face her. "I'm sorry, too. Sorry that happened to you and Del and your mom." She stood on her toes and kissed his forehead. "And no. I don't want you to go."

♦♦♦

In the lounge, the crowd seemed invigorated or at least well-lubricated, which Cheryl was glad for. So far, Lyle was a no-show, as was Rhoda, which would be okay, except they were the only people who knew how to operate the Korg sound machine. Renee had hooked the mike up to the karaoke, so that would have to suffice for now. This was a real test for her as a performer. She not only had to sing alone, she had to carry the whole night. Think what you like about Lyle, he was a natural showman with a line of bullshit that could go on for hours, including corny jokes, stories about the rivers they traveled, and stupid magic tricks.

"Good evening, fellow cruisers! Is everybody ready to party?"

The gang, comfortable with each other by now, screamed and whistled.

"Me, too! Did y'all have fun in St. Augustine today?"

More cheers, somewhat less enthusiastic, circulated around the room.

"Well, I don't know where you went, but we

had a great day. Of course, we drank from the famous fountain." She struck a portrait pose for a second. "Don't I look younger? Huh? I sure feel it."

Elmer clapped the loudest, then tried to do the two-finger whistle but blew his dentures out. Undeterred, he shouted, "I'd like to feel it, too, sweet thing!"

Cheryl, waved him off good-naturedly, and continued with her opening. "After our trip to the fountain, we found the best little shopping street, just one block from the main drag, and guess what I found? An alligator purse!" With that, she launched into Cheyl Wright's country song, "Alligator Purse."

Even without accompaniment, she had the crowd clapping and swaying with the music, joining in on the refrain. At the end, Dot raised her hand. "You're so wonderful, Cheryl. Do you have any albums or CDs we can buy?"

"Aren't you sweet, Dot! Thank you. As a matter of fact, our fellow passenger, Marvin, took us to a recording studio today, and I cut my first official CD! There're only four songs on it, but I did get fifty copies. It was so much fun!"

Cheers again filled the room.

"I want one!"

"Me, too!"

"How do we get one?"

With all the humility she could muster, Cheryl took a little bow and said, "God bless you all. You are too, too kind."

"WHAT THE HELL? YOU TRYING TO TURN A PROFIT HERE?"

Everyone turned toward the back of the room,

where Lyle, in yet another sequined jacket, glowered in the doorway. Renee rushed up behind him and patted his arm. "We've been waiting for you, Lyle. Haven't we folks?"

A smattering of assent and applause rose from the group.

Cheryl watched as his face turned from a scowl to a toothy grin. "Sorry, I'm a little late folks." He strode toward her and snatched the mike away. "I've been catching up on the happenings around here. Seems we had some excitement on board today. Does anybody know how to do the 'Alligator Stomp'?" Tossing the mike back to Cheryl, he launched into a rather threatening version of the old punk rock song by the Cramps. He ran around the room, clapping his arms in a chomp-chomp motion, more screaming than singing. No one joined in, and most recoiled in fear.

Desperate to save the evening, Cheryl suggested Lyle host and judge the karaoke contest. Her ploy worked, as he relaxed into full performance mode and even sang along with some of the guests.

While he commandeered the evening, she looked around for Maggie and Rhoda. Odd that they were both absent, though Maggie had mentioned something about meeting up with that Buddy guy around 9:00. Rhoda, though, was a puzzle. Cheryl realized now she hadn't seen her at all since they returned to the ship. Marvin had been at dinner alone, but he was nowhere to be seen now. Maybe they had hooked up again.

As the party started winding down, evidenced by the wheelchair and couch sleepers, Lyle announced Dot as the winner of the singing contest. Renee swooped in with a stuffed alligator as the grand prize, "and a free shore excursion tomorrow!" The few remaining revelers cheered and lined up at the bar for last call.

Cheryl, feeling a little adrift, searched the lounge one last time for Rhoda and Maggie. Disappointed that Ty had not shown for her performance, she returned to the room, hoping to find the girls. Unfortunately, the DO NOT DISTURB sign was on the door again. She headed to the nearest couch and waited.

Chapter 28

Lester thought he would relate how he saved the ship from a savage beast. He worked up a great story about kicking it in the nose and wrestling it into the elevator, but he didn't get a chance to tell the cops. They'd already seen the video of him stumbling backward, terrified, and landing up against the controls which closed the door. Oh well. He could tell his version when he got home. At least the captain and Renee praised his quick reactions.

But the real issue at hand was apparently the number of people getting sick. The police were interviewing the crew and had summoned him to the office. As he listened to the hospital reports, he learned that the last passenger to be transported was pronounced dead on arrival. Information gleaned from the passenger's wife was that he had been unable to find his seizure medication and had missed all but the first day's dose. They planned to visit a pharmacy in St. Augustine, but he suffered the catastrophic event shortly before they could go. The wife knew she had packed the pills because he had used them the first day of the trip and the bottle had been full.

Interviews with the room steward determined that no pills had been found on the floors or other surfaces in the room.

Lester squirmed in his seat like the suck-up kid in class who knew all the answers. "Excuse me, sir."

Heads swiveled in his direction.

The captain spoke. "We'll hear from you in just

a minute, Lester. Let the policeman finish his review of the facts first.

"Yes, sir." He listened to them drone on about the other two hospitalizations, both related to missing medications.

The captain shared that, on those occasions, the cleaning staff indicated the presence of pills dropped on floors and counters and empty prescription bottles scattered throughout the room. "As you know, our business model caters to an older crowd, and unfortunately, many of them combine alcohol with their meds, so it's not unusual for them to lose track of things."

The detective raised an eyebrow. "What do your room stewards do with the dropped pills?"

"They report immediately to Renee, who supervises them while they place all loose medications on the desk. It's not foolproof, but it does give us some liability protection."

The detective wrote on his pad and then spoke. "It sounds very possible that passenger negligence is the issue here, but you understand we have to explore all possibilities before we allow the *Forever Young* to leave port in the morning. I want the ship put on lockdown immediately. No one else has to know, unless they try to leave the ship."

Lester finally jumped from his chair. "Someone is stealing the pills, and I have a good idea who it is."

In the ship's office, all heads turned toward Lester. The captain spoke. "What makes you think you know who it is, and why have you waited so long to report this?"

Perspiration sprang to Lester's forehead and

upper lip. "I didn't really make the connection until just now. I've been seeing a woman in the halls a lot, helping all kinds of older people back to their rooms. And then the other night, I followed her and another man as they went to retrieve medication for a guest at their dinner table." He looked at their faces. Did they believe him? "I thought she looked suspicious from the start. She was checking doorknobs before the boat even left port in Jacksonville." He shoved his hands in his pockets to hide his trembling and felt his phone. "Oh yeah. I forgot. About two or three this morning I saw her sneak out of someone else's room." He pulled up the grainy video he had taken on his phone.

The captain watched. "Do you know who this person is?"

"Her last name's Mason."

Renee immediately jumped from her seat and pulled up the passenger manifest. "Rhoda Mason? It says here she's rooming with our performer, Cheryl Lennon, and a Maggie Lennon."

One of the policemen stood and looked at the video. "How do we know this is the same woman?"

"There's only one Mason on the ship. Plus, look," Renee showed him the manifest. A thumbnail photo was next to each person on the list. "This is the welcome photo we take as people enter the ship. It looks like the woman in the video."

"I'd like to talk to Ms. Mason."

Renee nodded. "Let me check the cameras. She could be in her room, but she might also be at the floor show. We'll check every room if we have to."

The group huddled in front of the monitor.

Lester scanned the crowd in the lounge. "Nope,

not there." The hallways were empty as were the stairwells. Finally, on the top deck, he noticed a woman lying on a chaise and a man sitting next to her. "There she is. I'm positive."

The cop stood upright. "Let's go."

The group sprinted up four flights of stairs, burst through the door, and surrounded the chaise. "Excuse me, sir," the first cop said. "Is this Ms. Rhoda Mason?"

Marvin jumped up, eyes wide, hands wringing. "Is there a problem, Officer?"

"Just answer the question." Right then, the other policeman noticed Rhoda's purse on the floor. He opened it and removed the wallet from inside.

"Don't you need a warrant or something to go through someone's personal belongings?" Marvin stood taller now, arms folded across his chest.

"Not with probable cause." The cop looked at the license. "It's her, all right. Somebody try and wake her up."

Marvin wedged himself between Rhoda and the group. "What's this all about?"

"We have reason to believe this woman has been stealing drugs from other passengers. Other passengers who have become gravely ill from having missed their medications. In fact, one person died this evening."

As if all the air was let out of him, Marvin slumped to the floor, his arm protectively around Rhoda. "I'm sure this is a mistake," he whispered.

"We just need to take her in for questioning. What's the matter with her? Looks like she's OD'd."

At that moment, Renee, who had been gently

shaking Rhoda's shoulder, noticed some movement. "Ms. Mason. It's Renee, your cruise director. Are you okay?"

Rhoda slit open one eye. "Hmmm?"

The policeman took over. "Ms. Mason. Have you taken any drugs tonight?"

Lifting her head off the lounge, she grinned. "No, g'dammit. Ya got any?"

"You're going to have to come with us for questioning, Ms. Mason. But first we're taking you to the hospital for a full toxicology workup." They shoved Marvin aside as they helped Rhoda to her feet, grabbed her purse and the bottle of Everclear, and steered her toward the elevators.

Before the doors closed, Rhoda managed a wobbly grin and yelled, "Tell the girls I'll be back soon." Her knees buckled as the door slid shut.

◆◆◆

Maggie reluctantly said goodbye to Buddy at midnight. Within seconds, there was a knock on the door. She pulled it open.

Cheryl rushed into the room. "Good God, woman. Two nights in a row?"

Maggie smiled. "Making up for lost time. And where have you been?"

"Doing an emergency karaoke night with Lyle."

"Emergency? Why?"

"I'm not sure. Renee asked me to, said the cops were investigating something. I assumed it was about the alligator on board. Anyway, the show was actually fun. Nut-bag Lyle only blew up once when he heard people asking me for copies of my CD." Cheryl smiled at herself in the mirror while she talked.

Maggie picked up her phone and checked for texts. "Have you heard from Rhoda? I haven't seen her all night, but," she did a little shimmy, "I've been pretty preoccupied."

"You're incorrigible. But no. I haven't seen or heard from her. She wasn't at dinner or the show. Maybe she was with Marvin."

"Could be, though I saw him alone at dinner." Just as Maggie finished the sentence, there was a knock on the door. "Maybe that's her." She turned the knob. "Marvin? What are you doing here so late? Where's Rhoda?"

"We've got to talk. Can I come in?" he asked as he stepped through the doorway. "Rhoda's in trouble. Possibly big trouble." He relayed the story of her showing up drunk, the police hauling her off, and their suspicions that she was the drug thief who was possibly responsible for three people getting sick on the ship. "The person they took off the boat tonight didn't make it."

The girls gave each other an oh-shit look. Maggie spoke first. "Drugs you say?"

He nodded.

"I don't know if you're aware, but Rhoda has had some issues with prescription medications in the past."

Cheryl narrowed her eyes at Maggie and added, "But she seems much better. Especially on this trip."

"I know all about it," Marvin said. "In fact, she did ask for a few of my antidepressants, but I personally saw her toss them overboard a few days ago. She said she didn't need them anymore."

Maggie sighed. "That's a relief. Why would they suspect her?"

"I don't know. They didn't say. When they took her away, they were going to the hospital to do a blood test—I assume to look for specific drugs in her system. Then they were going to take her in for questioning."

Cheryl had started pacing in the small room. "We have to find her. Poor thing. She must be terrified."

Marvin nodded. "And very hung over. For some reason, she really tied one on with a bottle of grain alcohol. That stuff is like gasoline."

"It's not like her to get really drunk. I mean, she'll have a drink or two, but rarely does she drink until she passes out, as far as I know." Maggie started scrolling through nearby hospitals on her phone. "I wonder where they took her?"

"Renee and the captain were there with the cops. Maybe they'll know something," Marvin said. "I'd like to go with you, if you don't mind."

"Sure," Maggie said. "Let's go to the office and see what they know."

The sign on the office door read "Closed until 6:00 a.m. For emergencies call 911."

"I could try calling Ty, though I hate to get into this discussion with him," Cheryl said.

"I can't believe they leave this place unattended at night. What kind of a goddamn cruise is this?" Maggie said.

Cheryl frowned. "Hey. I didn't see you winning

any deluxe cruises. You sure seemed to be enjoying it a few hours ago."

"Ladies, ladies. Take a deep breath," Marvin interjected. He'd refereed many a fight between his daughters. "It's okay. That's only a few hours from now. We know she's safe. Let's all go back to our rooms and try to get some rest. We'll meet back here at six and see if we can get some answers. Who knows? She may even be back by then."

"You're right. That sounds like a plan," Maggie said. "Sorry Cher. I'm just upset."

"Me, too. See you later, Marvin."

Chapter 29

The ringing in her ears, the dryness of her mouth and the pounding in her head threatened to kill her. Her face stuck to a vinyl cushion of some sort. She opened her eyes and took in her surroundings. Shit. Bars, stainless steel crapper, lumpy mattress. This was a first.

"Good morning, Ms. Mason." An ogre in a police uniform stared down at her. "How are we feeling today?"

She knew better than to say a word. "Don't I get a phone call?"

"Been watching crime dramas, have we?"

"Please?"

"Maybe, maybe not. We'd like to ask you some questions first."

Rhoda slumped back against the wall. Shit.

◆◆◆

The meeting with Renee was unpleasant but informative. She knew which hospital Rhoda had been taken to and promised to get Cheryl the address of the precinct where she was currently being held. "The police are waiting on the bloodwork before they talk to her and decide whether to press charges."

Cheryl gasped. "What about the ship? What time are we supposed to sail today? You don't intend to just leave her here, do you?"

Renee pursed her lips. "We don't hold a ship

231

for criminals."

Maggie cut her off. "You bitch. She's not a criminal. This is all a misunderstanding. In fact, we can probably sue you for making unfounded, false accusations. Do you even have any evidence? There are all kinds of people on this tub who could have done this, if a crime even has occurred. My god, everybody's so decrepit, they probably can't keep track of their room, much less their suitcases full of medicine."

Cheryl pulled Maggie back. "Let's assume she's not a criminal, Renee. Will the boat wait until we get this resolved? We're heading to the police station now."

"We have adjusted our schedule since the ship was on lockdown until after Ms. Mason was taken in. We plan to sail by noon. And by the way, Ms. Lennon," she stared at Cheryl, "you are still expected to perform this evening, as per your contract. If you'll be leaving the ship this morning, you should inform Lyle in case he has a rehearsal planned." Renee pivoted and headed to the back of the office.

Cheryl balled her fists. "So much for Ms. Sweetise Cruise Director. You're right, Maggie. She is a bitch."

Marvin cleared his throat. "I suggest we head to the station right away and see if we can talk to Rhoda. I have an attorney friend I can call if we need one."

Cheryl took a deep breath. "You're right. We don't have much time. But first I, apparently, have to ask Lyle for permission." They found him in the dining room.

"Hello, ladies and gentlemen." He swooped

into an exaggerated bow.

Such big white teeth so early in the morning. "Good morning, Lyle." Cheryl put on an equally fake smile. "I just wanted to find out what time rehearsal is today. I have some business to attend to this morning."

"Business? What kind of business? Are you still trying to sell your CDs on this boat? That's against the rules, you know."

"No, no. I'm not selling anything. I just have someplace I need to go."

As Lyle puffed out his chest to respond, Renee approached and interrupted. "Excuse me, Cheryl, but here's the address of your police precinct."

"Precinct, huh?" Lyle's eyes bulged as he expelled an exaggerated laugh. "Having a little legal trouble are we? Well, guess what? Rehearsal is now and if you miss it, your contract is void, and you have to pay for this entire cruise." His volume was such that the dining room fell silent and all heads turned in their direction. As if sensing his audience, he turned. "Seems like Little Miss Perfect has gotten herself in trouble with the law!"

By now, his voice boomed, and his laughter bordered on hysteria. Cheryl tried to reason with him. "Lyle," she whispered. "Let's take this out in the hall."

"Ha! We're not going anywhere. I want the world to see what happens when a fucking white trash amateur tries to take over for Lyle!"

Renee grabbed him by the arm and dragged him out of the room.

Cheryl looked at all the shocked faces and, with tears in her eyes, mumbled, "There's been a terrible misunderstanding. I'm sorry." She turned to Marvin and Maggie who escorted her off the ship.

♦♦♦

Maggie checked her phone. "The Uber driver is only three minutes away, according to the app. He's in a white Toyota Camry."

"There it is," Cheryl said, as she waved her arms over her head. "YOO HOO! Here we are."

"Good lord, Cher. He sees us. It's not like we're stranded on a mountain top. We're the only three people standing by the RIDE SHARE sign."

"I know. I'm just so nervous. I've never been to a prison before."

Marvin threw down his cigarette and ground it out. "It's a police precinct, not a penitentiary. They probably have her in a holding cell." He opened the door to the car. "Hop in, ladies. We don't have a lot of time."

The station appeared empty. Not one desk was occupied. Phones rang unanswered.

"Excuse me." Cheryl leaned over the front desk. "EXCUSE ME. Is anyone here?"

Maggie crossed her arms over her chest. "Good going, Cher. Piss everybody off before we get to see her."

A stout policeman, square jawed and clean shaven, came through a door at the back of the room, leather holster creaking as he walked. "Yes, ma'am. We're here. Just finishing up roll call for the first shift. Can I help you?"

Maggie tried to step forward, but Cheryl angled

her out of the way. "I think my sister, Rhoda Mason, may be here. Apparently she was taken off the ship *Forever Young* by police late last night. I'm not sure why she was arrested. There's no way she's committed any crime. This has to be a complete misunderstanding."

Without looking at or responding to Cheryl, the policeman tapped incessantly on a computer keyboard.

Cheryl leaned over the counter toward him. "I was hoping we could straighten this whole thing out and take her back with us. You know, bail her out or something?"

"Just hold your horses, Ms…"

"Lennon. Cheryl Lennon. And this is Rhoda's other sister, Maggie."

After several more minutes of tapping, the officer finally looked up. "Mason, Rhoda. Yes. We brought her in for questioning last night, but she was so inebriated, we had to let her sober up. She has not been arrested, though she is being held on some pretty serious allegations. We're waiting for her to come to."

Marvin edged in front of Cheryl. "Serious crimes? Since when did it become a crime to get drunk and pass out? She wasn't causing any kind of disturbance."

The policeman glared. "And you are?"

"Whitcomb. Marvin Whitcomb. I'll have you know I'm an upstanding citizen and successful business owner here in St. Augustine, and I demand that you either let her go or allow us to call a lawyer before any questioning takes place."

"Mr. Whitcomb, huh?" Fingers flew to the keyboard again. "Well." The cop grabbed the mouse and began scrolling down the page. "Marvin Whitcomb? Owner of Ann's Cluttered Closet?" Taptaptaptaptap.

"Yes, that's me."

The officer's lips curved into a smile. "The same Marvin Whitcomb who was arrested about a month ago for drunk and disorderly conduct and assaulting a woman? The one we had to Baker Act? That outstanding citizen?"

Maggie looked at the policeman. "What's Baker Act?"

He smirked. "It's a Florida law permitting involuntary commitment for those deemed a danger to themselves or others."

Blood drained from Marvin's face as the Lennon sisters stared at him with mouths open. "Achhh. That's all behind me. I paid my fines, did my stint in Halos of Help, and have faithfully attended all therapy sessions to work through my issues." He looked at the floor and stepped back.

The cop raised his head. "Good for you. However, your standing in the community and your criminal record have little relevance here. You can call any lawyer you want, but until we get those results back from the hospital, there won't be any questioning." He turned to walk away.

"Excuse me, sir," Cheryl said. "You mentioned serious allegations. What is it you think she's done?"

The policeman again clacked away on the computer and began reading. "The ship's security guard alleges Ms. Mason has been stealing drugs from other passengers, many of whom, coincidentally, have become quite ill. Last night, one of them could not be revived."

"That's just ridiculous," Cheryl said. "Most of the people on the boat have one foot in the grave already. There could be any number of reasons why they became ill."

The cop looked at her, nostrils flaring, face beginning to flush. "We are doing all we can to investigate the allegation. What exactly do you want?"

Maggie finally spoke up. "Can we see her?"

He looked them over. "Okay. For a few minutes, if she's awake. Step this way. You'll have to go through the scanner." He led them to the metal detector and searched their purses. "We'll keep these here until you're done."

Down a hall there were six small cells, complete with iron bars. "Mason? You got company." The officer turned and walked away, holster creaking with each step.

Rhoda looked up from the edge of a cot, eyes bloodshot and puffy. "Oh, thank God you're here," she sobbed. "I've been scared to death. They won't tell me anything or let me call anyone." She tried to stand but swayed and slouched back down on the mattress. "Plus, I feel like shit, and I can't remember a goddamn thing from last night. What happened?" She wiped tears on her sleeve.

Marvin stepped up and reached for her hand through the bars. "We don't really know. You disappeared when we got back to the ship. After dinner, I found you staggering up the gangway. You were pretty liquored up on EverClear."

Scooting toward the bars, she grabbed Marvin's hand and closed her eyes. "Oh, God. How'd I end up here?"

"After you passed out, the police showed up, started asking questions and hauled you off."

Maggie stepped forward. "They say you're suspected of stealing drugs and people are getting sick from missing their medications. They don't really have any proof, although apparently you had a blood test to determine if you had any of the drugs in your system." She checked the room for cameras or other cops, then leaned closer and lowered her voice. "Have you been using again?"

Rhoda put her face in her hands. "I swear to you, I have not been using drugs. I mean, I took some of Marvin's Celexa a few days ago, but that was it." She looked down. "I did not steal them. Marvin gave them to me. But we had a long talk, and I threw the rest away."

As soon as the words were out of her mouth, the burly cop clomped toward them holding a sheaf of papers. "Well, Ms. Mason. The results are in." He adjusted his holster.

Chapter 30

"ARE YOU STILL SLEEPING?"

Jesus, Ma. Lester rolled over and threw a pillow over his head.

"Nusbaum? Where the hell are you?"

Lester's walkie-talkie jolted him to full consciousness. Not Ma. Renee.

He checked his watch. Damn. 9:30 a.m. He was supposed to go on duty at 7:00. Of course he was up until almost 4:00 dealing with the pill thief. But it was worth it. He'd probably get a special commendation for being so observant and leading them to the prime suspect. He picked up the walkie-talkie. "Yes ma'am. This is Nusbaum."

"I repeat. Where the hell are you?"

"Um, sorry. I, uh, woke up and decided to make detailed notes of what I said last night that led to the arrest. I guess I lost track of time."

"Nice try. Meet me at the office, stat."

Renee hadn't sounded happy. But then she never did unless she was in front of passengers. He jumped up, scraped a toothbrush over his teeth, put on a clean polo and bounded out the door. He was not going to let this job get away from him.

Renee was pacing when he got to the office. Her eyebrows touched her hairline and her lips were pursed. She didn't look like she was about to congratulate him on a job well done.

"So, Nusbaum. You've been taking notes about your observations. Did you happen to mention there

239

are often people wandering the halls at night? That these geezers often go into the wrong rooms because they're too drunk or batty to know where they belong? Or did you just pounce on the one woman you've seen a few times and decide she was a criminal?"

"Uh, um, well. I guess Ms. Mason is the one I've seen the most, and I did actually witness her get pills from a woman's room and take the bottle to her in the dining room."

"So she got someone else's pill for them. Big deal. Sounds like a good Samaritan to me."

"Has something happened, Ma'am? I mean the police did take a super drunk Ms. Mason to the police station last night. They must have had good reason."

"Their reason was based on your accusations. But guess what? I just got a call from the station. They're releasing Ms. Mason. The toxicology results showed none of the drugs in question. In fact, besides the alcohol, her blood screen was clean."

His heart sank. "I'm sorry. I mean, I'm glad she's okay. So you don't think she did it?"

Renee was white with anger. "I don't know if anybody's been stealing pills. Do you realize we could get sued for this? She is the sister of our star attraction, after all. Unbelievable, Nusbaum. This is going in your file."

The captain entered the office while Lester was being scolded. "Settle down, Renee. Lester here just reported what he had witnessed. I think we all may have acted hastily."

Lester hung his head. "Thank you, sir."

"We will make note of it in his file, but no disciplinary action needs to be taken. I would advise,

Mr. Nusbaum, that you be very careful about making assumptions in the future. If you see something suspicious, report it to me directly, and I'll decide how to handle the situation."

"Yes sir. Thank you sir."

◆◆◆

Rhoda laid her head back on the seat of the Uber and closed her eyes. "The first thing I'm going to do when I get back on the boat is stuff myself in that tiny shower and scrub until the hot water runs out. Then I'm going to pitch these clothes. I feel like I've been sleeping in a toilet bowl."

"Looked like you kind of were," Maggie said. "What a bunch of crap. I can't believe they hauled you off to jail because of that stupid security guard."

Cheryl patted Rhoda's leg. "All's well that ends well, right?"

Maggie leveled a we-do-not-need-Pollyanna-right-now look. "I think the ship's staff owes her an apology. I mean, all she did was get drunk."

Rhoda opened one eye. "Really drunk."

"Whatever possessed you to do that? You're not normally a big drinker."

Looking askance at Marvin, Rhoda sighed. "I'd rather not talk about this right now. My head is killing me, and I could puke at any moment."

Everyone scooted as far away from her as they could in the small car, rolled down windows, and rode the rest of the way to the boat in silence.

When they arrived, Marvin asked if she'd like to come recover in his room.

"Thanks. For everything. But I think I'm going

to slink back to our room and collapse for a while. Maybe we could meet for lunch or dinner."

He nodded. "Sure. I'm glad you're okay. Let me give you my number so you can call if you need anything."

They watched him walk off as they waited for the elevator.

"Too bad about him. He seems like such a nice, normal guy," Cheryl said.

Rhoda frowned. "Seems like? He is a great guy."

Maggie elbowed Cheryl and mouthed, "Not now."

They filed off the elevator and into the room where Rhoda, as promised, headed straight for the shower.

After a few minutes, Cheryl whispered to Maggie, "I don't know why you stopped me. Shouldn't we tell her that Marvin has a rap sheet?"

"Oh, for chrissakes. A rap sheet? So he made a mistake. Who hasn't?"

"Most mistakes don't land you in detox."

"And some do." Maggie pointed to the bathroom. "Just leave it alone. Rhoda doesn't need to deal with your judgment right now." Maggie did not want to get into a conversation about the vices and virtues of the men they had chosen on this trip, especially since she had no intention of calling it quits with Buddy. "Let's just try to enjoy the last day of this cruise together."

"You're right. What's on the itinerary for today?" Cheryl asked just as the bathroom door opened.

"Whatever it is, count me out," Rhoda said. "I'm going to take a handful of Advil and Tums. But I'd better do it out of sight of that snoop security guard. Don't want him thinking I'm stealing shit again."

"The schedule says there's a tour of Green Cove Springs. Isn't that near your town, Rho?"

"Don't care." She collapsed on the bottom bunk.

Maggie nodded her head. "Me either. How about a nice, quiet day? We all deserve it after yesterday. I think I'm just going to find a sunny spot and try to finish that book I started."

"You're right. We'll go for normal. I guess I'd better get to rehearsal for my last big show, if that whack job, Lyle, will have me. I hope he's calmed down by now." Cheryl grabbed her lanyard, a bag and her phone and headed out the door. "You two stay out of trouble."

"Back at ya', Sis."

◆◆◆

Stripped of his gun, Lester hung his head as he shuffled away from the office. Bunch of ingrates. He'd only tried to help by suggesting that Mason woman might be the pill thief. Now he was the one in trouble. Less than twenty-four hours ago, he was the big hero for saving everyone from the alligator. He could hear his mother now, "Always remember, your greatest achievement is yesterday's news." He hated when she was right.

Grabbing a cinnamon roll from the kitchen, he started his patrol. He had the rest of today and tomorrow morning to prove himself worthy of a permanent position. Licking his fingers and brushing the crumbs off his shirt, he headed for the gangway. There were only a few hours left before they disembarked, but he would be super-vigilant making sure all passengers were on board and all vendors were not.

The cloudless sky was neon blue and the sun white hot. He could already see heat waves shimmering off the asphalt across the gangway. He donned his aviators and stood at attention swiveling his head in all directions. Who knew when another critter might try to board the boat?

The first hour passed with little activity, though Lester felt compelled to stay near the gangway in the event someone tried to sneak on board at the last minute. Catching a potential stowaway would surely boost everyone's opinion of him.

Finally, a group of passengers headed toward the boat from the shore. They were a passive group, all holding their lanyards out so he could check them against the manifest. Sure enough, they were all legit.

Settling back against the frame of the doorway, he checked his phone. Only twenty minutes to go. Renee's voice came on the loudspeaker announcing their imminent departure and asking guests to ensure all members of their party were on board and accounted for. "As you know, we'll be traveling down river to Green Cove Springs where you'll have three hours to explore this historic small town. Then we'll spend the rest of the evening sailing, arriving in Jacksonville in the morning. Don't forget to take advantage of all the activities listed in your itinerary for the afternoon and evening. As usual, cocktail hour will begin at 5:00, dinner at 7:00 and our grand finale, 'Thanks for the Memories,' by Lyle and Cheryl in the Peacock Lounge at 8:00. Enjoy every moment of your last full day aboard the *Forever Young*."

Momentarily distracted by the announcement, Lester looked up to see a frail old woman tentatively finding her footing on the gangway. What a string bean. These seniors were either obese or walking skeletons. Amazing they still wanted to travel.

He watched her grab the handrail and take a collapsible cane from her bag. She struggled to open it as she approached the first connector of the walkway. Just as she reached the joint where two sections were bolted together, the cane shot open, catching in the gap between the handrails. As she tried to free it, he could see her heel catch in the joint and, off balance, she slipped like a limp noodle through the rail, arms flailing, mouth open in a soundless scream.

Lester reached the end of the dock seconds after she hit the water. "HELP!" he screamed. "Somebody call 911!" Where the hell was everybody? Shouldn't someone be out here getting ready to cast off? He raced to the edge of the water, took a step down the embankment and slid to the bottom. "Hold on, Ma'am. I'm coming!"

The old woman gasped for air, arms thrashing, cane drifting away from her. Lester grabbed and extended it toward her. After a few failed attempts, she grabbed on. "Hold on, tight, Ma'am. Relax, and I'll pull you in."

At that moment, her head went under, though her hand still clung to the cane. He slogged through the silty bottom and pulled her ashore. Red with exertion, shaking from adrenaline, he too, gasped for air. Why hadn't he taken that CPR course? He was supposed to watch a training video on YouTube while he was on the boat, but it just seemed like there was never enough time. As he reached for his walkie-talkie to signal for help, he spied it floating away on the current. No help there.

All he could do was get her on the boat fast. Finding his footing, he swept her up in his arms—she couldn't have weighed a hundred pounds, literally soaking wet—and ran up the gangway.

♦♦♦

Cheryl dreaded rehearsal with that slithery eel, Lyle, but she would not let his obnoxious behavior keep her from singing. The fans loved her and she them. Plus, who knew when she'd get another chance to perform before a live audience?

She did have a stop to make on the way. She'd gift-wrapped one of her CDs for the captain. He'd said many times how much he loved her singing. Now he would think of her every time he played it. Did she dare risk another long-distance relationship? There was no way he'd be sailing to landlocked Tallahassee any time soon. Best not to get ahead of herself. They'd only known each other less than a week, but it seemed like they had a real connection.

After stopping at a mirror in the hall to fluff her hair and check her lipstick, she took a deep breath and knocked on his stateroom door. Was that voices she heard? Children's voices?

"May I help you?" A stunning blonde with

246

crystal-blue eyes smiled like a Vogue model from the doorway.

Three mini-models scampered up behind her. "Who is it, Mommy? Is that my lunch?"

Cheryl, blood draining to her feet, swayed. Another deep breath. "Isn't this Captain Cabot's room?"

"Yes. I'm Dana Cabot. Can I help you?"

The flawless family tableau shimmered through tears in Cheryl's eyes. "Uh, I uh…" Unable to form a coherent sentence, she turned and ran.

Chapter 31

The slam of the door woke Rhoda from her hangover coma. "What the hell, Maggie?"

A scowl squared Maggie's jaw. "Son of a bitch. SON of a bitch. I can't believe that rat bastard just left the ship without so much as a see you later, goodbye or go to hell."

Rhoda raised her head slightly. No headache. Good news. She sat up, taking full inventory. Stomach settled, head cleared, shakes stilled. Praise Jesus. "Let me guess. The guy you've been shagging ditched you."

"Looks like it. I just saw him walking from the boat with a backpack. And I haven't heard from him since last night."

"Did something happen then?"

Wham. The door slammed again. Cheryl threw herself at Rhoda and sobbed. "I can't believe it! That lowlife scumbag! How could he lie to me like that?"

In seconds Rhoda had a sister crying on each shoulder. Just like the old days. Many a time she had soothed their teenage angst, despite her own problems. Tears welled in her eyes. No matter how bad her own situation, these girls would always need her and vice versa. How lucky they were to have each other. "Okay, ladies. Let's all settle down and see if we can straighten this out. I'm guessing we've all just been jilted in some way. Let's review." She looked at them both. "Cheryl, you start."

The normally composed and perfect Cheryl looked up, mascara streaming down her cheeks, nose running, voice hiccupping. "He's married!"

"The captain? How do you know?"

"I just met his gorgeous wife and kids when I went to his room. The room we," she buried her face in her hands. "I can't even say it. That lying cheat."

"They're all lying cheats." Rhoda turned to Maggie. "And yours just ran off?"

"I guess. Like I said, I saw him leaving the ship. I can't believe it. Last night he really opened up to me. I thought we were really getting close."

"Opened up about what?"

Maggie took a deep breath. "He's done time."

Cheryl ceased blubbering as hers and Rhoda's mouths dropped. "Time? As in jail?"

"Prison, actually. But it was almost justifiable. Anyway, he's paid his dues. He's even going back to school."

Rhoda unwound herself from both of them. "Guess we've all had a bad day."

"What happened to you, anyway?" asked Maggie.

Rhoda relayed the story of seeing Ben, who not just ignored her, but hid from her, which led to her rot-gut binge and her subsequent incarceration. "So yeah. Bad day."

Cheryl wiped the streaks of mascara from her face. "Bad day? Some Lemon Sisters' Adventure. I've landed a cheater, Rhoda's been pussy-footing around with a senior citizen from the looney bin, and Maggie's fallen for an ex-con. I'd call that some pretty low-hanging fruit, girls." She blew her nose and squared her shoulders. "We can do better than this, can't we?"

"You know me," Maggie said. "When all else fails, lower your standards." She stood up and opened the sliding door. Air washed over the stuffy room. "There's something special about Buddy. Maybe he's just running an errand or something."

"And there's nothing wrong with Marvin." Rhoda arched her brow at Cheryl. "In fact, he's about the most decent man I've ever met. I like that he's not perfect. The good thing is, he knows it, admits it, and tries to do better. I'm not used to honesty in relationships, but I kind of like it."

Cheryl nodded. "You're right. I'm sorry. He is a good, caring man. He was very concerned about you and helped when we were trying to find you. I don't know about Buddy, but I'll give him the benefit of the doubt."

Rhoda patted her on the shoulder. "And you never know about the captain. Maybe this was all just a misunderstanding."

"Highly doubtful," Cheryl walked to the bathroom. "But I'm not going to let it ruin our last night together or my last night on stage. Let's wash up, get ready and rock this ship!"

♦♦♦

Lester scrambled onto the boat, the frail woman in his arms, and ran to the office. The door was locked. "Help! Is anybody in there? Help! Emergency!"

What seemed like minutes passed and no one answered. The bridge. He'd head for the bridge. He turned to run toward the stairs and slammed into an open door.

A scream came from the other side. Stepping

250

around the door, he found Lyle splayed on the hall carpet, surrounded by dozens, no hundreds, of pills of all shapes and colors. "RENEE! HELP, RENEE! ANYBODY!"

Lyle struggled to his side, frantically scooping up as many as he could reach.

"Not so fast, mister," Lester said, as he stepped on Lyle's arm. "HELP!"

People began migrating from their rooms to see what was happening.

"Excuse me. Excuse me." Renee muscled her way through the hall. "Go back in your rooms. Everything's under control." She surveyed the area. Lyle writhing on the floor, specks of something scattered around him. Lester standing on his arm, holding an ancient woman. "What's going on? Why are you so wet? Why are you standing on Lyle?"

"Call the captain. Quick. This woman fell off the gangway. I got to her, but she was under water for a while. Then I ran into this bozo. There's all your missing pills."

Renee again reviewed the situation. "Why didn't you use your walkie-talkie?"

"It floated away. Hurry. I haven't done CPR. I can't remember it all."

"Is she breathing?"

"I don't know. I think so, but I can't tell."

"Give her to me. I'll do the compressions; you take my walkie-talkie and call for help. And don't let him get away." She nodded toward Lyle as she placed the woman on the floor and began CPR.

"Get off me, you fat-ass. I'm innocent. These aren't pills," he screamed shoving them in his pockets.

"They're Tic-Tacs. Part of my magic act."

As Lester contacted the captain to call 911, a wild-eyed Lyle wriggled out from underneath his foot.

"I'll show you fat-ass, you son of a bitch." Lester hurled his sizable frame at Lyle, flattening him with a force that shook the walls.

The EMTs and the police arrived minutes later and sprung into action. By the time they had the patient loaded on a gurney and Lyle tased and handcuffed, the passengers were making their way to the final cocktail hour.

The girls readied for the night in a perfume-clouded room.

"Jesus, Cheryl. Your hair's as straight as a stick. Why you do you need all that spray?" Maggie choked and grabbed the can from her. "I, however, look like Marge Simpson, despite my expensive Brazilian blowout last week."

"You look fine," Cheryl said. "You both do. We ALL do! I'm so glad we ran to that cute shop in Green Cove Springs and got these fabulous gowns."

Rhoda shook her head. "Quite a contrast from last night when I sat in the slammer, sweat-soaked and reeking of booze."

"You see," Cheryl said to the mirror, "there's always something to be thankful for. In fact, instead of bemoaning the bad things that have happened, I think we should make a Glad List."

Maggie and Rhoda rolled their eyes and said in unison, "Okay, Pollyanna."

"No, I'm serious. Let's see…well, of course, I got to sing for a live audience almost every night, and they loved me! Maggie?"

"Um, the food was good? Rhoda?"

"Tough one. Let's see. At least I didn't become somebody's bitch in jail."

Cheryl frowned. "Let's change that to 'you got exonerated.' Come on, girls. You can do better. My turn again. I made my very own CD. Maggie?"

"I guess we all found someone we liked, at least for a little while. I did enjoy the sightseeing tours...and the warm weather. Your turn, Rhoda."

"I got flashed by a lecherous nonagenarian. Is that a good thing?" She shook her head. "Oh, I did enjoy the watercolor class, and despite his past, I like Marvin."

"See there? I told you there were things to be glad about. Neither of you mentioned the best part. We got to be together for almost a whole week while a host of people cooked and cleaned for us!" She gathered them both and turned toward the mirror. "And we all look fabulous. Selfie time! Cheese." She snapped the picture. "Now let's go out there and show everybody how fierce we are."

Chapter 32

Sir Marvin surveyed the blood-thirsty rabble from atop his loyal mount, his lance readied at his side. He would not let the fair Rhoda pay for a crime she didn't commit. It was because of him she arrived late for the queen's coronation and was not only dismissed from the court, but accused of stealing precious gems. Their innocent trip to the Mayfest had turned into an extended afternoon of gentle lovemaking on the banks of the River Arun. Her tardiness provided the perfect opportunity for a covetous lady-in-waiting to set her up for banishment.

The crowd swelled around the gallows as the gate to the palace was lowered. Framed in the doorway stood Rhoda, shrouded in a gray cape, hands tied behind her.

Time to make his move. He spurred his steed and moved behind the crowd, readying to charge in and grab her before the executioner prepared the noose. As she climbed the scaffold steps toward the gallows, he reared his horse and broke into a full gallop...

"Hey there, big fella."

He felt a bump against his hip and turned to see Dot, her sunburned scalp shimmering through her comb-over.

"I was kind of hoping we'd get to know each other better on this trip. You are the most handsome, virile man here, you know." She batted crooked false eyelashes and flashed him a lipstick-stained smile. "And it's not too late. How about we end this trip with a bang!" She leaned in, pressing her prodigious breasts against his arm.

He backed away. "Only if I had a gun."

◆◆◆

Cheryl fidgeted on the way to the dining room. "I don't know if I can stand this. Not only do I have to face the captain, I'll probably get publicly humiliated by Lyle again. I never did make it to practice."

"I think I'd worry more about Lyle than the adulterer. He was unhinged this morning. What is wrong with that guy? If we never see that sleaze-bag again it will be too soon."

"I agree, Mags. But some show biz people are like that. Really high strung. I hope I get to perform tonight."

Rhoda caught up with them after reading a text. "Do you two mind if Marvin sits with us at dinner?" She looked pointedly at Cheryl. "Is that okay with you?"

"Of course it is. He's no crazier than anybody else on this boat."

Maggie laughed. "Amen to that."

As they searched for a table, Cheryl felt someone tap her shoulder.

"Excuse me, Ms. Lennon," Renee said. "Do you think you could handle doing the final show by yourself tonight?"

"What about Lyle? Will he let me? I missed rehearsal today."

"That's the thing." Renee leaned in and whispered. "He's no longer with us."

"Is he dead?" Cheryl blurted louder than she intended.

Rhoda circled in. "Dead? Who's dead? Man, Renee, people are dropping like flies under your watch."

Renee shook her head. "Shhh. Please. No, he's not dead. And I'd like to apologize to you both." She looked around. "It turned out that Lyle was the one stealing people's medications. He was caught with the evidence this afternoon. I'd appreciate it if you didn't say anything to the other passengers."

Fists clenched, Rhoda leaned within an inch of Renee. "God forbid we should besmirch someone's reputation."

Renee took a step back. "Again, I'm sorry, Ms. Mason. Truly. And we'd like to make it up to you."

"Oh really? How do you make up for a night in a revolting jail cell?"

"How about a week-long cruise for two from Port Canaveral to the Keys, Ms. Mason?"

Rhoda's jaw dropped. "You have my attention."

"The captain and I discussed it. He's having the voucher made up for you now. And again, our deepest apologies." Renee returned to greeting guests.

Cheryl arched a brow. "So you get a free cruise, and I get a broken heart."

"Ah, my three favorite ladies," Marvin said. "Why don't we find a table?"

Rhoda grabbed his arm and nodded toward Cheryl. "Let's make it as far away from the captain's table as possible."

As the wait-staff scurried around the dining room taking drink orders, Cheryl noticed the absence of Renee and the captain. Coward. He probably heard about her visit and was too embarrassed to show up with his wife and kids. Good. Served the schmuck right. Hopefully they'd skip dinner altogether, so she could eat in peace.

◆ ◆ ◆

When Renee asked him to meet her and the captain at the beginning of dinner service, Lester worried. Was he in trouble again? He'd tried his best to do a good job. Well, almost. He'd watch that CPR video as soon as his shift was over tonight, so he'd never have to pass off that job again. And the pill thing had been an innocent mistake. He'd just been trying to help.

When he arrived at the staff lounge, Renee and the captain stood before the entire crew, minus those covering dinner.

Renee spoke first. "I guess you're wondering why we called all of you together like this. We have some very important information to share with you tonight, but we'll make it brief so we can all return to pampering our passengers."

Captain Cabot took the floor. "As you may have heard, this has been a bit of an unusual sailing for us. We've had the removal of two staff for drug use, an alligator on board, a rash of clients taken to the hospital, police intervention for a suspected pill thief, and just this afternoon, one of our very own saved a woman from a potentially deadly fall off the gangway. What you may not have heard is that our Entertainment Director, Lyle Broadmoor, has been arrested for stealing medications from passenger staterooms.

"While we applaud those of you who have helped keep the cruise going smoothly despite these anomalies, I feel that we need to heighten our diligence while on board. Therefore, we will be offering training on proactive strategies to ensure the safety of our passengers and crew. To lead that effort, we will employ a permanent safety instructor who will also work as head of our security team." The captain scanned the room. "And that person will be...Lester Nusbaum.

"I realize he has only been with us a week, but despite a rocky start, Mr. Nusbaum has been alert to all potential problems and has moved quickly to minimize the threat of harm to those on board."

Lester, flushed red from ear to ear, rose from his chair, mouth agape.

"Congratulations, Lester." The captain motioned him to the front and shook his hand.

Mom would never believe this. Not in a million years.

Anemic applause scattered throughout the room as a cabin steward raised her hand. "Can we go now?"

♦♦♦

By the time dinner was served, Cheryl's nerves were calming. Possibly because of the three wine spritzers or the fact that the captain hadn't shown up. If she quit drinking now, she would be sober enough for her performance. Screw that pig. He didn't deserve one more minute of her time or attention. She had an audience to please.

As the busboy cleared the first course plates, the waiter brought her another cocktail. "Chardonnay spritzer, right?"

She held up her hand to refuse just as the captain entered the room trailed by his adoring family. "Yes, thank you." She grabbed the drink. "And keep 'em coming." She could sing drunk.

Maggie also ordered another glass. "But none of that spritzer stuff. Cabernet, straight up." She grabbed Cheryl's hand. "Sorry, Sis. I guess you and I are the last two members of the lonely hearts club."

They looked at Marvin and Rhoda, heads together, giggling like teenagers.

"Here's to us, Maggie. May we spinsters age gracefully in a little cottage in the woods with no friends except our three hundred cats."

They toasted just as the captain stood and clinked the side of his glass. "Ladies and Gentlemen, I'd like to thank you all for being one of the best groups we've had on the *Forever Young,* and from the looks of all the canoodling going on, I'd say our first Boomers/GenXers Mixer was a success.

"I'd like to take this time to recognize some very special people. First and foremost, how about a round of applause for Renee Reinhart, our number one Cruise Director."

Hoots and whistles filled the room.

"And of course, our wonderful crew who provided and served you these gourmet meals, kept the ship in tip-top shape, and catered to your every whim."

Boisterous applause.

"Sounds like they're doing their job keeping the drinks coming, ha ha. I'd be remiss if I didn't mention our star attraction who entertained us with such passion and talent, Ms. Cheryl Lennon. Take a bow, Ms. Lennon."

Cheryl stood briefly, only because those diners who could gave her a standing ovation.

"And finally, I'd like to introduce you to my family who joined me as a surprise just this morning. Please meet my sister, Dana, and my nephew and niece, Victor and Hayley."

"I'll be damned," Maggie said.

"His sister. And her kids." Cheryl stared in disbelief. "So, is he married or not?"

"That's the first thing I'd ask him, if I were you," Maggie said, slamming back the rest of her wine. So she'd live alone in the woods with cats.

◆◆◆

Maggie stood in the corner by the bar during Cheryl's last show. The captain had come to their table during the dessert course, where Cheryl, emboldened by wine, pointedly asked if he had a wife. He did not. Not now; not ever. Of course. Gorgeous Sis won again. Even Rhoda, despite her numerous attempts at self-sabotage, seemed to be happily paired with Marvin.

Only she was destined to spinsterhood. What had gone wrong with Buddy? The last night they were together, she thought they'd connected. He knew she was willing to forgive his past. She thought they'd parted on good terms. Obviously, it wasn't enough to keep him from walking away.

The only thing left to do was get shit-faced and

endure the rest of this cruise. She sidled up to the bar and asked for a Cosmo, heavy on the vodka, light on the fruity crap. Just as she took a substantial sip, she heard her name.

"Maggie, Maggie, Maggie..." the crowd chanted. She looked up from the bottom of her glass to see Cheryl and Rhoda at the mike, whipping the crowd into a frenzy.

"Come on, Maggie," Cheryl said. "It's time for our theme song." She turned to the audience. "It's a tune by Irving Berlin made famous in the classic movie, 'White Christmas.'"

"Maggie, Maggie, Maggie..."

Oh for chrissakes. Leave it to Cheryl to try to drag her into a better mood. Not happening. Maggie upended her drink and turned to the bartender for another just as Cheryl and Rhoda hauled her to the front of the room.

"Stop it, you two. You know I can't sing a note."

Rhoda patted her on the back. "Oh, honey, you're much better when you're all liquored up. Come on. Have some fun. What do you have to lose?"

Good point. She was at rock bottom. Who cared if she could sing? If it made her sisters happy, what the hell?

The three took their positions, struck their poses and performed a full choreographed version of "Sisters."

The crowd, also well-lubricated, cheered like they were the Beatles.

"More!"

"Encore!"

"Sing it, girls!"

Since that was the only song Maggie could remember, she slipped away during the applause. Her head was spinning and her stomach churned. Lots of Cosmo sloshing around in there. She leaned against a wall in the back, desperate to get the ship to stop swaying.

After thirty seconds, her stomach started to cramp. Damn. She ran to the elevator, got to their floor, dashed from the door to the toilet and lost the contents of her stomach. Surrounded by darkness, she sat back on the floor, holding her head against the wall. Too many drinks, too much food, too much dancing, too much drama. What a perfect ending to her part of the Lemon Sisters Adventure.

Finally able to stand, she felt for the faucet, splashed water on her face, rinsed her mouth, and headed out of the bathroom. She needed to open the window and get some fresh air before hitting the sack. As she stumbled through the room toward the sliding door, she sensed a presence. Hair rose on the back of her neck, and her heart pounded. She could see the outline of someone on the edge of the bed.

Barely moving, she reached for the nearest thing she could find. Her hand closed on Cheryl's well-equipped make-up bag which she swung with all her might toward the intruder.

Chapter 33

"Good morning! This is your cruise director, Renee. I hope everyone has recovered from last night's fantastic show by the one and only, Cheryl Lennon.

"A few housekeeping tips. Double check to make sure you have all your possessions. Please place all tagged bags outside your room before you head to breakfast. And don't forget to stop by the bursar's office to settle any outstanding costs, including tips for our terrific crew. Our staff will carry your bags down to the debarkation area where you can retrieve them as you head for home or whatever adventure awaits you. You've been a terrific group, and we'll miss you here on the *Forever Young*. We hope you'll book with us again soon. In your farewell packet, you'll find coupons for special savings on future cruises only for veteran passengers. It's been our pleasure to serve you on our inaugural Boomers/GenXers Mixer. We'd like to take pictures of those who have made new friends here for our promotional materials. Stop by the photo booth in the debarkation area as you leave. Farewell friends."

"Okay," Rhoda said after they ordered their breakfast. "Give me a full report. Where was everybody last night, with whom, and what happened? Maggie, you start, since you ducked out before we could do an encore."

"All that damned dancing and singing made me sick as a dog, thank you very much. I raced to our room and puked my guts up. The room was dark, and when I went to open the window, I thought I saw someone in the shadows. Scared the shit out of me."

"Oh my God," Cheryl said. "Are you okay? It wasn't that Lyle creep, was it?"

"I didn't know, so I grabbed your make up bag and belted the guy with it. Turns out it was Buddy. He'd gotten a room steward to let him in to surprise me." She was aglow with contentment. "I broke his nose."

Rhoda snorted. "Way to reel him in, Sis."

"Good lord, Mags. I thought he'd left," Cheryl said.

"Turns out he got a call from his brother, Delmont, in Eugenia begging him to come visit, so he hitched a ride over there. Del's getting married this summer, and Buddy asked me to be his date."

"So you didn't get dumped," Rhoda said. "Way to go, Mags! By the way, that Delbert kid is the one who bought my old mobile home." She turned to Cheryl. "All right, Lady Gaga, spill it."

"As you know, Ty is not married, praise the Lord. I met his sister, and she is delightful. Must run in the family." She did a little shimmy. "She and the kids returned home after that, so we had the Captain's Suite all to ourselves. He even asked me to be the star attraction for a future cruise."

"To sum up, then," Rhoda said, "Cheryl and I both get a free cruise, and Maggie gets to go to a trailer-park wedding."

Maggie stuck out her bottom lip. "Hey."

"Joke," Rhoda said. "I thought this cruise was going to be a real dud when we first got on, but it looks like we all came out okay."

Cheryl raised her coffee cup. "Let's toast to another successful Lemon Sisters' Adventure!"

They laughed as coffee slopped everywhere.

"How about I meet you both down at the debarkation area? I want to say goodbye to Tyler. Then we'll drive you home, Rhoda, and Maggie and I will get back to Tallahassee."

"Oh, I forgot," Rhoda said. "Marvin offered me a ride. He's got a big van, so we're going to load up all the stuff I tagged in his store and go decorate my new double-wide."

"He really is a nice guy," Maggie said. "Good for you. Sounds like a brand new start."

Rhoda smiled. "It is the Year of Rhoda."

"I guess this is goodbye then?" Maggie teared up.

"Not yet," Cheryl said. "Wait for me by the photo booth so we can get a commemorative picture."

"Okay. See you there."

Marvin stood to the side as the women hammed it up for the camera, then grabbed their bags and walked toward him.

"We'll have to plan another trip soon," Maggie said. "I miss you guys already."

"I know," Cheryl said. "Let's Google Duo when we all get settled and start planning."

"Perfect," Rhoda said. "Love you guys."

"Me to you," Cheryl said.

Maggie hugged them both. "Love you more.

Acknowledgements

My deepest thanks to Anna Southard, Adrienne Cronebaugh, and Karen Mueller for your encouragement, beta reading, and input. To Ellen Binkley Hill for her title and story ideas. As always, thanks to my incredible writing group—James. R. Nelson, Gayle Lambert, Olive Pollak, Susan Wood, Maureen Gallagher, and Gene Luke Vlahovic—for your amazing insights and, mostly, for your laughter.

A Preview of the first Lemon Sisters' Adventure by Phoebe Richards

Relatively inSane

Prologue

June 20ᵗʰ

The taste of bile was his first conscious sensation, the pounding in his left temple the second. Forcing one eye open, he realized he lay on a concrete floor in a pool of befoulment so ripe, vomit again rose in the back of his throat. Despite the pain and vertigo, he pushed himself up on one elbow to lean against the steel post beside him. He could barely make out his surroundings in the black night. Adjusting to the dark, he remembered where he was.

What had happened? Someone... That's right. Someone hit him; knocked him out. The effort to remember made his head throb so hard his eyes bulged. Oh yeah. That bitch. That goddamned bitch had clubbed him. He'd kill her for this.

What was that? Footsteps? Yes, behind him. By the swamp. It had to be her.

Lifting his chin from his chest, he turned his head toward the noise.

Chapter 1
Saturday, June 8, morning

Pls, don't bother coming down. I'll be okay. Dr. said I'd only be in a cast about 3? months. Lute found me a scooter thing at the pawn shop. Sorry if I sounded desperate in the ER, but I'm okay. Really.

Maggie Lennon reread her sister's text from the night before as a man climbed over her to reach the middle seat. "Sorry," he said, hoisting his huge, mud-caked shoe over her knees. "These seats ain't half the size they used to be."

He wedged himself between the armrests. "You goin' to Florida for vacation?"

"I wish. I'm going to help my sister. She broke her leg."

"Aw, that's too bad. Them casts is a pain in the butt. Broke my ankle once when I jumped off the back of my daddy's pickup. I dragged that cast around half a my senior year."

She pulled out her book and pretended to read. When Rhoda called from the ER, she didn't say how she broke her leg. Well, she did, but as usual, Maggie didn't believe her. She had that airy tone she used when she was lying. "Oh, you know my stupid giant toe. I had on flip flops and caught it on the edge of the threshold just as I stepped out. Threw me right down on the sidewalk."

Maggie suspected another argument with Lute. Before the accident, Rhoda said he was "collaborating" with a guy for his new business venture. Lute usually conducted his so-called business at the pawn shop or The Broken Cleat Bait and Bar down by the river. Maggie's bet was on the bar. Most of Lute's get-rich-quick schemes hatched after a few bottles of Ron Rico.

She also suspected he wouldn't be much help to Rhoda. He'd prop her up in that sweat-slick, broken down recliner with the remote control and a big glass of RC before he headed out.

"I finally got that cast off just after baseball started, sos I missed the tryouts."

Maggie had forgotten about Big Foot. "Mmm. That's too bad," she mumbled.

"Ladies and Gentlemen, we are beginning our final descent into Tallahassee. Make sure your seat belts are fastened and all seat backs and tray tables are in their upright position."

She stuffed a bag of chips and the book in her carry-on. Rhoda would be surprised, but hopefully, pleased she came down. It was the beginning of summer, so Maggie had eleven weeks before the new school year started. Surely, Rhoda's cast would be off by then.

After talking all the way from the gate about how good he would have been in baseball, Big Foot was kind enough to pull Maggie's bags off the carousel. She dragged them into the nearest bathroom to freshen up before her other sister, Cheryl, came to get her. The trip was so last minute, Maggie didn't have time to put herself together before she left. Her ash brown hair had already started to frizz. By the time she stepped outside, its volume would double. Her short bob with blunt bangs that was so pretty and sleek in the salon now looked like a character in a Dilbert cartoon.

She leaned in toward the mirror; definitely should have bothered with makeup. Her skin showed signs of aging – a few brown spots, worry lines, and blue-black circles under her eyes. She didn't even look in the full-length mirror. There was no doubt she would not only outweigh her middle sister, her Walmart shorts and Greenville Devildogs polo would look dowdy next to whatever designer Cheryl was wearing today. Screw it. She didn't care about all that stuff. But her shoulders slumped as she grabbed her bags and rolled them outside.

"Yoo-hoo, MAGGIE," sang her sister from the loading zone. "Over here."

She spotted Cheryl a few cars down; her glossy, golden hair had grown to her shoulders, accenting her emerald eyes. Damn. She looked thinner than the last time Maggie had seen her. No matter how hard Maggie tried (which was never very hard) she could not lose that last ten (fifteen?) pounds.

"Hey, Cheryl." Maggie hugged her. "Thanks so much for picking me up and taking me to Rhoda's. How far is it from here?"

"Oh, it's a ways, but I love to drive. I want to help you with Rhoda at least for the weekend. Plus, I don't want to miss anything. I took Monday morning off, so I'll drive back then. Thank God you're here. Maybe we can figure out what happened."

Cheryl also doubted Rhoda's story. "I figure she was either so hopped up on pills she just fell down, or she and Lute had a fight. But I really don't think he'd hurt her."

"The hell he wouldn't," Maggie said.

"Oh, now, Maggie, he's not that bad."

Rather than challenge Cheryl's rosy viewpoint, she changed the subject. "Where's Chief?" Maggie couldn't believe Cheryl was traveling without her beloved teacup poodle, Chief Osceola. The dog had all the necessary gear - Gucci carrier, jeweled FSU leash and collar, canopied dog bed, and Royal Albert dishes.

"With such short notice, I hated to cancel his spa appointment, so my dog-walker, Pete, is staying with him for the weekend."

"I wish I were Chief Osceola," said Maggie.

Cheryl continued, "Are we staying with them?"

"I guess we'll have to. There's no hotel for miles, and that one B and B is way out of my price range. Plus, we won't be much help if we stay over in Starke."

Cheryl sighed. "I guess you're right. Their house kind of gives me the creeps - I mean there's not much room, and, well, you know."

Yes, Maggie knew. Neither Rhoda nor Lute cared about housecleaning. She shivered. "I don't know. We'll see how it looks. I think that sleeping porch has twin beds, but who can tell? Does Lute still have all those huge cans of pork and beans stacked to the ceiling in there?"

"Oh, I think it's worse now. He talks more and more about the revolution. God knows what all he has stockpiled," said Cheryl. "Last I heard, he was burying stuff in the yard."

Maggie shook her head. "How did Rhoda end up like this? Why does she stay with him?"

"Come on; you know why. Rhoda always was a rebel. Nobody was surprised when she ran off with Lute after just two dates. Plus, let's face it. He is incredibly charismatic."

"Says you. But he did seem like a real catch," said Maggie. "Back then, he looked like Hugh Grant, plus he had a solid business. Things seemed so promising. Who would have thought he'd go bankrupt in engine and fiberglass repair? In Florida, no less. Everybody has a boat, and boats always break down."

"He just can't seem to get along with anybody for more than a day or two. I don't know why she stays with him. They have some sick bond they can't break. As Dad used to say, 'I'm just glad they found each other, instead of ruining two more peoples' lives.'"

Maggie sighed. "I guess. Remember that time she tried to leave him? He followed her all over the state until she gave in and came back. So, here they are stuck in a swamp in the armpit of Florida."

"I know. At least she has her own money now since she went on disability."

This was news to Maggie. "She's on disability? What for? Why haven't I heard about this?"

"Oh, you know Rhoda. She didn't want 'the baby' to worry about her. The only reason she told me was because I know some attorneys through work," said Cheryl. "She claimed that fibromyalgia and depression made it impossible for her to do her job."

"Does she have those conditions?" Maggie was astounded she'd never heard any of this.

"Who knows? But she got it, so she must have had a pretty convincing case."

"So, how does it help her to be home all the time? Won't he still take her money when she cashes the check?"

"No. For once, she listened to me. I told her to

have it direct-deposited into her personal account, so he can't get to it. The doctors she used to work for paid her in cash, and Lute always managed to get his hands on most of her money. Even better, though, being on disability, she actually has health care."

"God, what a life. It's so depressing. Let's change the subject or turn on the radio."

"There aren't really any stations out here in God's country, but, did I tell you about the Golden Chiefs reception I went to? It was just after the spring game..."

Cheryl talked the rest of the way. Maggie couldn't remember exactly what she said. Cheryl's lilting chatter and the monotonous landscape of northern Florida's scrub pines lulled her into a twilight sleep. Maggie heard something about the society events Cheryl attended and how many times she managed to get on the FSU JumboTron during football season. After a while, Cheryl just sang which was a pleasant break.

Three hours later (Cheryl always drove just below the speed limit), they arrived southeast of Starke in the small town of Eugenia. Rhoda and Lute lived in a fish camp by the Oolehatchee Swamp. Their home was a rusty double-wide. Actually, it was a single-wide attached to a camper with a wooden sleeping porch built on. This place did have running water and indoor toilets, though, so it beat their last one.

Maggie tried not to judge. She lived in a simple tract house, but at least she kept it clean and the yard mowed. No need to worry about mowing grass here, though. The canopy of live oaks prevented much lawn, and the black sandy soil stayed hidden under fallen leaves.

"YOO-HOO – Rhoda, guess who?" trilled Cheryl as they scrambled up the steps and burst in the door. "SURPRISE!"

From her recliner, Rhoda looked up to see her sisters. They ran toward her, arms spread wide. Rhoda's heart surged; no matter where it was, no matter what the reason, being together made everything better.

"Don't get up," Maggie said, as they stooped over the walker for a group hug.

"What are you guys doing here? I told you not to come," Rhoda asked, eyes glittering with relief.

"What, are you kidding?" said Cheryl. "Of course we're here. You're hurt; you need help - the 'Lemon Sisters' to the rescue."

Rhoda laughed. "The Lemon Sisters? I haven't heard that name in forever. I hated when Mom called us that. We were just trying to sing."

"Oh, Rhoda, she was just joking," said Cheryl, defending their mother.

"Go ahead and say it," said Maggie. "I was the one who couldn't carry a tune." She had been told that often by their music-teacher mother.

Cheryl, always ready to show off her singing, started in:

> It takes a worried man to sing a worried song...

Maggie and Rhoda helped her finish -

> ...Well, I might be worried now, but I won't be worried long

Maggie laughed. "I told you I'm the lemon." She was glad for the ice breaker. She had been startled by

Rhoda's appearance when they walked in. Despite a refrigerator build, Rhoda looked fragile and ashen. Her stick-straight salt and pepper hair, always poorly cut, hung to her chin in greasy strings. Her once smooth skin was now etched with lines and her big, bedroom eyes were puffy and dark. It broke Maggie's heart to see the statuesque, doe-eyed sister she grew up with in such a state of decline. "Okay. Enough chit chat," said Maggie. "Tell me what really happened."

"I already told you; I stubbed my toe and tripped." Rhoda looked down.

"Bullshit. Your toe looks fine." Maggie was determined to get to the truth.

Cheryl started humming to cover the tension between her sisters. Having survived a miserable marriage and bitter divorce, Cheryl was phobic about conflict.

"Come on, Sis. What happened?" pressed Maggie.

Rhoda glanced toward the door and the driveway.

"Lute wasn't out there when we pulled up. Go ahead; spill it."

Rhoda collapsed against the back of the recliner. "Well, I'd been at the doctor's. My back's been acting up. It was after lunch, and Lute was out in the carport when I pulled up. He'd been drinking."

Rhoda's hand shook as she sucked on the straw of her Big Gulp cup. "He started yelling at me for no reason, asking where I'd been, who I'd been with. You know how he gets."

"Focus, Rhoda. What happened to the leg?" Maggie demanded.

Cheryl simultaneously broke into hives and a chorus of "Nearer my God to Thee."

"It was all my fault, really. I told him I'd been at the quilting club at church. He hates Dr. Stout, so I don't tell him when I go there. Anyway, he said I was lying and shoved me, which, I don't have to tell you, pissed me off. So I charged at him. He stepped aside and tripped me, and I fell over that goddamn prop stick/boom thingy from his stupid crab boat. I landed on a pile of concrete blocks and heard it snap."

Maggie's eyes widened. "What did Lute do?"

"He said I deserved it and went in the house. Luckily, I still had my keys, so I dragged myself to the car and drove to the emergency room."

Maggie and Cheryl stood dumbstruck.

"No one ever deserves that." Cheryl's voice quavered with anger and sympathy. She had spent many hours in therapy to reach that essential truth.

Silence stretched on until they all became uncomfortable.

"Well, you know Lute," Rhoda finally said. "He gets in a mood. He's frustrated now with this new business."

"What is it this time?" Maggie asked.

"Crabbing." They all rolled their eyes.

"He says this is the big one," said Rhoda. "He got a great deal on an old crabber. It just needs a little engine work and some patching, and it'll be ready to go. In fact, that's probably where he is. He said he was going to try and hire a crew today down by the docks."

Made in the USA
Monee, IL
24 November 2021